FIREWATER BLUES

CAIMH MCDONNELL

Caimh McDonnell

Visit my website at www.WhiteHairedIrishman.com

First edition: March 2022

ISBN:978-1-912897-33-9 (Paperback)

ISBN: 978-1-912897-35-3 (Hardback)

AUTHOR'S NOTE

Hi there reader-person,

Normally, these notes are intended to prepare North Americans for the horrors of reading things spelled correctly or to apologise to everyone for the fact that I have even less respect for chronology than I do for the meaning for the word trilogy. To be honest with you though, I've already covered that in the previous notes. If this is your first Bunny book, firstly, welcome, and secondly, where the hell have you been? Thirdly, if you're wondering why this note is here, it's mainly because my wife told me to write one, and she can be surprisingly scary.

Having said that, just so you know, the majority of this book takes place in the year 2000, straight after *Dead Man's Sins*, which itself followed on from the events in *Angels in the Moonlight*. If current trends continue, the 16-year gap between *Angels* ending and *A Man with One of Those Faces* starting will require a further ninety-three books. And yes, don't worry, I've already planned them out.

The next twenty-six will be great. There's going to be a tricky patch around book thirty where Bunny gets into the didgeridoo and while books fifty through to fifty-nine – which will be set entirely in space – will be hugely unpopular, it'll be nothing compared to the backlash towards books sixty to sixty-eight which are just rehashes of earlier tales told from the perspective of a hurling stick.

Luckily, book ninety-three will be when Bunny wakes up in the shower and realises that all of the other books were just a dream.

In the meantime, I hope you enjoy this book as much as I will enjoy the sausages that I have been promised for writing this note.

Mmmmmmmm, sausages!

Sláinte!

Caimh

In memory of Michael McDonnell & Karl Jones.
The best of fathers, the finest of men.

PROLOGUE – WHAT A TANGLED WEB

Sometime in 1999

The Spider sighed. It should really be a smoke-filled room. That's where this sort of meeting would have taken place in the good old days. He wasn't old enough to have been around back then, but he'd heard stories. When he'd realised that this was his vocation – making and breaking careers, doing deals, changing the fates of entire nations – he'd imagined conducting his business in a smoke-filled room, possibly with a well-aged and extortionately priced single malt set before him. As it was, the meeting was taking place in the juice bar of an obscenely expensive gym in the City of London, and the drink in front of him was something he'd selected from the menu at random, and he had no intention of touching it. For all of that, it was still that kind of meeting.

The man the Spider had been waiting for took the seat opposite. Eric Stringer. *His* juice abomination looked even worse. A bit of celery was sticking out of it. The Spider wouldn't have been able to pick Stringer out from the legion of other middle-aged men in Lycra that infested the place, all exercising with an air of sweaty desperation. Collectively, they appeared to be putting more effort into fighting their middle-aged spread than some countries had put into the Second World War.

The Spider didn't need a gym. While he didn't look it, he was ex-military and a tad old school when it came to his fitness regime. He looked nondescript by design. He liked to blend in. He also viewed excess muscle as an utter waste of space. Speaking of which ...

Stringer was Scandinavian, but not the tall, good-looking sort. No, he'd come from the shallower end of that gene pool. He had a 2000-krona haircut over a twenty-krona face. Fresh from the shower, he offered the Spider a glib grin by way of a greeting. He was almost of a slim build, nearly attractive, and had an air of ostentatious wealth about him that he probably thought made up for the absence of personality.

"Did you find the place okay?"

"Have I ever given you the impression that I'm the type of person who can't find a building without assistance?"

Stringer drew his head back, unused to such sarcasm from someone he considered an employee. "I was just making conversation."

"The time for that was" – the Spider glanced at his watch – "seventeen minutes ago, when this meeting was supposed to start."

Stringer leaned forward and jabbed his finger in the Spider's direction. "I think you're forgetting who the client is here."

"Your bosses are. So, do you have a message for me from them?"

"Not as such."

The Spider tilted his head to one side. "Excuse me?"

"I just wanted to chat through a few things."

The Spider picked up his briefcase and got to his feet. "We're done."

"What?" said Stringer, looking shocked.

The Spider turned to go.

"Look, I think we've got off on the wrong foot here."

"Have we?" asked the Spider, still facing the door.

"I apologise for my lateness. I appreciate your time is valuable."

The Spider relented and sat back down. "Right, prove it. Why am I here?"

Stringer glanced round to make sure they weren't being observed. They weren't. There were just three other customers in the juice bar. One was a man who was tragically trying to pick up the girl working behind the counter, despite their age gap being such that it would've been more appropriate for him to be picking her up from school. The other two were a couple the Spider guessed had been screwing but were now discussing why they no longer were. Human nature, in all its grubby glory, was his business.

Risk assessed, Stringer lowered his voice. "I have concerns about the candidate."

"What concerns?"

"They've only been a minor political player up to this point."

The Spider ran a finger down his silk tie. "I'm aware of that. That is precisely the point."

"But—"

"But nothing. We are gifting someone the highest political office in their country in exchange for them doing something they very definitely will not want to do. The bigger the ask, the bigger the get. You need someone who very definitely needs you. If it was going to be easy, then you wouldn't need me." He gave a smile that also served as a warning for how little patience he had left for being questioned. "And trust me, you do need me."

"The budget—"

"Is the budget. This is a complicated endeavour. Making a prime minister costs money."

Stringer sat back and picked up his juice. "It's actually *'taoiseach'*."

"Excuse me?"

"The Prime Minister of Ireland is known as the Taoiseach."

The Spider raised his eyes to the ceiling. "Yes, I know that. I have a rule of not using words from languages that I do not speak. After the three months my team and I have spent prepping for this, rest assured that I know more about the Irish political landscape than anyone who is in it. Now, will there be a pop quiz, or can I go about my day?"

"What about the timeline, then?"

"Eighteen months to two years."

"Can it be moved up?"

"Of course," replied the Spider as he pulled a pen from the inside pocket of his jacket and clicked it on. "Very easily."

"Okay. Good."

"Yes. I'm going to give you a phone number. It's for a general in the Korean People's Army – fourth biggest in the world, if memory serves. You'll need to see how much he'll want for invading a rainy island on the outskirts of Europe, and I don't imagine it'll come cheap."

"There's no need for sarcasm."

The Spider clicked his pen off. "You're right, but it's either that or I put this pen through your eyeball. Ever seen someone do that?"

Stringer paled.

"No, I don't imagine you have. Fine, here's what we're going to do. I'm going to leave here and do the job your employers have contracted me to do – in the timescale I have specified, for the budget we agreed. You try and pull another power move to prove to your bosses how invaluable you are by strapping a saddle on me, then I will terminate our relationship. What do I mean by that? Well, let's leave that to your imagination. I want you to savour every meal you eat, every car key you turn and every window you pass as if it is your last, because trust me, one time it will be."

Stringer had started to sweat again, and looked like a man in need of a second shower. "There's no need for threats." His voice cracked as he spoke. "We were merely looking for some reassurances."

"Fine. I am very good at what I do. How do you know that? Well, people who do what I do and aren't very good at it don't remain people for very long. There is no scenario here in which failure isn't fatal for me, because while people think knowledge is power, it really isn't. Knowledge coupled with failure equals an unacceptable liability. Console yourself with the prospect of my failure resulting in it becoming your job to hire the people to kill me. Incidentally, they will be incredibly expensive and I strongly suggest that you don't try to renegotiate the price with them either, as believe me, they will be worth every penny." The Spider picked up his briefcase, got to his feet and strode towards the door. "We're done here."

Chapter One

DEMONS

Eighteen months to two years later

Arnie tilted his chin towards the sky and felt the light rain kiss his face. Waves of electricity ran up and down his arms. They'd taken some pills as well as a few bumps of coke, so he couldn't be sure what was causing it, but something was kicking in. He felt as if his feet might leave the ground at any second and he'd rip right through the cloud-filled sky.

Maybe it wasn't the drugs at all. It might just be the thrill of anticipation. He'd been looking forward to this all week. It was 3am on a Tuesday morning. He and Ricardo had picked that time deliberately. The streets needed to be quiet for what they had planned. A rainy night in the arse-end hours of the morning was perfect – nobody would be hanging around who didn't need to be.

They'd been careful, scoping out the location earlier in the week and finding a CCTV blackspot where they could change into the black hoodies he'd bought specially, which were to be dumped and burned immediately afterwards. (He'd briefly considered getting the hoodies with a special logo on them, but he'd realised how stupid that would be and was glad he hadn't mentioned it.) When it came to trying to identify them, the cameras dotted round the city centre would be useless.

It had all started a few months ago. Some drunken old tramp had asked Ricardo for a cigarette and then got all aggressive when Ricardo had told him where to go. They'd all given the guy a few slaps – even Karl, although he'd been drowning in remorse the next day. Pussy. Arnie had played along, of course, agreeing that what they'd done had been out of order and while they'd been drunk, that was no excuse.

The next time, it had just been him and Ricardo, and on that occasion, the homeless bloke didn't do anything to start it. They'd given him a right kicking. At some point, without much being said, he and Ricardo realised they'd found a kindred spirit in each other.

As Ricardo explained it, what they were doing was almost a public service. All these wasters were lying about, scrounging for money, making the place look bad. The pair were simply giving them an incentive to get their lives in order.

A couple of weeks ago, they'd cranked things up a notch. The lighter fluid had been Arnie's idea. It didn't work the first time because, irony of ironies, Ricardo's lighter failed and the guy stumbled away. Bloody but unignited.

Last week, though – *whoosh!*

All over the newspapers the next day, too, and the day after that.

It had been weird on the DART into town, as people had sat around him, reading about what he'd done. The article itself was full of all the pant-wettingly tedious outrage you'd expect – as if it were the first crime ever to have been committed in Dublin. Please! Arnie saw three lads laughing and joking about it too. They were a cool underground thing now. Like *Fight Club*.

He and Ricardo had talked about it and decided on one farewell trip before they'd knock it on the head. They'd walk away as mysterious legends – the bogey men that tramps told one another about. Ricardo was already at college over in Galway and Arnie was heading to UCD in September after finishing his gap year. The last thing they needed was to mess up their futures with a bit of fun that got out of hand.

They were in Temple Bar, up behind the Central Bank, with its determinedly dull, grey-stoned façade. It always seemed as if it were trying to look too boring ever to be doing anything naughty with your money.

Ricardo slapped Arnie on the shoulder and pointed. Huddled in one of the corners sat what looked like a large bundle of rags. It moved. Arnie looked round to check there was nobody about, then smiled and nodded. They sauntered over.

As they approached, he could see the bundle was a man with a raggedy old sleeping bag wrapped around him.

"You alright there, brother?" asked Ricardo, all sweetness and light.

This only elicited a mumbled reply.

Ricardo leaned in and tapped the knee of the guy's stained trackie bottoms. "Y'alright there?"

The knee was jerked away and a slurred response came from beneath the sleeping bag.

Ricardo stood up and pulled a face. "Feck's sake, man. The stench of booze off him. I might not even need this." He drew a bottle of BBQ lighter fluid out of his pocket and smiled.

Arnie checked round them again and pulled the camcorder out of his hoodie pocket. They'd debated whether to film it or not. On the one hand, it was a risk. On the other, this was their last time. If they were careful, made sure not to show their faces or say anything, they should be fine.

"Are you ready?" whispered Arnie.

"Hang on a sec."

Ricardo turned away and started fiddling with something.

"What?" hissed Arnie. "What's the hold-up?"

"The cap on the thing. It's hard to get off with these gloves." They'd decided gloves were a sensible choice. No fingerprints. You couldn't be too careful.

Arnie leaned in to help. After struggling for a few seconds,

Ricardo eventually used his teeth to pull the cap off the bottle of lighter fluid. It struck Arnie as a bad idea, but screw it, too late now. It was go time.

Ricardo snapped open the fancy Zippo lighter he'd bought after the first cock-up and flicked it into life. The flame ignited his grin. He looked at Arnie with a demonic glint in his eyes.

As Ricardo turned, the lighter was walloped out of his hand. It flew through the air, and the flame was extinguished as it skittered across the cobbled street.

"What the—"

They must've been so focused on the lighter-fluid bottle that they hadn't noticed the homeless guy getting to his feet. The fella now seemed very, very awake. And big. So much bigger than they would have expected. Not only that, but he was also holding a hurling stick.

The man looked down at the lighter and back up at the two young men. "Sorry, lads, how rude of me ..."

Arnie froze as the man gave him a wide grin. Somewhere deep inside him a little voice screamed that he was in real trouble.

The big man seemed to have one eye on him and the other on Ricardo as he pulled a lighter from his own pocket and sparked it into life. Then he held it against the hurling stick. Arnie leaped backwards with a scream as the thing burst into flames.

The sleeping bag fell away. The suddenly massive man held the flaming hurl above his head and roared, "Were you boys looking for a light?"

Chapter Two

THERE IS A FLAME THAT NEVER GOES OUT

Bunny sat and stared into the Styrofoam cup he'd been given. Having drunk its contents, he still couldn't say with anything close to certainty whether it had been tea or coffee. Beggars couldn't be choosers, though – even temporary ones.

He looked up as the door to the interview room opened.

"Detective Inspector Fintan O'Rourke, we have to stop meeting like this."

"Never a truer word spoken."

O'Rourke held his coat draped over his arm and wore an expression that indicated bonhomie might be in short supply. He was a few years older than Bunny, but the man was the embodiment of the word "svelte" – the result of being the kind of smug bastard who somehow finds the time and energy to go jogging. In his mid-thirties now, Bunny only ran when he had somebody to catch, and in those situations adrenalin compensated for all manner of sins. Still, he'd been alarmed at how out of puff he'd been after just a relatively short run through Temple Bar. It was time to have a serious think about ordering the occasional salad.

"What are you doing here at four in the morning, Detective Inspector? Did you piss somebody off?"

"I'm beginning to think I must've done, Bunny. Possibly God." The DI pulled out the chair opposite, sat down and tossed a copy of an arrest report onto the table in front of him. "As you well know, I'm here because you're here. Again."

"So, I suppose the question should be – what am I doing here?"

"Yes. Or more precisely, what were you doing sleeping outside the Central Bank at three in the morning?"

Bunny shrugged. "I wasn't actually asleep. I was only resting."

O'Rourke rolled his eyes. "Thing is, while the pay might not be what any of us consider fair, you're a detective in An Garda Síochána and, although you're currently on sabbatical, you're not homeless. I've been to your home."

"You have," agreed Bunny. "In fact, you were part of a raid on it a few months ago."

"You know that wasn't me."

Bunny drummed his fingers on the table. "Would you believe they've still not paid me for the new front door, or that ceramic duck they broke? That was a present."

"A good one?"

"No, but 'tis the principle of the thing."

"Even for you, this is one hell of a way to lodge a complaint." O'Rourke leaned forward, put his elbows on the table and held his face in his hands. "I am so far beyond tired at this point, Bunny. I could really do without this shit."

"Don't blame me. I didn't call you."

"No, but the powers that be have decided that you're a problem. What's worse, for reasons I don't understand, they've made you my problem." He raised his hand to stop Bunny's objection before it started. "I know. You don't see it that way. What a shock. How about —" O'Rourke drew back and wrinkled his nose. "What the hell is that smell?"

Bunny folded his arms. "I'm undercover."

O'Rourke waved a hand in front of his face and gagged. "Nobody needs to be that convincing. Besides, a minute ago you were 'only resting', and now you're deep undercover. Which is it?"

Bunny said nothing to this.

"Condolences, by the way," said O'Rourke. "I hear your little hurling team got demolished in that final you made."

Bunny's eyes narrowed and O'Rourke sensed that maybe there were some buttons you didn't press.

"Fine," O'Rourke conceded. "Moving on. First off, other than being an awkward sod, why did you feel compelled to get involved?"

"Involved in what?"

It was clear from O'Rourke's face that the jousting section of their chat was over.

Bunny shrugged. "Micky Flynn is a friend of mine." This elicited a blank expression from the DI until Bunny added, "Homeless gentleman. Currently in the Mater with second- and third-degree burns over sixty percent of his body."

O'Rourke nodded awkwardly. "It isn't my case."

"Whose is it?"

"There's a task force of about two dozen bodies working it."

"Is that right?"

"It is," said O'Rourke. By way of explanation, he added, "It got a lot of press and it might be an election year."

Bunny laughed. "It's Ireland. Every year is an election year."

"Ain't that the truth," said O'Rourke, "but seeing as our current taoiseach is hanging up his expense-claiming pen, and with the party conference this weekend to decide the next one ... Well, everything's a bit political at the moment."

"Still, it's great to see we're pushing the boat out to take care of the homeless community in these stressful political times. Two dozen officers on this task force, is it? I think I met a couple of them yesterday."

"Did you?" asked O'Rourke. "Let me guess – as a fellow officer, you offered to assist them in their investigation given your invaluable connections garnered through years on the beat?"

"I never got the chance. One of them opened the conversation by nudging me with his foot, and the other threatened to arrest me for public intoxication. Quite the case study in community policing."

O'Rourke leaned back and huffed at the ceiling. "Oh, for fuck's sake."

"Might be a bit of a training moment, that."

"Like I said – not my investigation."

"Whose is it?"

O'Rourke paused and Bunny could tell the precise second at which the DI decided that lying would be too much effort.

"Grainger's."

"And how is the Minister for Justice's nephew?"

"He had a journo embedded in his task force, and given that you've embarrassed him and them, I'd imagine he's over the fucking moon. I've to ring him back after we're done here. Safe to say, you can add him to your extensive list of enemies."

"Oh, he's been on there for a while."

"Why am I not surprised?"

"I'm shocked he's not here himself. Up grafting every hour God sends to get a result. His work ethic is legendary."

O'Rourke gave Bunny a knowing look and left it at that. "Moving on" – he indicated the arrest report on the desk in front of him – "can I just clarify a couple of the details about what happened tonight?"

"What's there to clarify? I was sitting there, minding my business, and two scumbags tried to flambé me."

"Yes," said O'Rourke. "And thank God they were unsuccessful in their endeavour. Still though, am I reading this correctly? You chased them with a flaming hurling stick. I mean, I assume Garda Wilkes, who wrote this report, isn't using colloquialisms there."

"No," said Bunny, "my hurley was on fire right enough."

"Did they ..."

"I set it on fire myself."

O'Rourke sighed. "Course you did. Do I want to ask why?"

"Have you read any George R. R. Martin?"

"Let's assume I haven't."

"You should. I've been trying to widen my reading choices. Tried a bit of epic fantasy and I'm enjoying it. One of the characters has a flaming sword. The idea had a certain *je ne sais quoi*."

"I bet it did," said O'Rourke, flipping the report over. "Maximum bang for your buck in terms of putting on a show. Are you trying to get yourself booted off the force? Is that it?"

"For catching criminals?"

O'Rourke clenched his right fist in frustration. "When you're on sabbatical? Yes!"

"At no point did I attempt to arrest the suspects. They attempted to assault me and I defended myself. They ran. As a concerned citizen, I gave chase while endeavouring to get the attention of a serving member of the Garda Síochána."

"And how were you doing that, exactly?"

"Well, I figured a lunatic running through Temple Bar waving a flaming hurl about – that's the kind of thing that traditionally gets everyone's attention, including the gardaí's. And, to be fair, it did."

"Oh yes," agreed O'Rourke. "No arguments there. Gardaí Wilkes and Murphy were on the opposite side of the Liffey. They came running over the Ha'penny Bridge when you and your quarry appeared out of the Merchant's Arch laneway. By the time they reached you, one of the suspects – an Arnold Canavan – was in the river."

Bunny stabbed the table with his finger. "Ye can't pin that on me. He jumped in of his own accord. Didn't even try for the bridge. Maybe he's afraid of bridges. That's a thing. I've seen a TV programme about it."

"Sure," said O'Rourke, flipping to page two of the report. "Or maybe he wasn't thinking straight. If memory serves ... Yes, here it is." He ran his finger along a line of text and read it aloud. "Mr Canavan thought he was being chased by a demon."

"The fecking nerve," muttered Bunny. "What those two scumbags were up to and he thinks *I'm* the demon."

"Well, I believe he was on drugs at the time. Probably explains why he jumped into the river, too."

Bunny laughed. "Between you and me, he leaped straight in without looking. The gobshite is lucky it wasn't low tide."

"True, although that would have at least removed the problem of him not being able to swim."

"How is that my fault?" asked Bunny, stretching his arms out wide. "I mean, in this day and age, I thought everyone could swim. His mate certainly could."

"Yes. A Richard Drake. According to Officer Murphy, you threw him in after Mr Canavan."

"I most certainly did not. It may've looked like that from a distance, but he was actually mad keen to save his buddy. I was trying to hold him back."

"Right. So you didn't" – O'Rourke scanned the report again – "lift him up off the ground and physically hurl him into the Liffey?"

"Absolutely not. That young man deserves great credit for that unassisted act of heroism. After we're done locking him up and throwing away the key, I reckon he should be up for some kind of award or something. Or at least one of those swimming badges they give you if you can rescue a brick from the bottom of a swimming pool in your jimmy-jammies."

O'Rourke snatched up the arrest report, folded it in half and shoved it into his inside jacket pocket.

"Alright, Bunny. Enough nonsense. Just so I know, how did you happen to be in the right place at the right time?"

"Off the record?"

"For fuck's sake, what part of this conversation did you think was *on* the record?"

Bunny puffed out his cheeks. "I asked about. There've been incidents stretching back a few months. Assaults. Hassles. Always late at night from guys in their late teens, early twenties. Once you started to pay attention, it was fairly clear there was a set area and an established pattern. I figured the most likely spots, and for the last few nights I've been moving between them."

O'Rourke pursed his lips for a moment. "Sincerely, that is an outstanding bit of policing."

"Thanks."

"The only problem is, you're not currently a member of the

bloody police. A lawyer could have a field day with this, and you know that."

Bunny shrugged. "The last I saw of our two twisted firestarters, they were singing like canaries. Is that not the case?"

"Yes, it is," conceded O'Rourke. "Not only have they both given full confessions, but one of them has also asked to see a priest. Then, of course, there's the fact the other one helpfully videotaped the whole thing."

"Really?"

"Even more helpfully, the thing cuts out as you're chasing them."

Bunny stretched out his arms and yawned. "So, job's a good 'un. What are we doing here? Doesn't seem like there's any reason for you to have been dragged from the loving embrace of your wife. How is she, by the way?"

"Still hates you."

"Hate is a very strong word."

"You got into a fight with a large wading bird at our wedding."

"Seriously, is she still going on about that?"

O'Rourke tilted his head to one side. "Women get very touchy about people fucking up their wedding day. Until she has another one, don't expect to make the Christmas card list."

Bunny scratched his armpit. "So, can I get out of here, then? I'll be honest, I've never appreciated the idea of my own bed more, and even I think I could use a shower."

"We can all go home once you've seen sense."

Bunny raised his eyebrows. "How so?"

"The good news is that no less than the Commissioner himself has agreed we can say your sabbatical ended four weeks ago, and your pay will reflect that."

"While I've always fancied the idea of time travel, let me stop you there. No. No, I'm not going to pretend that I was part of that useless gobshite Grainger's task force."

O'Rourke exhaled loudly. "Are you deliberately trying to be awkward?"

"Deliberately? No. I'm just doing what comes naturally."

"Alright. As your friend, can you explain to me what the hell is going on? This sabbatical of yours ... I mean, initially, I got it. Gringo died. You needed some time away. But it's been what? Four or five months now? Are you punishing yourself? Having some kind of breakdown? Or have you just decided you'd rather not be a copper any more? Instead, you'd rather be a pain in our collective arse?"

Bunny paused for a few seconds and looked down at his fingers. "Honestly, I'm not sure myself."

"Then just come back."

He shook his head. "I'm not ready yet."

O'Rourke drew a breath "Any idea when that will be?"

Bunny shrugged.

"Of course not. Fair warning – after this morning's little adventure, I'm pretty sure I'm going to be dragged in front of the Commissioner in a few hours. At a guess, he might decide to force the issue. There's only so long he's going to be willing to have you outside the tent pissing in."

"Jesus, what I'd have given to have had a tent for the last few nights. You ever tried to sleep in the middle of a city, Fintan? I've never felt more shattered in my life."

O'Rourke got to his feet. "You and me both, Bunny. You and me both."

"Any chance of a lift?"

"And have you stinking out my brand-new car? No way. I'll ask one of the uniforms to drop you home."

Chapter Three

HUSBANDRY

"He's in a 'bit of a mood'."

As far as DI O'Rourke knew, Carol Willis had been Commissioner Ferguson's personal assistant since the days when the position was known as "secretary". Come to that, she might even have been his PA since birth. Certainly, O'Rourke had never walked into the Commissioner's outer office not to find her there. She had literally been there longer than a couple of the walls. Now that he thought of it, presumably the woman did take holidays and days off, but he'd never seen any evidence of this. There was every possibility that when the Commissioner shuffled off this mortal coil, she would be buried at the front of his tomb to manage his eternal schedule and prevent the unwashed and unworthy from gaining access.

This morning was, however, the first time Carol had been moved to warn O'Rourke that the Commissioner was in a "bit of a mood". This was Commissioner Gareth Ferguson, the highly respected and beloved leader of An Garda Síochána. A man who could make veteran police officers tremble simply by staring at them for long enough. A man who had once, while questioning a junior officer about how a television presenter had somehow evaded a speeding ticket in exchange for an autograph, caused the unlucky sod to turn and run into the wall of his office. The mark beside the door was still visible today. Not only did the Commissioner not have the plaster repaired, he also placed an empty frame around it as a not-so-subtle warning to others who might incur his wrath.

O'Rourke forced a smile onto his face, thought again, and abandoned it as an unnecessarily provocative gesture. Best to look unhappy going in, as there was every chance that was how he would be coming out. He steeled himself, glanced over his shoulder at Carol, who gave him a worryingly encouraging nod, and knocked on the door.

"Come the hell in."

A bit of a mood indeed.

O'Rourke entered the Commissioner's office to find Ferguson sitting at his desk, staring morosely out the window beside him at the kind of unremarkable grey drizzly morning that Dublin does so well. His shoeless feet were up on the desk and, unusually, his tie was hanging loosely around his neck. While he was a large man in all senses of the word, he was never usually slovenly.

"Commissioner."

Ferguson spoke without turning around. "Fintan, as an officer with your extensive experience in the field, how many times, give or take, do you think you've been lied to in your career?"

"Well..." started O'Rourke, trying desperately to buy himself some time to consider which supposed lie the Commissioner might have caught him out in. "It's impossible to say. I've done an awful lot of interviews in my time and, as we all know, even the people who are innocent still manage to find stuff to lie about."

O'Rourke braced himself for the counterpunch that didn't come. Instead, the Commissioner nodded forlornly and pursed his lips.

"Indeed. And however many lies you have been told, we can double that number for me, given my advanced years. In fact, we could safely triple it, seeing as so many of my days now are filled with meeting after meeting with politicians and civil servants. There is one individual from the Department of Justice, with whom I have worked for four years, and honestly, I am not one hundred percent certain that he's even told me his real name. You'd think with all that experience, I could spot a lie from a loved one pretty easily, wouldn't you?"

O'Rourke opened his mouth to speak then shut it again. He had no idea what was going on here, but even allowing for the possibility that the Commissioner had skulled a bottle of brandy for breakfast, O'Rourke still couldn't see any way that it was him being referred to as "a loved one". The entire force could be divided into people the Commissioner either despised, tolerated, or hadn't yet met. Love did not come into it.

Ferguson took his feet down from the desk and swung himself back under it. He looked up at O'Rourke for the first time since the DI had entered the room.

"Is everything alright, sir?" O'Rourke was used to the Commissioner as a blazing inferno of rage and indignation. This morose version of his boss of bosses was becoming very unsettling.

Ferguson sighed. "Yesterday was my beloved's fiftieth birthday."

"Oh no," said O'Rourke, temporarily forgetting himself. "You didn't—"

"Forget it? No, Fintan – despite what you might have read in a certain newspaper, I am not an idiot. I bought her a selection of fine gifts, some of which I am sure she liked."

"I see ... Actually ... sorry, sir, I don't see at all. I mean, I don't see what the problem is."

Ferguson puffed out his cheeks. "The problem, Fintan, is that a year ago, I asked my beloved if she wanted a big party for her fiftieth and she was adamant that she did not."

"Ohhhh."

"Yes. I double checked a few months ago. I triple checked a few weeks ago. I even quadruple checked last week."

O'Rourke winced.

"How on earth did I miss this? I swear to God, we went out for an early dinner at her favourite restaurant and she was in sparkling form. In hindsight, the clues were all there. Last month she had several of our downstairs rooms repainted. She got the carpets cleaned. The dog even went for a trim yesterday." Ferguson slammed his fist on his desk, causing its contents to vibrate. "I didn't catch a sniff of the fetid turd I was brewing until our car pulled in to the driveway last night. Have you ever watched somebody prepare to feign surprise, only to see it replaced with genuine surprise and heartbreak? She walked through her own front door to be greeted not by an assembled mass of family and friends there to celebrate a massive moment in her life, but by one mentally deficient Labradoodle – Kevin – who was destroying the obscenely expensive cashmere sweater I'd bought as the one present I was confident she'd definitely like."

"Sweet Jesus."

"I'm beginning to think salvaging the situation might be beyond the son of God's considerable powers. I lost count of the number of times she told me last night that she was fine and how much she enjoyed her birthday."

"I appreciate this might be a ridiculous question, but is it possible … she did?"

"Don't be an idiot, Fintan. When I left this morning, the woman was listening to an entire Joni Mitchell album. At 7am. This is an utter disaster." Ferguson fixed O'Rourke with an alarming glint in his eyes. "Speaking of utter disasters … Would you care to explain to me the other catastrophe that occurred last night?"

O'Rourke resisted the urge to throw up his hands in frustration. It was beyond unfair for Ferguson to segue from his own epic matrimonial fail to asking him to deliver his report. There needed to be at least five minutes of padding between the two – a discussion about the weather, some sports results, a chat about reality television, perhaps. O'Rourke didn't watch it and he would bet his left nut that Ferguson didn't either, but for the sake of his own well-being he would be willing to give it a go. His mind flitted from one bad idea to another as he stood there in silence.

"Not to hurry you, Fintan, but I have just a few small hours to come up with the most romantic gesture in the history of humanity in order to save my marriage. While I enjoy you standing there doing this delightful impression of a goldfish who somehow managed to jump out of his bowl, I would rather have you report on why a certain Detective McGarry is somehow inserting himself into the middle of high-profile investigations while on sabbatical."

"Yes, sir. Have you thought about flowers?"

Ferguson arched an eyebrow. "To be honest with you, Fintan, I was leaning more towards an official reprimand."

"I meant for —"

"I know what you meant. Please do not use my private life to distract me from your failure to manage a straightforward situation."

O'Rourke was genuinely outraged. "With respect, sir, that is spectacularly unfair. That was not my investigation and Bunny McGarry is not my responsibility."

"Yes, he is, Detective Inspector. I know this because I made him your responsibility." Ferguson raised his hand to stave off O'Rourke's objection. "Blah, blah, blah, blah. Welcome to the curse of basic competency. When you reveal yourself not to be totally inept, the powers that be" – Ferguson pointed his thumbs towards his chest to emphasise where the aforementioned power lay – "will pile more and more on your plate. It is how one becomes cursed with promotions until the day an unimpressive cheese-and-wine reception is held to announce that you are in charge of everything. The downside of your shameless flaunting of your own abilities, Fintan, is that people will insist on you putting them to good use. Responsibility is the curse of the capable."

"Thank you, sir. To be clear, the investigation we are discussing is the one headed by DI Grainger."

Ferguson ran his tongue expansively around his mouth and nodded. "Well played, Detective Inspector. The dim-witted nephew of the Minister for Justice is obviously the exception to everything I just said. Have you spoken to him?"

"I was supposed to talk to him after I met with McGarry last night, but he didn't answer the phone when I rang. I got a text this morning which informed me that he'd fallen asleep."

Ferguson pushed back his chair and lowered his forehead until it was resting on the desktop. He stayed that way for several moments until, without raising his head, he reached out and pressed the intercom on his desk. "Carol."

"Yes, Commissioner. Do you need something?"

"Not really. However, I do feel compelled to use some very bad language at a very high volume, and I don't feel it is appropriate for you to hear that kind of thing in the workplace. Would you be so kind as to put on your headphones for the next fifteen seconds, please?"

"Of course, Commissioner."

"Thank you, Carol."

By O'Rourke's reckoning, the Commissioner went over by a good three seconds, but he did use the time to scream into the floor a thorough, if colourfully worded, assessment of Detective Inspector Grainger's abilities, shortcomings, and what can best be described as a vivid, if unlikely, theory about the man's parentage. Given that half the building must also have overheard Ferguson's diatribe, O'Rourke reckoned that DI Grainger's fellow officers would be dropping oblique references to it for weeks to come. On the upside, at least Grainger was too dim to catch any of them.

Commissioner Ferguson straightened himself up, seemingly feeling much better for the soul-cleansing properties of a bit of primal-scream therapy. "So, what do you suggest we do about the McGarry problem?"

"I'm not sure there is anything we can 'do', sir."

"I don't understand. How did he come to involve himself in the situation in the first place?"

"He knows the victim of one of the previous attacks."

Ferguson steepled his fingers. "I see. I feel ridiculous even for suggesting this but, given McGarry is a member of the Garda Síochána and, despite the impression DI Grainger gives, it is in fact our job to investigate such crimes, would it not have occurred to McGarry to assist us in that endeavour?"

"Apparently not."

"And the offer to have him assigned to the task force

retrospectively, with the financial and career benefits associated with that?"

"Zero interest. I'm afraid he is that most dangerous of things – a man seemingly determined to follow his own code. Bunny McGarry is a law unto himself."

When Commissioner Ferguson thumped the desk this time, the vibrations were enough to knock to the floor a pen holder he'd been presented with by the Dublin Chamber of Commerce, and a framed photograph of the time he and Mrs Ferguson met Tony Bennett.

He spoke through gritted teeth at a volume most people would require a megaphone to achieve. "This is exactly my point, but neither you nor McGarry seem to have fully grasped it ... He cannot be a law unto himself because I am the law."

O'Rourke was genuinely curious to know if the Commissioner quoting Judge Dredd was entirely accidental or not, but even DI Grainger would have realised that this moment was not the time to ask. Instead, O'Rourke opted for silence being the better part of valour.

Commissioner Ferguson jabbed a chubby finger in O'Rourke's direction. "Let me be crystal clear, Fintan. Since he has been on sabbatical, McGarry has insinuated himself into not one but two major investigations. Mark my words, there will not be a third. I would bet your career on it." As the Commissioner sat back in his chair, the considerable movement of his girth caused it to creak alarmingly. "Now, hot-air balloons?"

O'Rourke found himself discombobulated by the sudden change of tack. "I'm sorry?"

Ferguson shook his head. "Never mind. I just remembered she doesn't like heights." He waved a hand to dismiss O'Rourke. "Be gone, Fintan. Be gone."

All things considered, that could have gone worse, thought O'Rourke. Ferguson barked his name just as he placed his hand on the door handle to make good his escape, and he cursed himself for jumping the gun.

"One more thing ..."

"Yes, sir?"

"Did the lunatic really use a flaming hurly stick?"

O'Rourke did not turn around. "I believe so, sir."

"In the name of all things good and holy, why?"

"It's hard to say, sir, but best guess? He doesn't own a sword."

Chapter Four

FOR WHOM THE BELL TOLLS

Bunny awoke to the sound of his doorbell ringing. As his level of consciousness rose, so too did his level of confusion. He looked around and double checked that he was definitely in his own bedroom. Through a gap in the curtains he could see a cloud-filled sky offering a half-arsed threat of rain to anyone who might consider leaving the house without an umbrella.

He guessed it was mid-morning. His bedside clock had given up the ghost a while ago, and he'd decided he preferred it that way. Time was very over-rated. He'd been trying to have a lie-in – if you can even call it that, seeing as it had been almost 6am by the time he'd got home. Last night had been eventful, but the two before that had been just as exhausting – he had no idea how anyone managed the sleeping part of sleeping rough, given the inhospitable nature of a modern city.

Not only was Bunny not expecting visitors, he was actively trying to avoid them. Fortunately, his endeavour was made easier by the fact his doorbell didn't work. It had packed up a week before the bedside clock and Bunny had found the absence of interruptions liberating. Some part of him did wonder if he might end up living in a cave eventually, albeit one with access to a good local pub.

The non-working doorbell rang again, and again – at exactly ten-second intervals. It stopped only when Bunny roused himself and came clattering down the stairs.

"Alright, alright, alright!" he shouted. "Keep your bollocks on."

He expected it to be one of the lads from the team. If it turned out to be that evangelical loon with the pamphlets again, the guy was going to have his beliefs about the afterlife verified. Bunny threw open the door but his invective-laden rant about improper doorbell use didn't make it past his lips.

The woman standing there was sporting a pink mohawk and a Ramones T-shirt.

"Hello, Bunny."

Somewhere in his sleep-deprived brain, Bunny's synapses were slowly firing. It was the distinctive set of her jaw that did it. "Rosie?"

She nodded. "Yes."

The last time Bunny had met Rosie Flint, she had been a mousy-looking girl who wore a selection of unmemorable cardigans. She now looked as if she was on her way to pogo her brains out at CBGB. It suited her.

"I almost didn't recognise you with the hair."

"I've always had hair."

It had been years since they'd spoken but Bunny was now remembering what an interesting experience conversations with Rosie were.

"You have," he conceded. "I meant that it wasn't pink the last time I saw you."

Rosie gave another curt nod. "I dyed it on October twelfth, two years ago."

"'Tis very nice."

She must have been nearly thirty now, but still had the fresh-faced complexion of a child. Her eyes, which had been fixed on Bunny's right shoulder, looked briefly into his face before returning to his shoulder.

"I'm not very good at knowing if people are being sincere or not."

"I was," Bunny assured her.

She gave the same brief dip of her head, then paused before adding, "You look older."

"Well, it's been, what? Ten years?"

"Eight years and four months."

"Really?"

"Yes," replied Rosie. "I have a very good memory for such things." She really did.

Bunny had first come into contact with Rosie Flint when she was a student reading economics at Trinity College Dublin and writing her dissertation on the ways in which financial hardship could lead to prostitution. She'd been frequenting what could be loosely termed as Dublin's red-light districts, although Bunny always hated that term. One of Bunny's old mentors, DI Roger Plummer, had a daughter who was at Trinity with her, and he'd become concerned. It wasn't safe for a young woman to be in those areas late at night. Rosie had countered that she was in those places precisely because they were already frequented by lots of women, and if they weren't safe then something should be done to protect all of them. That was Rosie; the woman had an innate ability to repeat your words back to you in such a way as to strip away all of the bullshit and leave your logic standing there naked and embarrassed.

Plummer had asked Bunny to shadow Rosie out of hours, as a favour to him. Unofficially, it had been Bunny's first bit of plainclothes work. The bit where he followed her hadn't lasted long, as three nights into Rosie's research trips, a self-styled pimp had objected to her presence. He had then been treated to Bunny's presence, which had resulted in a stay in hospital for the guy and Plummer's assurances that when he got out, he would be subjected to the undivided attention of the Garda Síochána.

Bunny had never actually said to Rosie that he'd just happened to be passing, but he also hadn't corrected her when she'd assumed that's what had happened. While she was positively antagonistic in her interactions with the police, he had offered her a lift home as her bike had been damaged in the confrontation with Dublin's answer to Huggy Bear, and she'd agreed. On the drive home, she'd explained her research to him and he'd offered to help. A little shaken by her experience, she'd accepted, and so he'd unofficially become Rosie Flint's chauffeur, on and off, for the next few months.

Bunny being Bunny, he'd got involved. It had been an eye-opening experience. He'd never been a big fan of the gardaí hassling women on street corners. It wasn't as if they were there by choice. The whole thing seemed to be symptomatic of a bigger problem that nobody wanted to deal with. The experience had helped to form in Bunny's head one of his unofficial rules – he wanted no part of any policing that came down to locking up the poor for being poor.

"So, to what do I owe the pleasure, Rosie?" Noticing her look of confusion, Bunny remembered to rephrase his question. Rosie had a truly brilliant mind, it just didn't run along the same track as everybody else's. "By which I mean, why are you here?"

"I was looking for you but I didn't know where you lived. I knew it was in Cabra, though, so I got the 38 bus here and just started ringing doorbells."

"Really? How long did that take?"

"Far less time than I had anticipated. Cabra has a population of approximately twenty thousand people, according to the last census. I assumed this would take all morning. I found somebody who knew you on my third door."

"You don't say." said Bunny, oddly proud of the fact.

"Yes. A gentleman in a blue tracksuit three roads over referred to you as 'that prick from Cork'."

Bunny's feeling of pride quickly dissipated. "Did he? Well, ye can't please everybody. What's so urgent that you came out here ringing doorbells at random?" Bunny's memory kicked in. "Hang on a sec – my doorbell doesn't work?"

It was hard to tell, given Rosie wasn't making eye contact with Bunny, but he thought she looked embarrassed.

"It does now," she said. "I tried to ring it and it didn't work, so I opened your door and fixed it."

"You opened my door?"

"It's actually quite easy to do with some very basic tools. I watched a video on the internet once, when I lost my keys."

Bunny paused for a second while he replayed Rosie's words in his head. "You broke into my house, fixed the doorbell, and then went back outside and rang it?"

Rosie gave the same almost robotic nod. "Yes. Technically, I didn't fix it. It just needed a new battery." She indicated the record bag she was wearing on her hip. "I always carry spare batteries with me."

Bunny was flummoxed as he considered what the correct response to this admission might be. He settled for moving on. "So, why are you looking for me?"

Rosie stared down at her ripped jeans and Doc Martens. Then, as if remembering something that she had disciplined herself to do, she raised her eyes to Bunny's shoulder. "Could we discuss that in private, please?"

Bunny looked behind her at the empty path. Seeing him do so, Rosie pointed to her right. "Your neighbour is standing behind her front door, listening to us."

"I most certainly am not," came the instant response from behind Cynthia Doyle's front door. "As it happens, I'm doing some dusting. I'm not listening to anything."

Bunny raised his voice slightly. "Howerya, Cynthia."

"I'm grand. How's yourself, Bunny? Do you want me to drop over some lasagne later?"

"I've actually got plans, but thanks for the offer." Bunny stepped to one side and opened his door wider. "Come on in, Rosie. We can have a cuppa and a proper catch-up."

Rosie took a step forward then hesitated. "Are you aware that you smell terrible?"

Bunny blushed. "Yes, sorry. I was working undercover and only got back a couple of hours ago. The immersion wasn't on so I thought I'd wait until later for a shower."

She gave that nod again. "Okay. If it was me, I would prefer if somebody told me."

"Me too," agreed Bunny. "Actually, I'll nip up and have a quick shower while the kettle's on."

Rosie trudged past him and made her way down the hallway towards the kitchen. Before Bunny could close the front door, Cynthia Doyle was out of her house and leaning over the low garden wall. "Is that the girl off the telly?" she whispered.

Bunny was confused. "Who? Rosie? I doubt it."

"It is," insisted Cynthia. "I'm sure of it. She was on that political programme last week. You know, the one with what's-his-name with the squint and all those revolving chairs. She got stuck into that awful minister. Yer man – that hairdo from Kildare. He thinks he's JFK but has the brains of a bucket of KFC."

Bunny peered down the hallway towards the door that Rosie Flint had just disappeared through. "I don't think that was her, but I'll ask."

"I'm telling you it was. By the way, she's right – you fecking stink."

———

Eight minutes and a hasty shower later, Bunny placed a cup of tea on the kitchen table in front of Rosie and sat down opposite her. He was aware the smell hadn't gone entirely – that would take a bath, minimum – but at least it had been beaten back to the point at which it would hopefully no longer be a topic of conversation.

"There you go, Rosie. Actually, before we get to your thing – have you been on telly recently?"

"Yes. I was on *Question Time* as the Head of SWIT."

"What now?"

"SWIT. Sex Workers of Ireland Together. I set up the organisation two years ago to campaign for the rights of sex workers. There was also a lot of discussion about violence against women."

Bunny nodded. "Fair play to you. I know it's a subject close to your heart. How did it go?"

She looked down at the tabletop. "Okay. I was very well prepared. I'm good when I'm well prepared, and this was important."

She didn't need to explain why.

On those long nights spent driving Rosie around the city, she'd eventually opened up to him about her unfortunate family history. Her father had passed away from cancer a couple of months after she was born, and then, when Rosie had been thirteen, her mother had been murdered. As if that wasn't bad enough, her murder had been at the hands of an ex-partner who she had reported to the police on numerous occasions. It had prompted a review at the time, which only rubbed salt in the wound as the gardaí was absolved of any blame. Incredibly, nobody found fault with a desk sergeant advising a woman with a broken jaw that maybe she and her ex should sit down with the parish priest, to see if they could save their relationship.

Rosie had been left alone to work her way through the foster-care system, with nothing but a burning hatred for the Garda Síochána to keep her warm. Luckily, she'd ended up with a brilliant pair of foster parents and she'd managed to get her life together. She'd gone to college on a full scholarship. In fact, there had been competition between universities to enrol her. Trinity had won, as it was closest to the flat off Parnell Square where Rosie and her mother had lived.

"So, Rosie, what's all this about?"

Bunny's guest rotated her cup of tea twice, then left it where it was. "I need you to find my boyfriend."

"Why? Where's he gone?"

"If I knew that, I would not need you to find him." From anyone else, the response would have been decidedly sarcastic in tone, but from Rosie it was merely a statement of fact.

"Right. Why don't you start at the beginning and explain what's happened?"

Rosie fixed her eyes on the cup in front of her as she spoke. "Two nights ago, Mark was supposed to be coming round to my apartment but he never showed up. That is very unusual. He is very reliable. I tried ringing him and got no response. The next morning, I dropped over to his apartment and there was no answer. I ... let myself in and he wasn't there. I had never been there before but some furniture was smashed and there was blood on the floor."

"Oh dear," said Bunny.

"Yes. That is when I rang the gardaí again."

"Again?"

Rosie pursed her lips. "Yes, I rang them the night before – when he didn't turn up. They laughed at me."

Bunny winced. Given her history, that was particularly unfortunate. "Ah. Right."

She flicked her eyes up to meet Bunny's briefly. "As I told them, he is very reliable."

"I'm assuming they took it a lot more seriously when you told them about the blood?"

She shook her head. "Not really. Two gardaí came round to the apartment and took a statement. Then a detective showed up and he kept asking me questions about how I'd got in."

"Really?"

"I explained to him like I explained to you – I had seen a video and it is actually pretty easy to do."

"Ah, I see. You didn't have a key to your boyfriend's apartment?"

She shook her head again. "No. He said my place was a lot nicer and he preferred to come and see me there. I didn't mind as I prefer to be at my place too."

"Fair enough. What did this detective say about the blood?"

"They spoke to some neighbours but nobody heard any kind of disturbance. They also went to the building site where Mark told me he worked, but they didn't know who he was. They said a Mark Smith had never worked there. They said the blood on its own could have lots of explanations. They suggested I keep trying to ring him or else I get a new boyfriend."

"Feck off," said Bunny. "They didn't really say that?"

"I think the detective was trying to be funny."

"Sounds like a right gobshite. What was the guy's name?"

"Detective Tierney."

Bunny resisted the urge to roll his eyes. "Owen Tierney?"

Rosie's eyes darted to Bunny's for a moment before she looked away again and gave a quick bob of her head.

"Well, that figures. He's a monumental prick. 'Tis hard to tell if he's completely incompetent and a bit lazy, or incredibly lazy and only a little incompetent, but the results are the same. He's an embarrassment to the uniform he inexplicably got out of. Him making detective is the eighth wonder of the world."

"That is why I came looking for you. I need you to find Mark."

Bunny was alarmed to see that Rosie's eyes were spilling over with tears, causing her mascara to run.

"Ah, here now. No need for that."

He twisted around in his chair and scanned the kitchen. There was no chance of a box of tissues but there might be some kitchen roll. When he turned back, Rosie had already produced a tissue from somewhere and was dabbing at her eyes.

"How long have you known Mark?"

"Almost six months."

"How did you meet?"

"I saved him."

"Excuse me?"

"It was outside Trinity. I'm a lecturer there now."

"Really? Fair play to you."

"Yes. I give lectures. I am good when I am well prepared." Bunny noted her repetition of the words from earlier. As if it were a rote phrase by which she lived.

"And you saved him?"

"Yes. I was crossing the street, then I turned round and happened to notice him stepping in front of a motorbike. I grabbed him and pulled him out of the way. Without me, he could have been killed." Rosie wasn't bragging in any way. As far as she was concerned, she was simply imparting facts.

"And do you know much about him?"

Rosie shrugged and rotated her untouched cup of tea once more. "I thought I did. I am confused as to why the building site had never heard of him. I even went there with a picture and asked around, but nobody recognised him." She pulled a photograph from the pocket of her jeans and held it out to Bunny. "The people there laughed at me too."

Bunny took the image and looked at it. It was of a well-built man in his early thirties, with shoulder-length brown hair and an angry red mark on his neck, possibly from a burn. He had his arm around Rosie, but it was neither the Rosie Bunny had known in the past nor the one that sat before him now. He had never seen her smiling so broadly before. She looked so happy.

"Okay. If you want, I can make a few calls and talk to a couple of people. I'm on sabbatical from the force at the moment, but I'll try to pull a few strings, see if I can get a better detective assigned to your case. Or, at the very least, get a boot put up the arse of the one you have got."

Rosie reached across and grabbed his hand. "No. It has to be you, Bunny," she insisted. "You're the only one I trust. I need you to find him."

Bunny was taken aback. He tried to pat her hand sympathetically, but she pulled it away.

"Listen, Rosie. I know this isn't what you want to hear, but there might not be a happy ending here. Sometimes people aren't who they tell us they are."

"Not Mark. Whatever's happened, I need to know. He is in trouble."

"But—"

"Do you know what it's like to love somebody completely and one day, without any real explanation, they just disappear?"

She might as well have punched him in the solar plexus. For a moment, all the air left Bunny's body and he closed his eyes, blindsided by a wave of emotion as a memory washed over him. He opened his eyes again to see Rosie staring straight at him.

He spoke in a soft voice. "As it happens, I do."

"Then you have to help me."

"Alright," said Bunny. "Let me make some calls."

Chapter Five

ANIMALS OF ALL KINDS

It was an established fact in certain areas of Dublin that it was impossible to stare down Bunny McGarry. Many had tried, none had succeeded. It looked as if that might soon change. Bunny wasn't sure for how long this staring contest had been going on, but he was damn sure he was not going to look away first. A precedent could not be set.

"Hiya, Bunny," came a familiar voice from behind him.

"Butch Cassidy, as I live and breathe," he replied without looking round. "How's it going?"

"Same old. Same old. Sorry I'm late. They had me sitting outside the court for three hours, waiting to testify, and then that dipshit of a prosecutor, Delaney, cuts a deal just before I was about to do my bit. I was up all last night practising my testimony. You know how I hate doing that."

"This is why you have to beat a signed confession out of every suspect," said Bunny. "It really cuts down on the admin."

"It's amazing they don't have you training new recruits down in Templemore."

"Well, I have offered."

"Are you okay? I've been standing here for, like, a minute and you haven't looked at me. Are we having a fight? I mean, it's cool if we are, but you should really let me know."

"If you must know, that cheeky little sod over there is staring me down, and I'm not going to let him win."

"Are you referring to the ring-tailed lemur?"

"I am. 'Tis the principle of the thing."

The lemur won an unexpected if well-deserved victory when Butch slapped Bunny soundly on the ear hole, forcing him to look away.

"Jesus, Butch!"

The diminutive yet dangerous figure of Pamela "Butch" Cassidy was looking up at him with a devilish grin. Behind her, a mother and three hyperactive children she was trying to corral were staring at them in utter horror.

"Mammy, that lady hit that man on the head."

Bunny smiled and waved at the children to show no harm was done. "'Tis alright, kids. She's a police officer. Violence is a necessary part of her job."

"Bunny!" hissed Butch under her breath. "Don't mind the silly man," she called over to the family. "We're only playing."

The dirty look the mother shot the pair, as she hurried her children away in the direction of the lion enclosure, made it clear she did not find their antics amusing.

"Are you trying to get me thrown off the force?"

"Well, I could use somebody to hang around with during the day. They don't half drag on."

Butch entirely failed to keep the exasperation from her voice. "Well, stop pissing about and come back to work, then. Is this what you're doing with your time? Mooching round Dublin Zoo, trying to get into fights with ring-tailed lemurs?"

"He started it."

Bunny held out the massive bag of popcorn he was halfway through, but Butch waved it away.

"Why are we meeting here?"

"What do you mean?" replied Bunny, a tad defensively. "Not only is Dublin Zoo widely regarded as one of the finest zoos in the world, but it also happens to be across the road from your office. Seeing as you're the one who asked to meet me, I think it's a very considerate choice of location."

"God, you're an awful sensitive lump of a man, aren't you? I actually meant the lemur enclosure. I'd have thought the gorillas would be more your speed?"

"Here, now – no slagging off the lemurs. They're a good bunch. Also, they're a matriarchal society, which I thought you'd appreciate."

Butch nodded approvingly. "I've always thought they had a distinct air of intelligence about them."

"Besides," continued Bunny, "as it happens, I'm banned from the monkey and ape area. Grossly unfair. The little buggers can chuck poo around all day, but you dare to throw one back ..." He bobbed his head in the opposite direction towards the reptile house. "Come on, let's go see some lizards."

"After being down at the courts all day, it feels like a bit of a busman's holiday, but okay."

They started walking slowly down the path, side by side. Around them, tourists sauntered along while parents chased after overexcited offspring, save for the occasional teenager moping in their wake.

Butch looked up at Bunny. "You look like shit by the way."

"Thanks. I'm giving up sleeping entirely."

"Nice. Suits you. Bit of heroin chic. Really brings out the massive bags under your eyes."

"Is this how lesbians flirt?"

"With men? Yes."

"So," said Bunny, changing tack. "Do you want to get your bit out of the way first?"

"Alright, yes." Butch sighed. "Rigger O'Rourke asked me to have a word with you. For such a smart bloke, he seems to cling on to the stupid idea that I might be able to talk you round."

"If it's such a waste of time, then why are you here?"

"Because for different reasons I want the same thing. Come on, Bunny. Stop pissing about and come back. The office is no craic without you and I'm sick of being lumped with Carlson all the time. I'm convinced Rigger keeps dumping me with him to punish me for not being able to convince you to come back. Look, I get it – you needed a break. But look at yourself. If you weren't ready to come back, would you be chasing scumbags around Temple Bar in the middle of the night with a flaming hurly?"

"You heard about that?"

"Are you kidding? I'd estimate there are, at most, three guards in the entire country who haven't heard about it. It's quite the story. I imagine they had to pull in a few favours to stop the newspapers from giving a full account. Consider yourself lucky nobody had any photographs. Oh, and before I forget …"

Butch jabbed Bunny in the gut with enough force to render any point she was making not entirely playful.

"Ouch. What the feck was that for?"

"You're pulling shit like that and you don't call me? What the hell, Bunny? What would've happened if you'd needed back-up?"

Bunny rubbed his stomach. "You've a peculiar way of showing you care. Besides, I didn't want to get you in trouble."

"And I don't want to see you re-enacting the cover of a Pink Floyd album. Next time you pull a stunt like that and don't tell me beforehand, it'll be me setting your stupid arse on fire."

"Noted," conceded Bunny. "I have to say, I never had you down as a Pink Floyd fan."

"Ex-girlfriend. Let's just say it was very easy to divvy up the albums." Butch leaned in, lowered her voice slightly, but failed to keep the excitement from it. "Seriously, though? A flaming hurly?"

Bunny could feel the broad grin breaking across his face. "I know it was a bit OTT, but fuck me, it looked amazing."

"I'll bet."

"Not the most practical of things to be running around with, in fairness. I think I singed my eyebrows."

"Worth it. I believe Detective Inspector Grainger is spitting feathers. Useless waste of space that he is."

"Actually," Bunny began, as he nimbly stepped around a toddler who was making a break for it, "speaking of useless wastes of space, you used to work with Owen Tierney, didn't you?"

Butch dodged the stressed-looking father who was attempting to hunt down his errant child.

"You know I did," she said, her voice filled with suspicion. "Why do you ask?"

"I need to have a chat with him. Could you maybe find out where he'll be in the next few hours?"

"Bunny!" Butch shook her head in exasperation.

"What?"

"Don't 'what' me. You know what. Your shenanigans from last night pissed off a lot of people. If you're so determined not to hop back on board, you need to stop messing around with Garda business."

"I just want to have a little chat with the man, that's all."

"So why don't you ring him, then?"

"I would do, but he hates me."

Butch rolled her eyes. "What a surprise. You've got more beefs on the go than Tupac and Biggie ever had."

"Who and what now?"

"Never mind."

"Fair enough. Besides, this is one of those chats you really need to have in person."

They came to a stop outside the door to the reptile house.

"D'ye know what," said Butch. "Do you mind if we don't do this? I'm not a massive fan of snakes." She caught the glint in Bunny's eye and jabbed a finger at him. "Don't."

"What?"

She broke out in an alarmingly good impression of his Cork accent. "Fear of snakes – is that a lesbian thing? Ha ha ha."

"Maybe I was going to say that. Maybe I wasn't. You'll never know," he said huffily, before shoving a fistful of popcorn into his mouth.

Butch studied the map of the zoo on the wall. "Let's go see the penguins instead. They're always good value."

Bunny shrugged in agreement and they moved off in the indicated direction.

"Before I tell you how to find him," Butch began reluctantly, "what business do you have with the legendary Garda Detective Owen Tierney?"

"The boyfriend of Rosie Flint, an old friend of mine, has disappeared and—" Bunny broke off as Butch twirled round and blocked his path.

"Rosie Flint? The SWIT woman?"

Bunny nodded.

"How the hell are you friends with her?"

Bunny waved his hand. "Long story. Doesn't matter. 'Tis no big deal. I'm just doing her a small favour."

"Are you sure? She happens to be quite a big deal. She may even have already had an effect on who's going to be the next taoiseach."

"What are you talking about? Isn't that what's-his-face?"

Butch shook her head in disbelief. "Do you ever read the front pages of the newspaper? Or do you just go straight to the GAA news and then use it to wipe the tomato sauce off your T-shirt?"

Bunny rolled his bottom lip out in a look of mock hurt. "The big words make my head hurt."

"That or the booze. Anyway, What's-his-face, as you refer to him, is a dead man walking. Dodgy expense claims. He's agreed to stay in power for a few weeks until they elect a new leader at this weekend's hastily convened convention. The presumptive heir to the throne was that shiny-faced so-and-so from Kildare – McCarty – until your mate got hold of him."

"Rosie?" asked Bunny. "Are you sure we're talking about the same woman? I mean, she's so smart that I actually couldn't tell you how smart she is because I don't understand half the things she says, but she doesn't strike me as the greatest of public speakers."

"That's exactly how she got him – lulled him into a false sense of security. They were both on that debate programme last week, with the decriminalisation of prostitution being one of the topics, obviously. McCarty says it's a blight on the country and makes some crack about organised crime controlling it. Rosie responds by saying that's precisely why it needs to be legalised, because history has proved time and again that the sex industry isn't going anywhere. If it's decriminalised, though, it'll be far safer for the sex workers, and the gardaí can focus their efforts on running the gangsters out of it."

"Reasonable point, I suppose," said Bunny. "At least, in theory."

"Yeah," agreed Butch. "But then McCarty – big smug grin on his face, like he thinks he's about to be really clever – makes a dig about wondering how SWIT is funded. Reckons he was going to throw her on the defensive. Herself responds by saying she's more than happy to show their accounts to anybody who wants to see them, as financial impropriety isn't acceptable anywhere, particularly in politics. She then goes on to point out how McCarty is very buddy-buddy with the gambling industry, and asks is he happy to confirm that he's never received any donations or gratuities from them?"

"Ouch."

Butch laughed. "Oh, yes, indeed. On the spot, McCarty goes for the deny, deny, deny approach. You could see it in his eyes as soon as the words left his mouth. Blood was in the water and every journalist with a pulse was on the phone before the show had even finished. They've now got him attending Royal Ascot, several matches at United, and skiing in the Alps, would you believe? All on the dime of those close friends he is now deeply regretting having. He's gone from being the next taoiseach to hanging on to his job for dear life and hoping the news cycle moves on."

"Is that right? Fair play, Rosie. I'm going to have to start reading the newspapers properly again. I gave up once the *Peanuts* cartoon stopped."

"You should, it's wide open now. There's five or six of them with their hats in the ring – including a woman aiming to be this country's first female leader as, embarrassingly, that hasn't happened yet."

"You seem very well informed about all this?"

"I've been on stake-outs for the last three weeks."

"Ah, right."

"My point is," continued Butch, "that your friend has just become a bit of an unlikely celebrity, and the last thing you need is your profile being raised. There'll come a point where the higher-ups are going to get sick of you grabbing headlines."

Bunny shoved the remnants of his bag of popcorn into a bin. "Ara, would you stop? Headlines. What headlines? The girl's fella has disappeared and she got lumped with that waste of space Tierney investigating. I just need to have a little chat with him – to make sure he's doing all he can to carry out his duties."

Butch folded her arms. "Right. So, why do I have such a terrible feeling about this?"

Bunny shrugged. "I dunno. Could be something to do with that massive snake behind you."

"Sure. I'm really going to fall for—"

Butch ended up giving him all the information he needed, primarily so that he'd promise never to tell anybody just how much she'd screamed at the sight of the poor zookeeper walking back from his show-and-tell with a large python draped around his shoulders.

Chapter Six

GOBSHITERY ON A BUDGET

Bunny held up the menu-that-wasn't-a-menu to his face. The reason you couldn't technically call it a menu was that, while it looked like one, it was a bill of dishes that were *possibly* available. The dining establishment in question was the Ken Chi all-you-can-eat buffet on Lower Abbey Street, and Bunny's current position was in the back corner booth. His vantage point offered a clear line of sight to the front door, and he was using the technically-not-a-menu to conceal himself from view. Normally, that would have passed for some solid basic espionage technique, except he was the only person in an all-you-can-eat buffet who wasn't eating. His day had worked out with some accidentally grim scheduling. After leaving the zoo – and once he'd stopped laughing himself to near death at the sight of the normally unflappable Butch Cassidy wetting herself following an unexpected close encounter with a bona fide snake – he'd paid a visit to the Mater Hospital. He'd received a message that Micky Flynn wanted to personally thank him for finding the two guys who had attacked him. It wasn't something Bunny would have expected, but turning down the request wasn't something he could do either.

Once at the hospital, he'd quickly realised that there was a world of difference between knowing what had happened to Micky Flynn and seeing the reality in the charred flesh. Even a couple of weeks after the event, nothing could prepare you for the damage inflicted upon the human body when a sadistic mind is given free rein with a bottle of lighter fluid.

Both he and Micky had done their best to keep the conversation cheerful, but the whole thing had felt wrong. A man lying in a hospital bed, having lost the sight in one eye and suffering burns to over sixty percent of his body, should not be thanking anybody for anything. He should be screaming at the sky, cursing God for being a bastard, and demanding unholy vengeance. Bunny didn't know the details but, given Micky's circumstances, it was a safe bet that he hadn't had the easiest of lives. Still, the fella had chatted and smiled, praised the doctors and nurses for all they'd done for him, and had even cracked a couple of jokes, but the knowledge of what he'd been through hung over everything like a thick black fog.

Bunny had felt embarrassed when Micky had grabbed his hand and thanked him tearfully. He had walked out the hospital doors with a roiling belly of bilious anger. The dark cloud had stayed with him for the rest of the day, and his mind had kept going over the events of the previous night again and again, only on these occasions the two scumbags either didn't make it to the Liffey or didn't make it out of the Liffey. Justice was a nice idea in theory, but in practice it disappointed more often than not. The courts would never give those maggots what they truly deserved. It wasn't the first time Bunny had felt this way. Far from it. The truth was, the police don't really fight crime so much as clean up after it.

With the above in mind, having to spend his evening sitting in an all-you-can-eat buffet that prided itself on its Korean barbecue section felt like some kind of sick joke. He wanted to go home to his bed, but he'd made Rosie Flint a promise. He also had zero appetite – an unprecedented state of affairs. He probably should have filled up a plate anyway, for the look of the thing, but after sleeping rough, the idea of wasting food seemed equally unpalatable.

In the half-hour he'd been sitting there, three different members of staff had approached him and explained the concept of a buffet to him in increasingly exasperated tones. He'd apologised on each occasion and had assured them that he was just deciding what he wanted to eat. In fact, he'd already resolved to slip the next server twenty quid and explain he just wanted to sit there for a bit.

He'd already paid the cover charge on the way in and, luckily, it being a Tuesday evening, the place was unlikely to get that busy. Capacity was currently hovering around the thirty-customer mark, and it didn't look as if it would rise much higher, but on weekends this place would be rammed with discerning diners on a budget. It was a good-sized space, mostly filled with long tables with wooden benches running along either side, designed to get people in, fed, and out again with the maximum of choice and the minimum of fuss.

The three members of staff out on the floor, who Bunny guessed were the husband and wife that owned the place and a daughter or a niece, were huddled around the cash register, quite possibly trying to decide who should take another crack at explaining how buffets work to the lunatic in the corner. At that moment, the husband spotted someone walking through the front door and nudged his wife. Bunny ducked behind his non-menu.

While Bunny might have proved a source of confusion for the staff, this new arrival clearly inspired a very different set of emotions in them. Bunny had once seen a dog owner pulling a poo out of the arse of her embarrassed canine companion, after the mutt had found some string that was too delicious not to eat. The memory of the expression on the dog owner's face came back to him as he watched the older woman take the cover charge from their latest customer.

The new diner, if anything, basked in the glow of their hatred as he pulled a large plate from his bag. He headed straight for the buffet, ignoring the concept of queueing as he did so, and began to load up. Bunny held up the non-menu menu to shield his face completely, although the person was so intently focused on his objective that there was every chance Bunny could stand up, take off his clothes, start dancing the "Hokey Cokey" and he would still go unseen.

Oddly, despite having stared at it for a considerable length of time, Bunny only noticed now that the menu didn't actually say "all you can eat". Either the result of a typo or a linguistic misunderstanding from somebody working in their second language, it actually read "eat all you can". It was amazing how one subtle change made the dining experience seem less like a fun treat and more like a grim attempt to gorge oneself into an early grave.

The man with the massive plate seemed to be interpreting the wording as a challenge, as he loaded up with a gluttonous serving that was almost exclusively meat. This was the man, the myth, the embarrassment that was Detective Owen "Tape" Tierney.

Tape – short for Tapeworm – came from the fact that Tierney's legendary appetite did not match his freakishly scrawny build. That being said, while you could say he was rake-thin, you couldn't describe him as looking healthy. His skin had a sweaty, jaundiced tinge to it, and his thinning hair hung over a face that was not designed to express joy. While he was capable of varying his expression, it seemed never to leave the sphere of a sneer.

Bunny peered over the top of the menu to observe the husband and wife in the midst of a rather heated, if whispered, discussion. Judging from the body language, he would bet a tenner that the wife was strongly suggesting that the one-man plague of locusts either play by the rules or take his business elsewhere, while the husband was countering that such an approach wouldn't be worth the effort. Bunny would go double or quits that they'd had this conversation a few times in the past, and it always ended the same way. Tierney was precisely the kind of prick who would wave his Garda ID around at the first sign of being challenged. The man had always been a small-minded little bully who took a perverse delight in gaming the system.

Bunny watched Tierney take a seat at the end of an unoccupied table and gave him a couple of minutes to wolf down a sizeable chunk of the mountain on his plate before making his move. As Bunny sat down opposite the human dustbin, Tierney didn't even look up from his plate.

"That seat's taken," he grunted through a mouthful of food.

"Now, Tape, is that any way to greet an old friend?"

Tierney flinched involuntarily, revealing how much the nickname irritated him. "Friend? I think you've got me confused with somebody else, McGarry."

"Ah, there's no need to be like that. Aren't we just two work colleagues bumping into each other in a social environment?"

"Is that what we are? What are you doing here, *Bunny*?" Tierney's heavy emphasis on his name mistakenly assumed that Bunny shared his aversion to the nickname life had assigned him. The man had no feel for people. If Tierney had really wanted to annoy him, he should have gone with his actual name – Bernard.

"Sure, haven't I come to eat all I can, same as yourself?" He indicated the plate in front of Tierney. "I take it you're a regular? You navigated that buffet like a pro."

Tierney jutted his chin before cautiously returning some of his attention to the food in front of him and resuming his consumption of it at a slower rate. "Yeah. The food isn't bad if you know what you're doing. Don't fill up on all that vegetable crap. That's how they get ye."

"Good tip," said Bunny. He'd decided to take the spoonful-of-sugar approach – at least initially, although it was doubtful that Tierney would taste it, given how much else he was shovelling into his mouth.

"Yeah," continued Tierney, warming to his subject. "And don't let them tell you there are limits, or any of that bullshit." He jabbed his knife in the direction of the front door. "If it says 'all you can eat' outside, then it's all you can eat. End. Of. Story. If it's out, then it's fair game." Tierney raised his eyebrows and licked his lips, turning the sneer dial to conspiratorial. "Last week, out in this place in Balbriggan, I nabbed an entire chocolate cake. They were spitting feathers about that."

"I'd imagine."

"Had to flash the badge, remind them whose country they were in. We didn't stage a revolution just to have some other bunch of foreigners coming over here and telling us what's what."

"Fair point," said Bunny. "I'm not sure that's exactly what Michael

Collins was fighting for, but I suppose the overall principle is similar."

Thankfully, Tierney was now so focused on ripping the flesh off a barbecued rib that the sarcasm passed him by. He sucked the sauce off his fingers and nodded. "You've got to watch these Chinks or they'll rob you blind."

In the interest of the softly softly approach, Bunny knew he should just let the slur go, but it'd been a very long day and he was running short of patience. "I'm pretty sure that's not the right word, Tape – and not just because I'm fairly certain the family that own the gaff are Korean."

"Whatever. Gooks. Call them what you want."

Bunny clenched his fist under the table. "Let's just stick with Chinese or Korean, shall we?"

Impressively, Tierney managed to change sneers while simultaneously shoving some kind of sausage into his mouth. He spoke around his mouthful of food, losing some of it in the process. "Oh, here we go with the political correctness," he mumbled, making air quotes around the last two words.

"You know," began Bunny, "they're a funny couple of words, aren't they – 'political correctness'? I'm a muck savage from the shitty end of Cork, and nobody's idea of diplomat material, but it strikes me that those two words are simply a derogatory label for what used to be known as basic manners. I live by a very simple rule because I'm a very simple man: people deserve respect until they prove they don't. I don't really care who they are, where they're from or what they look like."

Tierney swallowed and belched. "I didn't come here for a lecture."

"No," agreed Bunny. "You came here to eat a meal in the most dickish way imaginable."

Bunny caught Tierney's eyes flashing up to the corner of the ceiling and then back down to the plate in front of him. So that's how it was going to be.

He leaned forward and pushed Tierney's plate to one side.

"What the fuck are you doing?"

Bunny smiled. "I just need your undivided attention for a couple of moments, Tape. I believe you're the lead on an investigation involving one Mark Smith?"

"What's it to you?"

"As it happens, his girlfriend, Rosie Flint, is an old friend of mine and I said I'd help her out."

Tierney rolled his eyes. "Oh Jesus, I met her. The retard."

Bunny gripped the table so tightly that his knuckles went white, but to anyone who didn't know better his voice came out still sounding jovial. "The woman has a PhD in economics, is quite possibly one of the smartest people on the planet, and she might one day win a Nobel Prize or something like that, so I think you might have wrongly assessed the situation there, Tape. Perhaps your normally excellent detective skills have deserted you? How about you focus on giving me a quick update on the case and I can let you get back to enjoying your meal?"

"Why should I?"

"Call it a professional courtesy."

The two men locked eyes for a few seconds. Tierney blinked first. A little part of Bunny's mind was reassured to know that while ring-tailed lemurs might be beyond him, the McGarry stare was still maintaining a perfect record against humanity.

Tierney seemed to gather himself, if you could call it that, and summoned a bit of bravery. He gave what he mistakenly thought passed as a smile. "I was sorry to hear about your partner, Gringo, kicking the bucket. Still, not to speak ill of the dead, but he was always a bit of a reckless arsehole. No offence."

Bunny smiled back for several seconds. Tierney did his best to hold his grimace but couldn't quite pull it off. Laughing in the face of death is one thing but sounding like you mean it is something else entirely.

Bunny let out a noise that, to the uninitiated, might be mistaken for a chuckle. Those who knew him well would already be looking for somewhere to hide.

"Tape, Tape, Tape – you are a gas man. Always looking for a way to cheat the system, aren't you? Whether it be at work, where, let's be honest, you've somehow managed to keep your job despite your frankly piss-poor performance. Or coming to a buffet and being an arsehole just because you enjoy it. And now you've decided that you can get your revenge on me by winding me up enough that I'll give you the slap you so richly deserve." Bunny pointed back over his shoulder. "In full view of that security camera behind me. It's a fun little plan."

Bunny's smile widened as Tierney's fell away. "Got one teeny-tiny flaw, though," he continued. "I was here before you. I had a pretty good idea, seeing as I'm me and you're you, how this could go. That's why I asked Joe over there – that's the name of the nice man from Korea whose restaurant you're in – to turn off the cameras. I didn't even have to flash my Garda ID like I know you love to do."

Tierney started to move back but Bunny reached out and placed his hand over his. "Now, of course, you could still go looking for witnesses, but you have to ask yourself, do you reckon you've ingratiated yourself with the staff here?"

"You're full of crap." Tierney tried to sound confident but his voice cracked halfway through.

Bunny laughed again, louder this time. "Of course I am, and you are more than welcome to find out for sure. Or, you could just tell me what I want to know."

Tierney tried to pull his hand away but Bunny's grip was firm. "There's not even anything to know."

"You went into the guy's apartment and there was blood on the floor. I believe that in the business that's what we call a clue."

"The guy was an alco. The—" Tierney stopped himself. "Your friend even told us that. There was booze all over the place. Broken glass. Smashed furniture. Looked like somebody falling off the wagon hard."

"Is that so? And how many minutes did it take you to reach that conclusion?"

Tierney winced as the pressure on his fingers intensified slightly. "Listen to me. The whole thing was a waste of time. I contacted the landlord. He told me the apartment was paid for by some company or other, but the name of the guy staying there wasn't even Mark Smith – it was Daniel Poole. For fuck's sake – Mark Smith. It even sounds made up. My guess is the bloke is married and he's over here getting his end away, telling stupid bints anything they want to hear to get into their pants. Your friend was just a meaningless fuck."

Bunny drew a deep breath and slowly let it out again. "Is that it?"

"That's it."

He released Tierney's hand, stood and turned towards the door, just as the proprietor sidled up to the table, a nervous smile on his lips. "Is everything okay, gentlemen?"

Bunny turned and looked at Tierney, who had the appearance of a cornered animal, his eyes darting between Bunny and the owner. After a moment, Tierney drew his plate back in front of him and picked up his fork. He didn't look up as he mumbled, "Fine, thank you, Joe."

"Okay," replied the proprietor in the forced cheerful tone that anyone who deals with the public on a regular basis has learned. "Good, good, good. By the way, my name is Ben."

Bunny doffed an imaginary cap. "Enjoy your meal."

———

As he walked out onto the street, Bunny pulled his mobile from his pocket and scrolled quickly through his contacts to find the number he needed. She answered on the second ring.

"Gráinne – quick question for you. Would you happen to be free and fancy earning yourself a swift fifty quid?"

———

Fifty-four minutes and three mountainous plates later, Tape Tierney exited Ken Chi's all-you-can-eat buffet. Following the run-in with McGarry, he hadn't been able to enjoy the rest of his meal, but had still eaten it on principle. He never left a tip but on this occasion he didn't do so for a particular reason – he couldn't accurately express it, but he felt the staff had played a part in his humiliation.

As he headed towards the station to pick up his car, he noticed a black girl in a wheelchair, pushing herself down the footpath towards him. Bloody typical – between the bin bags out on the kerb for the morning collection and the wall there wasn't room for him to pass her. She was taking up the whole bloody footpath. No consideration for anybody else. Reluctantly, he stood to one side. What were the odds she wouldn't even thank him and apologise for the inconvenience? If she didn't, he was going to give her a piece of his mind.

As the girl drew level with him, she looked up and gave him a big smile. "Thanks very much, guard."

Even as he gave a nod of acknowledgement, a little alarm bell in the back of his head went off. How did she know he was—

His train of thought was interrupted by an unbelievably strong elbow being rammed into his groin. All the air left his body as he doubled over in more agony than he had ever experienced in his life.

Through tear-filled eyes he looked up to see the girl still smiling down at him. The only thing she said before speeding off was, "And you can shove that political correctness up your arse."

Chapter Seven

NOTHING IS EVER GOING TO BE REAL

Bunny sat and watched Rosie Flint pace back and forth across her kitchen floor. His old friend was blinking rapidly and rubbing the palms of her hands together.

He pinched the bridge of his nose and took a deep breath. He was all kinds of tired. After three nights of precious little sleep, he had fully intended to spend today in bed, followed by a dirty big takeaway and a few pints in O'Hagan's, but instead, he'd been involved in trying to investigate the disappearance of Mark Smith on Rosie's behalf. While the timing had been far from ideal, he'd been happy to help. He might not have seen her in a while, but Rosie was a good friend and, more importantly, a person who had made it her mission to help the kind of people that most of society either ignored or treated like lepers. A tad unusual she might be, but Rosie Flint was one of the good ones. None of which made Bunny any less exhausted.

Still, after pulling up a stool by the window in the pub opposite Ken Chi's all-you-can-eat buffet for just long enough to watch Gráinne Dolan, all-round bad ass and older sister of the St Jude's Under-12s full back, slam a beautifully placed elbow into the oh so deserving testicles of Owen "Tape" Tierney, Bunny had started fantasising about a glorious reunion with his bed. Then Rosie had rung him. He'd been considering waiting until the morning to call her to offer an update but circumstances had outrun him – as soon as she'd returned home, she'd been certain that someone had been in her apartment.

Bunny had grabbed a taxi and rushed over to find her in quite a mess. As a rule, he strongly disliked it when the unqualified offered diagnoses, but to his untrained eye, it was fair to say that the poor girl was in a near-manic state. From the little sense he got out of her, nothing had been taken and there were no signs of forced entry. Her reason for saying that someone had been in her apartment was that things had been moved around. She'd offered as evidence the fact that her DVDs were now in a different order and the knife block on the counter had been moved less than six inches to the left.

The apartment itself was a weird shrine to 1970s punk. The walls were adorned with posters of the Ramones, the Sex Pistols, the Clash, Stiff Little Fingers, and several bands Bunny had never heard of. They were all perfectly aligned and evenly spaced – down to the last millimetre, he was willing to bet. It was odd to see the most chaotic genre of music ever to birth itself into existence, kicking and spitting, being celebrated in the most anally retentive manner imaginable. Everything about the place screamed that it was tidied obsessively and kept constantly in a regimented state, and Bunny could well believe that Rosie might notice a DVD out of place or an object being moved six inches.

In the absence of any better ideas, Bunny had put on the kettle, sat down at the kitchen table, and waited for the water to boil and Rosie to cool off. It looked as if the kettle were a firm favourite to win the race. If Rosie kept pacing like this, there was every chance she would wear a groove into the wooden flooring.

"I'm not going crazy," she told him. "I know how it looks. I know what I know. I'm not going crazy."

Bunny spoke in a calm voice, essentially repeating the same assurances he'd already given her several times. "Rosie, sweetheart, nobody thinks you're going crazy – I promise. You need to take a moment to try and calm down. Just stall the ball for a second."

She stopped and looked him in the eye, before her gaze slid down to his shoulder.

"I will do everything I can to help," continued Bunny, "but you have to sit down and let me. Okay?"

Rosie worried at her thumbnail for a moment, then nodded several times before taking a seat on the edge of the chair opposite him.

"Good," encouraged Bunny. "Now, is there anything in the apartment that somebody might be looking for?"

"No. I don't keep cash here. I don't have much in the way of valuables. My laptop is still here. TV. DVD player."

"Right. Did Mark have a key to the apartment?"

She looked taken aback by the question. "He did, but why would he be here when I'm not here? I've been trying to ring him all day – every fifteen minutes. If he was here he would have left a note. He would have let me know he was okay."

Bunny scratched at his ear. "I'm sure he would have."

A rapid series of blinks flashed across Rosie's face. "What are you not telling me?"

Bunny held out his hands in a placatory gesture. "Nothing."

"What have you found out from your investigations today?"

He hesitated. In the cold light of day, all he'd managed to discover so far was what Tape Tierney knew, which effectively meant he was copying his homework off the laziest boy in school. "I spoke to Detective Tierney, just to see what the gardaí had so far." He hesitated. "He mentioned that Mark was an alcoholic?"

Rosie blinked twice and nodded. "I told him that. He's been on the wagon since before I met him. I didn't pry but I know he's going to meetings."

"Okay. Good." Bunny suddenly felt as if he should be taking notes, but he didn't have a notepad or anything else with him. He'd long ago learned that people always felt somewhat validated when you took down what they were saying, even if it was of little consequence.

"Did he ever mention a Daniel Poole?"

"No. Who is that?"

Behind Rosie, the kettle clicked itself off.

"The landlord says that's the name on Mark's apartment lease. At least, that's according to Detective Tierney, who admittedly is not the world's most reliable source of information. Still, do you have any idea why Mark might not be named on the lease?"

Rosie gave her head the briefest of shakes and stared down at the kitchen table where her fingers were nervously skittering out a rat-a-tat beat. She spoke without raising her gaze, her voice suddenly soft. "I know how this looks – a different name on the lease, the building site I thought he worked at not knowing who he is. Before you ask, no, I don't know a great deal about where he comes from or his past. He's from England, somewhere near Sunderland, but he said he hasn't been back in years. No family to speak of. He worked around the world but he hates to talk about it, so we didn't."

She ran trembling fingers through her pink hair. "All of that makes it sound like I don't know the man at all." Her eyes rose and caught Bunny in a ferociously intense gaze that she managed to hold. "But I do. You know my history, Bunny. I, more than anyone, get how somebody doesn't want to be defined by their past. And no, we didn't know each other for that long – but believe me, it was long enough. We were in love." Her breath caught in her throat for a moment before she corrected herself. "*Are* in love. I don't know why he lied. I guess he had his reasons, but the other things we said, the moments we shared – they were real." Her eyes fell and refocused on a spot on the floor. "Or if they weren't, then nothing is ever going to be real."

Bunny didn't know what to say to that.

She looked up at his shoulder, tears in her eyes. "So what's our next move?"

What indeed.

Chapter Eight

EXILES

Bunny stood in the centre of the room and slowly turned in a full circle. It was a trick he'd picked up from his old sergeant, Gearoid "Grinner" Morgan, in his early days on the force – take in the whole thing and then note what stood out, what was there, what was missing, what was unusual.

The room he was standing in was the front room cum kitchen of Mark Smith's one-bed apartment. Rosie Flint had offered to come to help gain access, but Bunny had assured her it wasn't necessary. She might have taught herself how to pick a lock using the internet, but Bunny had possessed the skill to do so long before the internet was a thing. He had learned from a man who was quite possibly one of the best thieves in Ireland – at least, hypothetically. That was the thing with someone who was that good at what they did – only they really knew for sure how many times they'd got away with their crimes. Bunny had been charged with bringing the man to and from court every day, and ironically, getting him talking about his favourite subject had been a good way of distracting him from engaging in any escapology attempts. The only reason he'd got caught in the first place was that he'd made the mistake of screwing around on his missus. Hell hath no fury like a woman scorned, and who knows where you store your stolen goods.

Bunny could see why Mark Smith had avoided bringing Rosie back to his place. Her apartment really was an awful lot nicer. This one was on the third floor of one of the many identikit redbrick boxes that had sprung up across the city in the last decade. When building anything, it is accepted wisdom that you can have two out of three from cheap, fast and good. This place reeked of the first two. As apartment buildings went, it wasn't poo-in-the-lift bad, but on his way up, Bunny had noticed a quartet of bin bags dumped in front of a rubbish chute that was out of order. The whole place looked as if it could do with a lick of paint too. At least he didn't have to worry about any nosy neighbours noticing that he'd let himself in. It was the kind of building where nobody knew anybody on more than a polite-nod-in-the-hallway basis.

The room all but vibrated to the bassline of the tedious dance music coming from the floor above. What it lacked in variety it more than made up for in volume. Bunny could feel a migraine coming on. As for the flat itself, whatever had gone on here, it was highly unlikely that the weapon used was a cat, as there was nowhere near enough room to swing one. A glass double door at one end of the room led to a balcony, on which there was barely enough space to stand. It overlooked the internal courtyard, which meant that, at least in theory, people in the flats opposite might have seen something. Bunny would bet several of his bodily organs that Detective Tierney's canvassing of the area had consisted of knocking on the doors to the neighbouring apartments on either side. Bunny took a mental note that checking in with those opposite was a possible avenue to explore. Before that, though ...

Bunny completed his three-hundred-and-sixty-degree turn.

The place didn't feel like a home. The paltry number of possessions and the absence of any personalised decor gave the vibe of somewhere someone did not expect to stay too long. That was the overview of the more mundane elements of the picture, but then there was the more arresting evidence. The coffee table lay crumpled on two legs. The cheap TV was on its side, a corner of its screen smashed. One of the two flimsy-looking chairs that went with the tiny IKEA table in the kitchen had been reduced to kindling. The signs of a violent struggle were clear. What was less clear was whether that struggle had been between two or more individuals, or between one man and his demons. A large bottle of cheap vodka lay on the floor, and under it, on the cheap off-white carpet, was an unmistakable circular bloodstain. A couple of empty bottles of red wine sat on the kitchen counter. Hallmarks of a bender.

Bunny took a handkerchief out of his coat pocket and hunkered down. He picked up the vodka bottle and examined the label. The name was something in Russian with a couple of letters in Cyrillic script to make it look authentic. Below it was an image of two angry bears wrestling. Maybe Mark Smith and whoever else had been recreating the branding and things had got out of hand? Something about the label bothered Bunny but he couldn't put his finger on exactly what.

He swore under his breath as his train of thought was derailed by his mobile ringing. He carefully placed the bottle back where it had been, stood up and dug the phone out of his coat pocket. He'd been expecting it to be Rosie, checking in to see if he'd come up with anything. It wasn't. Bunny didn't exactly recognise the number but he spotted the Kerry area code and put two and two together. He answered.

"Deccie Fadden – the one and only. Accept no substitutes."

Deccie, the assistant manager of the St Jude's Under-12s hurling team, was in the midst of a traumatic situation – at least, as far as he was concerned. His grandparents, with whom he lived, had won ten grand on the Lotto and were off fulfilling their lifetime ambition of going on a cruise around the Med. Initially, Deccie had been delighted with the news of their windfall, assembling what amounted to an early Christmas list of things he wanted, which Bunny noted included several items that were illegal for him to own, and a couple that were illegal for *anyone* to own. Bunny received assurances that the crossbow was solely for self-defence purposes and that Deccie would be a responsible archer. Bunny had taken him at his word, if only because the odds on Deccie's grandmother buying him such a weapon were about the same as her buying her twelve-year-old grandson a motorbike, a hang glider or the services of a bodyguard (all of which had also featured on the list).

Instead, what Deccie got was a month at a Gaeltacht school in Kerry to improve his Irish language skills. This wouldn't prove too much of a challenge as Bunny knew for a fact that such skills had been limited previously to being able to ask to go to the toilet, please, sir. In fact, Deccie's grasp of the language had already improved, seeing as he now knew what the Gaeltacht meant, although he was extremely unhappy about it.

"Boss," said Deccie, "you've got to get me out of here. These people are monsters."

"I'm fine," responded Bunny. "Thanks for asking. But enough about me."

"Boss, don't mess about. This is life or death."

"How exactly is it life or death, Deccie? Improving on your frankly piss-poor grasp of the national language is unlikely to do any permanent damage, although I have no doubt the process will be painful for all concerned. Have you even been there a day yet?"

"No," pleaded Deccie, "and that is precisely my point. This headmaster fella instantly decided that he hates me. Him and all the staff."

"I'm sure they don't," said Bunny, not entirely believing it. For better or worse, and it was normally for the worse, Deccie Fadden had a way of making a first impression.

"They have, boss. They have. These culchies – they're all inbred country bumpkins down here. They hate us Dubs."

"I can't imagine why," said Bunny. "And by the way, Deccie, I'm also one of those culchies."

"Ah, don't put yourself down, boss. Cork is almost a city. And you've done very well for yourself, given your rough start in life."

"You see, Declan? You can turn the charm on when you want to. Maybe try some of that on the staff?"

"It's too late – they've already made up their minds. Small-minded so-and-sos. I think they're intimidated by my sophisticated big-city ways. They can't even take a bit of constructive feedback."

"I'm afraid to ask, but ... What kind of constructive feedback did you feel compelled to give them on your first day?"

"All I said was the whole place smells of cow shit. You'd think they'd want to know that?"

"Were you able to say that in Irish?"

"Be serious, boss. This is an emergency. You need to come and bust me out. Tell them you need me for important police business."

"I'm a bit busy at the moment, Declan, but I'll send you a cake with an Irish dictionary in it as soon as I can. In the meantime, remember these three words and they'll get you out of any bother. *Gabh mo leithscéal.* Quick, say it back to me."

"What's it mean?"

"Those three words, Declan, will have you accepted into the sacred guild of Irish speakers, in spite of you being one of those hyper-sophisticated Dublin dilettantes. Listen carefully – *gabh mo leithscéal.* Say it."

"God my legs fail."

"*Gabh mo leithscéal.*"

"Gob my lips scale."

"*Gabh mo leithscéal.*"

"Gab me lets mail."

Bunny sighed. "Close enough. Go with God, Deccie."

"No, boss – wait!"

He hung up the phone and shook his head. "Other countries are sending monkeys into space."

He tried to refocus himself on the crime scene in which he was standing while also technically committing a crime by being there. Something was gnawing at the edge of his consciousness, a half-formed thought that couldn't find full expression. He scanned the room again then moved back into the cramped hallway, across which lay the tiny bathroom and bedroom.

Bunny moved into the bedroom. The double bed took up most of the available space. It was made – not a crease to be seen. The small wardrobe in the corner contained three shirts, an overcoat, and a small selection of T-shirts, all ironed and neatly folded. You could cut yourself on the corners. The drawer below contained underwear, fastidiously arranged in a similar fashion.

Bunny felt a slight draught. He moved across to the window and noticed that it wasn't closed properly. He pulled out his handkerchief again and as he carefully pushed the handle, the hinges gave a pained squeal. From somewhere below, cigarette smoke wafted up on the night air. The bottom hinge on the casement looked as if it had broken and an unsuccessful attempt had been made to fix it. Bunny leaned out and peered around. There, on the outer side of the window, he noticed a dark stain. He studied it more closely. Blood. Not just blood – bloody fingerprints.

He looked down. Down on the ground were some bushes. It wouldn't be a pleasant experience but it would certainly be possible to jump from this window and survive. The possibility raised more questions than it answered. What would cause Mark Smith, or anyone else for that matter, to jump from this window? You'd only do that if you couldn't leave by the front door. Even then, you'd jump off the balcony, wouldn't you?

Bunny closed his eyes and tried to conjure thoughts in his exhausted mind. He attempted to block out the thumping bassline from above. *Can't go out the front door – which means you think there's either somebody outside it or blocking access to it. Can't go out the balcony door because somebody is blocking that. The same somebody you've just had a fight with in the front room. The person who has wounded you. The one you've decided you desperately need to get away from. Either you'd thought it out beforehand or you improvise the emergency escape route by jumping out the window into bushes below.* Unless Bunny had missed it, there was no blood on the walls in the hallway or the bedroom. That seemed unlikely. Unless it had been cleaned and ...

The thought that had been floating on the edge of Bunny's consciousness finally made itself known. He hurried back into the front room, bent down and carefully picked up the vodka bottle again, examining it as he slowly rotated it.

It had been on top of the large bloodstain, but there was no blood on it – not a single speck. The bottle had been placed there a considerable time after the blood had been spilled.

Whatever had happened here, someone had felt the need to escape it by jumping wounded from a third-floor window, and then someone else had tried to cover it up after the fact by making it look like an alcoholic not only falling off the wagon but also tumbling down a cliff into the great abyss.

Perhaps Rosie Flint wasn't crazy after all.

Chapter Nine

ROAD SAFETY

The Spider enjoyed speed. He worked his way smoothly through the BMW's gears and moved into the middle lane to undertake some deadbeat who didn't understand what the fast lane was for, then floored it.

It wasn't just that he enjoyed speed, he found it helped to clear his mind. There was something about being in control of a superbly engineered machine travelling at well over 100 miles an hour that got the synapses firing. The problem with this godforsaken yet God-bothering little country was that it didn't have the roads to allow you to really open her up. He was currently travelling along the M50, which the Irish considered to be a motorway, despite the fact that it appeared to have only two lanes in most places. The only way he could reach anything like a satisfying speed was to do what he was doing now – go out at three in the morning.

Even in developing-world shitholes there was always some way to get a decent drive in. This crappy little island was barely a country at all – more like a car park with trees and an overabundance of pubs. Churchill had been right – push it off into the Atlantic and be done with it. Plus, if Ireland were to float away, there was no doubt an abundance of valuable resources located in the space it was occupying. Such an approach was impossible, of course, but he liked to think he was doing the next best thing.

He needed to be sharp. After all the preparation, research and subtle manipulation, they were now in the endgame. Finally. Once it was done, he promised himself never to take another contract on this grim little island. The last week had been challenging, though by no means all bad. He'd watched a few months of work become redundant as one of the main players had been removed from the board live on TV. While he would never admit as much to anyone else, it had never occurred to the Spider that a man accepting freebies to attend numerous sporting events would constitute a scandal.

Still, that was the Irish for you. Something that wouldn't even be worthy of a newspaper article across the Atlantic, or indeed the Irish Sea, was somehow something for them all to get worked up about. In his mind, it had little to do with morals and a whole lot more to do with basic grubby jealousy. Small people with small minds and small lives in a tiny little country, like crabs in a bucket, dragging back down any of their compatriots who dared to try to climb out.

The only reason the Spider had been watching the TV show in question was that there was somebody on it who definitely shouldn't have been. Maybe it was just a peculiar twist of fate, but the Spider hadn't got to where he was in life by believing in coincidences. The possibility that there were other players in the game couldn't be ruled out. If that was the case, it made the screw-up he was on his way to discuss all the more unforgivable. He decelerated, moving quickly down the gears. His exit was coming up.

Five minutes later, the Spider pulled in to the unlit car park of a public beach. Over the dark brooding dunes the wash of light from a distant lighthouse periodically brightened the sky. A car was waiting there for him and had been for over an hour. That was no accident. It was the way the Spider had chosen to make clear his displeasure to the individual inside it. One of the ways, at least.

Furkser, up to this point, had been an invaluable asset. The man was discreet, efficient, and unburdened by moral squeamishness. The Spider had used him on several projects and compensated him handsomely for his work. In truth, the Spider held himself partly to blame. He knew it never paid to mix the personal with the professional. When Furkser had come to him and told him he had an ex-army buddy who was looking for work, the answer should have been no. Instead, they'd taken him on. His CV had been on point. Ex-special forces, having seen plenty of action, only some of which was officially acknowledged – he had the kind of skill set that had proven useful in the past. The Spider's research also threw up some personal problems, but that was more or less par for the course when you're hiring the kind of individual who can put a bullet in somebody's head when instructed to do so. The plan had been to use him in a low-level role, carrying out some basic surveillance. Hardly taxing. Break him in – see if he could be of more use down the line. Instead, he had screwed the pooch.

The Spider pulled up his car alongside Furkser's so that the drivers' windows were side by side and the two men could talk without getting out. He buzzed his down.

"How could this happen?" he snapped.

"It happened," replied Furkser evenly.

The Spider narrowed his eyes. "Given that you vouched for this man, if I were you, I would be very careful with the tone I adopt."

Furkser's granite jaw tightened for a moment and there was a twitch of irritation in his face. The Spider imagined the man was dealing with something he was not used to: embarrassment.

They rarely met face to face. As he studied Furkser, he noticed the guy was greying around the temples. Maybe he was getting old? Losing his touch? The Spider had already been considering freshening up the team after this job. Yes, there would always be a place for experience, but fieldwork was still a young man's game. Luckily, there was never a shortage of young, highly skilled men who had become disillusioned with how the world treats those it so casually sends into the line of fire. Some people will never kill, others will find it a joyful experience. Neither of those types were useful to the Spider. What he needed was an individual who had found they could take a life then quickly realised that when you were good at something you should never do it for free or for government wages.

Furkser turned his gaze away for a moment then looked back. "I'm sorry. I misjudged the situation. Apparently, he became involved with subject five."

"How involved?"

The question was met with a grimace. "Very. He was screwing her, but he didn't tell her who he was or what we're doing."

"How can you be sure of that?"

"I'm sure." Furkser watched a car pass by on the road and head off into the night. "Besides, he doesn't know anything."

"Excuse me?" said the Spider, raising his eyebrows. "He doesn't?"

"He didn't. He's been dealt with."

The Spider paused to consider this. "You did so personally? Given your history together?"

Furkser refused to break eye contact with the Spider. "Yes. Business is business. His stupidity was unforgivable."

"The stupidity wasn't all his."

Furkser glared at the Spider, who matched his gaze. When dealing with men such as Furkser, backing down was not an option. After a few moments, Furkser turned away and ran his hands up and down the steering wheel. "It's done, and I covered it up in such a way that I don't expect the local boys in blue to show any interest."

"Yes," said the Spider. "I've checked with my sources. *Luckily*, that appears to be the case. You know how I feel about having to rely on luck."

The Spider turned away and scanned the dunes as the periodic light washed across them from left to right. "And the other thing?"

"We're doing everything in our power to check."

"Prove to me that your judgement isn't terminally flawed. I want a copy of that manuscript in my hands within forty-eight hours." The Spider started his engine. "Don't disappoint me again."

Furkser tried to reply but his words were lost as the Spider gunned the engine and threw the car into a one-hundred-and-eighty-degree turn before heading off into the night.

Chapter Ten

GUESS WHO?

DI O'Rourke looked at his watch. It was exactly 11am. He made sure always to double check his time of arrival as on the extensive list of things known to bother Commissioner Gareth Ferguson, poor punctuality was right up there. He disliked people being early for things almost as much as he disliked them being late. The Commissioner's PA, Carol, wasn't at her desk so, seeing as O'Rourke had been informed an hour ago that he had an 11am appointment, he straightened his tie and prepared to knock on the door to the inner office.

Normally, a detective inspector in the gardaí would be lucky to meet the Commissioner once a year; O'Rourke was about to have his second appointment in just over twenty-four hours. The reason for this was the Commissioner's growing obsession with Bunny McGarry and, for better or for worse, O'Rourke was inextricably linked to Cork's answer to a question no one asked. It was starting to feel an awful lot like for worse; as if McGarry was tied to him like a concrete weight used to sink a body so that nobody would ever find it.

It made him think of his current investigation into the Gerrard brothers, a couple of previously low-level scumbags whose rapid ascension to the top of the criminal underworld's unofficial charts had brought them to his team's attention. O'Rourke had had to request a section of the docks to be dredged following a tip that had resulted in the grim discovery of a corpse that had been disposed of in such a manner a few months previous. The memory of it, and especially the associated stench, remained fresh in his mind.

Before O'Rourke could knock, the door flew open and out charged the unflappable Carol. Behind her, the Commissioner could be heard barking the plaintive appeal, "How hard can this be?"

Carol rushed behind her desk, picked up the phone, put it down, picked it up again, and then looked to the ceiling, as if pleading with the heavens for help. She looked, in short, decidedly flapped.

"Is everything okay?" asked O'Rourke.

Carol considered him as if noticing his presence for the first time, then gave him an exasperated wave to indicate he was next to go into the breach.

He peered around the door before entering gingerly.

Commissioner Ferguson was standing behind his desk, staring down at a collection of twenty or so photographs arranged in front of him.

"Good morning, Commissioner."

"Is it? That seems very unlikely." Ferguson collapsed into his chair and sighed heavily. "How long have you been married, Fintan?"

O'Rourke stood in front of the desk. "Eleven years last anniversary, sir."

"And would you say you're good at it?"

"Excuse me, sir?"

Ferguson scratched his belly. "Being a husband – would you say you're good at it?"

O'Rourke paused, unsure of the correct answer, or even if there was one. "I don't know, sir. I guess you'd have to ask the wife."

The Commissioner grunted before turning to look out the large window at trees swaying in the light summer breeze.

"I take it this is about your wife's birthday, sir?"

"You just can't teach that kind of deductive reasoning. You've either got it or you don't. Yes, Fintan – it is about my beloved's birthday. I have decided to push out the lifeboat – tomorrow night I am holding the surprise party to end all surprise parties. There will be a string quartet, fireworks, a Frank Sinatra impersonator whose fee is so extortionate I had to double check it was not Frank Sinatra himself performing via the medium of a Ouija board. The food will be prepared by somebody who has his own TV show, apparently. I assume it's a cookery show, but it could just as well be a show where a man burns money while laughing hysterically. The guy costs so much that he could certainly keep that going for a couple of series on my back alone. And, most importantly, the event will be packed to the rafters with my darling wife's nearest and dearest. All of whom I am inviting today, under the admittedly flimsy pretence of a last-minute 'come as you are' theme to prevent the – and I'm quoting the invitation here – 'greatest detective in the family' from finding out and spoiling the surprise. When in doubt, play yourself down."

"That's a very clever idea," said O'Rourke, because it was.

"It is indeed," agreed the Commissioner. "It was Carol's. The woman is invaluable."

"I'm sure it will be a roaring success, sir."

Ferguson spun back around and leaned on his desk. "Are you? Are you really? Let me explain to you, Fintan, the ring of hell in which I am currently residing. My wife is a wonderfully popular woman. She can't walk from one side of a room to the other without making at least two new best friends along the way. She regularly updates me on all of these people. I nod and feign an interest I, frankly, do not have. I could not give any less of a shit about who is divorcing whom, who is screwing whom and whose children are now doing what – unless the what in question is illegal, and believe you me, in a display of just how unfair life can be, I have ended up in the doghouse on more than one occasion when the Garda Síochána have arrested the offspring of someone my wife knows from the golf club.

"My point being – I care about my wife, of course. I care about the people under my command, in a sort of general 'don't get shot, do the job to the best of your abilities, and for Christ's sake, don't ask anyone involved for sexual favours' kind of way. I care about the Leinster rugby team, the golfer Pádraig Harrington, and Plácido Domingo, whose voice is the only thing I have ever experienced that made me think there might just be a God. Outside of that, I have been pretending to be interested in my wife's myriad social circles for over three decades. That bastard chicken has now come home to roost."

The Commissioner waved a hand at the photographs in front of him.

"I swiped these from her photo album last night. You know that dream everyone has where they turn up to an examination and realise they haven't studied for it? I present to you my final exam as a husband, which I am failing spectacularly. I'm trapped in the world's shittiest game of Guess Who."

O'Rourke leaned over and studied the photographs. Even the wrong way up, he could see that each of them contained groups of people smiling at the camera, with the Commissioner's wife as the common denominator.

"I belatedly realised that I have to assemble a guestlist, and the mortifying ignominy of not inviting somebody important, or, indeed, of inviting somebody who my wife has fallen out with, now hangs over my head like the sword of Damocles. In short, you are looking at a dead man."

O'Rourke shifted from foot to foot awkwardly. "I see what you mean, sir."

"Good," Ferguson barked in response. "I'd hate to think I was imagining it. Luckily for you, none of this is your problem. Bunny McGarry, on the other hand, most certainly is."

For the briefest of moments O'Rourke considered pushing back on that assertion, but one look at the Commissioner's face suggested that running with the bulls in Pamplona on a pogo stick would be a much safer option. "And I can assure you, sir, I am attempting to deal with it. I already asked one of his colleagues to meet with him, and she did so yesterday."

"Excellent," said Ferguson. "Hopefully, the lady in question can give him an alibi for last night."

O'Rourke was overcome with a sinking feeling. "Sir?"

"By any chance, Fintan, are you familiar with one Detective Owen Tierney?"

"I am."

Ferguson nodded approvingly. "Well done, Fintan. You managed to pack the appropriate amount of disdain into those two small words. Tierney is a pus-filled boil on the arse of this sainted institution. I'd put him right up there with the reprobate from Donegal who managed to get caught on camera pleasuring himself in a patrol car with a copy of *Woman's Weekly* last year. I mean, Donegal, for Christ's sake. There can't be more than five cameras in the entire county. And quite aside from the morality of the thing, the basic stupidity boggles the mind. Still, in his own inimitable way, Tierney is worse."

O'Rourke was aware of what the Commissioner was referring to, both in terms of Tierney and the now ex-guard from Donegal. In Tierney's case, when he was not busy being awful at his job, he'd made a habit of winding up his colleagues so much that not one but two other officers had now been caught on film attempting to physically attack him. In one case he received a tribunal payout, and in the other, he managed to get a desk sergeant three years away from his retirement kicked off the force. Somehow, he'd found himself a very good lawyer, which meant that neither demoting him nor sidelining him entirely were viable options, for fear of further legal embarrassment. O'Rourke knew for a fact the man had been offered a sweetheart deal to take early retirement and, for reasons known only to himself, had turned it down. He was unique in that he was almost as unpopular with the rank and file as he was with management.

"What about Tierney, sir?"

"He claims to have been assaulted last night."

"By Bunny McGarry?"

For the look of the thing, O'Rourke attempted to sound shocked by the very idea. In reality, it was so credible that it was surprising it hadn't happened before now.

"Indirectly."

"Excuse me?" This time, O'Rourke didn't have to pretend to be confused.

"Tierney claims he was the victim of a vicious elbow in the meat and two veg on Lower Abbey Street just before 9pm. Apparently, the blow in question was delivered by a teenage girl in a wheelchair."

"I'm assuming we're not suggesting McGarry has become a master of disguise, sir?"

"No. Tierney is, however, claiming the attack was carried out under McGarry's instructions."

O'Rourke couldn't stop himself from laughing. "He is seriously claiming—"

"Yes," interrupted Ferguson. "He is. There is a sadly piss-poor bit of footage from a CCTV camera across the street that shows McGarry leaving the restaurant, then, about fifty or so minutes later, the assault taking place. I've yet to see it myself, but I'm reliably informed that it is both inconclusive and joyous. I'm having copies made as Christmas gifts."

"Are you asking me to question McGarry about this accusation?"

The Commissioner blew a raspberry. "I mean, technically, yes, but for the sake of argument, let's assume he will deny the allegation as soon as he finishes laughing."

"I'd imagine that is a very safe bet, sir."

"Indeed. On an unrelated note, if McGarry happens to know any differently abled teenaged girls who, in a few years' time, might consider joining the police force, tell him my door is always open and this building is wheelchair accessible."

"Understood," said O'Rourke. "Well, if that is everything?"

Ferguson shook his head firmly. "If only, Fintan. If only. Sadly, there is the matter of what McGarry was discussing with Tierney in the restaurant. It appears Tierney pulled a missing person's report for one Mark Smith, an Englishman who was acquainted in the biblical sense with one Ms Rosie Flint."

"Isn't that the woman who—"

"Nuked the career of a certain minister from Kildare live on national television last week? Yes. Yes, it is. She's also a high-profile lecturer at Trinity College Dublin and the Head of SWIT – the organisation representing sex workers who are campaigning for decriminalisation. The woman is a headline in waiting."

"Ah," said O'Rourke, as the penny dropped.

"Yes. It seems that, despite your best efforts and those of his erstwhile colleague, Mr McGarry is not exactly keeping his head down."

O'Rourke threw out his hands. "Respectfully, Commissioner, I don't know what else I can do here? You've seen the limited influence that I, or indeed anybody else for that matter, have on the man. Outside of locking him up ..."

"That thought has occurred to me, Fintan, but let's put a pin in it for now. In the meantime, I want you to assign a member of your team to quietly look into this disappearance, on the frankly inevitable assumption that Tierney has botched the investigation. I imagine he'll be on sick leave for at least a week nursing his traumatised testicles, so I'm sure he won't get in the way."

"As you know, we live in tricky political times. Now that the sports fan from Kildare is out of the picture, the first government in thirty years with a solid majority is going to tear itself apart at the weekend to see who gets to be its leader. That means we've got desperate politicians scrabbling around like crack addicts looking for a hit, trying to find an issue to pretend to care about. The last thing we need is a woman with a proven ability to kick up a fuss making us an issue. For once, I'd like to know what it feels like to be on top of a problem, as opposed to being run over by it."

"Understood. Do you want me to try and warn off McGarry?"

Ferguson stretched out his neck and scratched at it with both hands. "While I've never met the man, I'm going to hazard a guess that such an approach would be counter-productive. Just see if you can find out what needs to be found out, and then we'll take it from there. The whole thing might be nothing, but that isn't the kind of week I'm having."

"Yes, sir."

Ferguson stared down at the photographs between them. A few

seconds later he looked up again. "If I wasn't clear, Fintan, that was the point at which you could bugger off."

"I appreciate that, Commissioner. Only ..." O'Rourke hesitated.

"What?"

His hand hovered over the desk. "May I?"

"Yes, yes. Get on with it."

He picked up one of the pictures and studied it carefully to make sure he was right. "That's what I thought." He turned it round and pointed at the woman standing beside Mrs Ferguson. "That is Celine Dion, sir. The singer."

Ferguson snatched the photograph from O'Rourke's hand. "Christ, she was one of only two out of this line-up I thought looked familiar. The wife's sister got them a VIP package to see her in concert a few years ago."

"I thought it might be helpful to know that, sir."

"No, Fintan, it is not. Not unless you happen to have Ms Dion's phone number and know whether she is available to be fed scandalously overpriced vol-au-vents tomorrow evening. Failing that, get out of my office, and the next time I see you I expect good news."

"Yes, sir."

Chapter Eleven

THE IMPORTANCE OF PREPARATION

I am good when well prepared.

I am good when well prepared.

I am good when well prepared.

Rosie Flint repeated her mantra over and over in her head as she strode quickly down the corridor. She was good at her job when well prepared and, normally, she was always well prepared. That was until this morning, when she'd stepped in front of a lecture theatre of two hundred students and realised that she'd forgotten to bring her new slides with her. She never made mistakes like this. Never.

Duncan, her research assistant, had said he'd go and get them, but she'd refused his offer. It was her job. She was good when well prepared.

For three nights in a row she had barely slept. That was why she was making mistakes. Her world was falling apart. She needed to regain control of it. She needed her slides.

"Rosie," said Duncan, trailing in her wake. "Honestly, it's no trouble. I can get them."

"I will get them."

She turned the corner, circumnavigating a cluster of undergrads who had decided the narrow corridor was a good spot to stop for a chat. Her office was at the far end of the hallway with its damnable black and white square tiles. She had never told anyone this, but she had to walk down the hall on the white squares and back up on the black. She didn't know why.

She altered her gait. There was no point rushing – if she took a misstep, she'd have to start again.

"Rosie," repeated Duncan. "Would you like me to—"

"Everything is fine," she said through gritted teeth. "Just let me get on with it."

As she walked down the hall, she could sense Duncan dallying behind her. Oh God, had she just been rude to him? She didn't know. Maybe she had been. It was so hard to tell.

As she strode on, Dr Baker, the head of the school, appeared out of his office. "Ah, Rosie, do you have a second?"

She shook her head and kept walking.

"Right," he said, behind her. "No problem. We'll talk later."

She was nearly at her office. According to her watch, it was seven minutes past. She could grab the slides and be back at the lecture theatre in four minutes. The class could stay later to make up the time. Yes.

As she reached the door, she felt that familiar wave of relief wash over her. She liked her office. She didn't like walking around the campus. There were far too many people. In fact, she often wore her earphones as she walked. That way, people knew not to talk to you. She did not like crowds.

She opened the door to her office.

A tall man in a baseball cap was standing behind the desk, a pile of files in his hands. Was this the wrong office? Had she got lost?

No. As he put them down, she realised that the files were hers. The man nodded at her and gave a smile as he stepped out from behind the desk.

"This is my—"

The man rushed forward suddenly and barged past her towards the door.

"Hey, what the hell?" shouted Duncan, throwing out his arms to block the man's path.

Lightning fast, the man threw an open-handed jab at Duncan's throat, sending him sprawling backwards. Duncan's legs went from under him and, with a sickening thud, his head collided with the far wall of the corridor as he crumpled to the ground.

Rosie looked between Duncan and the back of the stranger who was now walking away hurriedly. She should do something. Duncan was coughing and gurgling as he struggled to breathe. He was also trying to say something.

She bent down beside him. "What is it?"

"Ambulance," came the guttural croak. "Ambulance."

She nodded. "Yes. You need one of those."

He gave her a pleading look. After a couple of seconds, she nodded vigorously and got to her feet, clutching her hands into fists by her sides as she looked up and down the now-empty hallway.

"Right. Yes. Ambulance." She raised her voice. "Ambulance!"

Chapter Twelve

STATUES OF LIMITATIONS

Bunny took a bite from his breakfast burrito and felt the need to stop walking immediately.

"Jesus, that's only gorgeous." He looked down at the cylindrical mass of sausage, scrambled egg, cheese, and some kind of spicy salsa thing wrapped in a tortilla that he held in his hand. "Baby, where have you been all my life?"

This last sentence earned him a rather startled look from a matronly looking woman walking in the opposite direction down Grafton Street. It was either that, or the overly sensual groan that followed it. She veered away from him as far as it was polite to do and quickened her pace. If she'd realised that the carrier bag he was holding contained nine more identical breakfast burritos, there was a very good chance she'd have broken into a run.

Grafton Street was teeming with the kind of peculiar mix of individuals that you only get in Dublin in the summer. By their clothing choice alone, you could clearly differentiate the people who believed it was summer and those who believed they were in Ireland. It was, of course, possible to believe those two things at the same time, but it would inevitably lead to some form of breakdown. Ireland was the only country in the world where a native could describe the weather as "fierce mild" and their brethren would know what they meant. Optimism to the true Irish person wasn't leaving your umbrella at home, it was believing that the stupid thing would work when you needed it. Not that Bunny was in any position to judge, having taken to wearing his thick overcoat year-round.

The person Bunny was looking for was a fixture on Grafton Street – not quite a permanent one, although he did give off that vibe. He was remarkably easy to locate because of his dress sense, which was distinctive regardless of the time of year. If the gold suit coupled with the gold body paint didn't make him stand out enough, he was also two feet taller than the crowds thanks to the box on which he stood.

Bunny weaved his way through the mid-morning throng towards his destination, munching appreciatively on his breakfast burrito as he went. His target was outside HMV.

Ivan Retton was good. Very good. It took a particular kind of mind to be a moving statue. When he'd first come to Ireland, Ivan's English had been minimal. Standing there, day after day, come rain or shine – and it being Ireland those two things happened simultaneously quite often – Ivan became fluent in the language by listening to snatches of conversation as people walked by.

He'd taken over the costume and character from a nice man called Paul, who had allowed him to pay it off over time in tiny amounts. The people who undertook such work became very emotionally attached to their alter egos and Paul had wanted to make sure the character lived on. He'd been retiring from the moving-statue game because of the curse of the profession – foot problems.

Ivan had been doing it for seventeen years now and was particularly good, as evidenced by the pigeon currently perching on his hat. His proudest moment was when he'd appeared on a "Greetings from Dublin" postcard, copies of which were proudly pasted all around his box.

Being able to stand incredibly still was only one part of the job. When you had a bucket in front of you containing your earnings for the day, you quickly learned how to sprint after any gurrier who decided to swipe it, or else you went hungry. A lot of moving statues incurred hamstring injuries after going from nought to sixty in pursuit of their rapidly departing paycheque. The secret to Ivan's success was a comprehensive stretching routine he undertook before beginning work.

Not that he caught every bolter. This was how he'd come to meet Bunny McGarry several years ago. While off duty, Bunny had been kind enough to clothesline an absconding thief. He'd even managed the feat without dropping the ice-cream he'd been eating at the time. Ivan had taken him for a drink to say thank you and what followed was a lot more drinks before both men had woken up in a fountain in St Stephen's Green the following morning. All of that was in the past now, though. Ivan was a new man.

"Howerya, Ivan," said Bunny, looking up at him. "You're looking well."

Ivan didn't move a muscle.

After a couple of seconds Bunny nodded. "Right. Yeah." He nodded to himself before remembering the half-eaten burrito in his hand. "By the way, there's a new Mexican place just near O'Connell Bridge. Sweet baby Jesus and the donkey he rode in on, the breakfast burritos will change your life. I don't know whether to eat this thing or take it away for a dirty weekend. Incredible."

Ivan didn't move a muscle.

Bunny considered taking another bite of his breakfast, but instead, he wrapped it back up in its silver foil and shoved it into the pocket of his overcoat to save for later. "I had to sort of go undercover there for a few days, sleeping rough, and I'm dropping a few of these around to some of the bods I met, as a thank-you for helping me out."

Ivan didn't move a muscle.

Bunny looked around awkwardly then moved closer and lowered his voice. "I'm really sorry to bother you at work, but it's important. It's about AA."

This time, Ivan did move. He brought up his right hand and formed it into a thumbs-up.

"Oh no," exclaimed Bunny. "I mean, sincerely, well done to you.

Fair play for, you know, turning your life around and all that. I'm—I'm very pleased for ye and all that, but I'm not asking for myself."

Ivan didn't move a muscle.

"I don't suppose you have a break coming up any time soon?" Bunny was feeling increasingly ridiculous.

Ivan didn't move a muscle.

"Right. No. Course not. You're a working man and I know this is your busy season. Me standing here talking to you, or at you, is probably bad for business."

Ivan nodded his head once. Impressively, the pigeon didn't move. It did, however, give Bunny what felt like a very judgemental beady-eyed look.

Bunny shuffled even closer. "You know I wouldn't ask if it wasn't important. I'm looking for a fella who's gone missing, and I think he's in big trouble. His girlfriend knew him as Mark Smith but I'm pretty sure he's using other names too."

Bunny had stopped by the printers in Cabra on his way into town that morning and run off a dozen copies of the picture Rosie had given him of her and Mark Smith. He pulled one of them out of the non-burrito-containing pocket and held it up in front of Ivan's face.

"I don't suppose he rings any bells?"

Ivan didn't move a muscle.

Bunny lowered the picture. "I knew 'twas a long shot. Thing is, though, I believe he attended meetings somewhere round the city centre, and I figured you might know a lot of the people who'd be at them."

Ivan didn't move a muscle.

"Now, I know what you're probably thinking – the word 'anonymous' is included in the name for a very good reason, and I respect that, I do. But like I said, this might be life or death. If it isn't, then at the very least we can put a good woman's mind at rest. So, for an old friend, I was hoping maybe you'd ask around and see if anybody recognised him?"

Ivan didn't move a muscle.

Bunny scratched at his stubble. A thought occurred to him. "I should say that this isn't a police matter. I'm on sabbatical at the moment for … Well, it's a long story, but what I mean is, nobody's going to get into any trouble with the gardaí here, rest assured. I'm just trying to figure out if this lad is okay or not."

Ivan didn't move a muscle.

"If it's alright with you, I'm going to leave a picture of the fella in question in your bucket?"

Ivan didn't move a muscle.

"Grand," said Bunny. "I'm going to take that as a yes." He bent down and dropped the photocopy into Ivan's bucket.

"I tell you what," said Bunny, standing back up. "You are seriously good at this statue thing. I mean, I knew you were, but it's unnerving. I feel like I'm having a conversation with a pigeon."

Ivan didn't move a muscle.

The pigeon gave Bunny a look you'd normally only receive from a bouncer for turning up in the wrong footwear.

"Right, so. I'll be off. If you can help, I'd really appreciate it. We'll leave it there."

Ivan didn't move a muscle.

Bunny gave a little wave and walked back the way he'd come.

———

Two minutes later, Bunny returned and stuck a tenner in Ivan's bucket.

"Sorry – for taking up your time and getting in the way of your business. Good luck. Hope the kids are doing well."

With another little wave, Bunny departed.

———

Another two minutes passed and Bunny returned.

"Sorry, I just remembered I changed my phone number a couple of years ago, and I'm not sure if you've got the new one. I've written it down on this." He shoved a piece of paper into the bucket. "Good luck."

Bunny hurried away.

———

Another two minutes later, and Bunny was back again.

"Apologies, Ivan. Here's me bigging up the breakfast burrito like it's the greatest thing ever – which it is – and I didn't even offer you one. You could be there mentally salivating at the prospect of eating one, and I've got you wound up about something you can't have. They stop doing them at eleven."

Ivan didn't move a muscle.

"Right," said Bunny. "Don't suppose you'd wink your left eye if you want a burrito, and your right one if you don't? Something like that?" He stared at Ivan's face. "Oh – there was a blink there. Doesn't really tell me anything. You have your code you can't break – the statues' code. I know you take this seriously – as, of course, you should. Sorry, I'm sort of rambling here, amn't I?"

Bunny took one of the untouched burritos from his carrier bag. He looked down at the bucket and then thought better of it.

"I'll tell you what – I'm just going to stick a burrito in your suit pocket and then you'll have it. And sure, if you don't want it, judging by the look the pigeon is giving me, I'm pretty sure he'll have it."

Bunny clumsily shoved the burrito into place.

Ivan didn't move a muscle.

Bunny nodded. Then, without a word, off he went.

———

Two minutes later, he reappeared for a final time and took the burrito back.

"Sorry, sorry, sorry, sorry. On third or fourth thought, or whatever one we're on now, I was thinking that worse than being told about this burrito and how great it is and then not having one, is having one in your pocket and you standing there for a couple of hours with the smell driving you mad. I'll hang on to this. Anyway, I look forward to hearing from you."

———

A minute later, as he walked back down Grafton Street, Bunny felt something hit him. As he glanced at the shoulder of his sheepskin coat he wasn't in the least bit surprised to see a dollop of pigeon shit.

Chapter Thirteen

PUT UP A SIGN

Bunny ran down the hall, his trainers squeaking on the marble floor. He turned the corner and was confronted by a wiry man wearing enough corduroy to pose a serious hazard to dry woodland should he move too quickly. He was also sporting the kind of beard that academics grew so they'd have something to scratch while contemplating.

The man held out his arms. "Please, no running in the corridors."

Bunny had an odd flashback to his schooldays, although this man carried none of the menace of the Christian Brothers who had educated Bunny.

"Sorry, I'm in a bit of a hurry and this place is a fecking maze. Would it kill you to bung up a few signs? Where am I now?"

The man had a rather put-out air to him. "As it happens, these are the academic offices for the School of Social Sciences and Philosophy."

"Is economics one of them?"

"Yes."

"Grand. I'm in the right place, so. I'm looking for Rosie Flint?"

The man shook his head. "I'm afraid now is not a good time."

"I know. That's why she rang me."

He lowered his voice and leaned in conspiratorially. "The gardaí are here."

Bunny matched his volume and tone. "That's because there's been a crime. They do that. Still, Rosie called me, so I'm going to talk to her. Now, where is she?"

The bearded man pulled himself back as his mouth opened and closed a few times, like a ventriloquist's dummy that was warming up for a musical number. Eventually, he found a few words. "And who are you, exactly?"

"I could ask you the same thing."

The man drew himself up to his full height. "I am Dr Steven Baker, head of the school."

Bunny extended his hand. "Bunny McGarry. Seriously, throw up a few signs."

Dr Baker gave Bunny's hand a confused look, torn between not wanting to be rude and feeling the need to make some kind of a point. Manners won out and he shook it.

"Now," Bunny continued, "if you'll please direct me to Rosie. She rang me and she sounded upset."

Dr Baker ran his tongue around his mouth and clenched his hands nervously. "Yes, but the gardaí—"

Bunny was fast running out of patience. "Has Rosie been arrested?"

"Good heavens, no."

"Then neither the gardaí nor anybody else can stop her from talking to whoever the hell she likes."

"Yes, but ..." The good doctor steeled himself. "Nevertheless, I'm afraid I'm going to have to say that she is unavailable."

"Be like that, then. And to think I was considering offering you a breakfast burrito." Bunny lifted up his carrier bag that still contained three breakfast burritos. "These things will change your life." He elected to cut out the middle man and raised his voice. "Rosie?"

His shout was met instantly with a response from down the hallway. "Bunny? Is that you?"

Dr Baker looked set to launch into a full objection but he was stopped in his tracks as one of the hallway doors flew open. Rosie's head popped out and she looked visibly relieved to see Bunny.

"Yes. Hello." Bunny raised his free hand in greeting and Rosie motioned for him to join her inside.

"I'm not sure this is a good idea, Rosie," fretted Dr Baker. "I mean, the gardaí are ..."

The rest of Baker's sentence was lost as Rosie closed the door on him. Then, much to Bunny's surprise, she threw herself at him, tears rolling down her cheeks.

"It's so awful."

"Here now, here now, here," said Bunny, patting her awkwardly on the back. "It'll be alright. Just tell me what happened."

They were in what appeared to be a rather grim lunchroom. A kitchenette ran along one wall and a half-dozen uncomfortable-looking chairs desperately in need of re-upholstering were arranged around a wooden table. Rosie slumped into one of the chairs, an untouched cup of tea on the table in front of her, and Bunny sat down opposite. She dabbed at her cheeks with the backs of her hands, looking embarrassed by her outburst of emotion. After a few seconds, she composed herself and looked at his shoulder.

"I was about to do my normal Wednesday-morning lecture as part of the summer school programme and I realised I'd forgotten the slides I had created to illustrate neoclassical principles. I came back to my office to get them. Only, when we got there, there was a man inside. He pushed by me, and when Duncan tried to stop him, the man hit him in the throat."

"Jesus," said Bunny. "Is he okay?"

"He took a blow to the back of the head but the paramedics said he should be alright. They took him away." Rosie tilted her head and clenched her pink hair in her fingers. "I should probably go and find him. See if he needs anything."

Bunny tried to sound soothing. "He'll be fine. They'll be taking good care of him."

Rosie turned and looked out the window. The room's only view was of the side of the neighbouring building.

"Rosie," said Bunny in an attempt to bring her back into the room. "Rosie," he repeated. He waited for her to turn her attention to him. "I know you're freaked out, but this is important. First your apartment and now here. Is there anything you're not telling me? Anything you might have that someone else would want enough to do this?"

She shook her head emphatically. "I don't ... I don't know what's going on. Honestly. Is this something to do with Mark's disappearance?"

Before Bunny could answer, the door to the lunchroom opened.

Rosie straightened herself up, as if trying not to show weakness to a stranger. A stranger to her, at least. "Bunny, this is the new detective assigned to my case. I'm sorry, I didn't catch your name."

"Don't worry about it," said Bunny. "We've met. Howerya, Butch?"

Chapter Fourteen

ARNIE OF ACADEMIA

Butch ushered Bunny into an unoccupied office and closed the door behind them. It looked exactly as you'd expect an academic's office to look, save for the massive framed photograph on the wall of Arnold Schwarzenegger in *Conan the Barbarian*.

"Well," said Bunny, "that's unexpected." He leaned against the desk and folded his arms. "What are you doing here, Butch?"

"What am *I* doing here? There's been a crime and I'm a member of the Garda Síochána. Turning up to crime scenes is, like, our thing. You, on the other hand ..."

"You know what I mean."

"Actually, Bunny, I don't." Butch shoved her hands into the pockets of her trousers. "Why don't you explain it to me?"

"I'm just saying that yesterday I told you I'm helping out Rosie Flint, and today, despite you still being a member of the serious crime task force, you're somehow working the case. Bit of a coincidence."

"Bit of a coincidence?" repeated Butch, her eyes wide. "Fuck you, Bunny."

"I'm just saying—"

"Oh, I know what you're 'just saying'. For your information, despite my objection, two hours ago I was pulled off the detail I'd been working for two months and transferred to a missing persons case by Rigger O'Rourke. He was directed to do it by the Commissioner himself, after the detective working the case became unavailable, owing to an incident."

"Ah. Right," said Bunny.

"This would be Detective Owen Tierney, whose Tuesday-evening whereabouts I happened to disclose to you, on the assurance you were just going to talk to the man."

"In my defence, I didn't lay a finger on him."

"Yeah," snapped Butch, her voice laced with sarcasm. "I believe it was a teenage girl in a wheelchair who left an indelible impression on him. For the record, Mr McGarry, would you happen to know such a girl?"

"No comment."

Butch placed a clenched fist against the wall. "By the way, criminal genius, should I remind you that last year I helped you flog hundreds of tickets around headquarters and the three different Garda stations to send a girls wheelchair rugby team to North Carolina to compete in a competition?"

"Ah," said Bunny, sounding a whole lot more contrite.

"Yeah, if memory serves, Gráinne Dolan is the big sister of one of the lads from the St Jude's team. If anybody does an actual investigation into that incident, how long do you think it'll take even a semi-competent detective to make that connection?"

"The prick was asking for it, Butch. You should have heard what he was saying."

Butch threw out her arms in exasperation. "I worked under the arsehole for two years and I'm a female and a lesbian – do you reckon him being a small-minded toad comes as a monumental surprise to me? He's literally made a career out of it, not to mention destroying a couple of other people's along the way. Thanks, though – both for lying to me, and then dragging me into your stupid little stunt. One of us still wants to have a career in the gardaí when you're done."

"I apologise."

Butch pulled a face. "Whoop-de-doo, I'll get that framed. Maybe have a think next time, before you go accusing me of running my mouth off."

"I wasn't—"

"You bloody well were," snapped Butch. "And while we're on the subject, when we're in the presence of members of the public, you know damn well not to refer to me as anything other than Detective Cassidy."

Bunny paused for a second. "What? Are you talking about Rosie?"

"Yes. The high-profile individual in a case that now involves breaking and entering, assault and a potential missing person. I'd like to give her the impression that it's being handled professionally."

"I'll have a word."

"No," said Butch, exasperated, "you will not. What you'll do is get out of the bloody way and let me do my job."

Bunny held up his hands. "Alright, Butch. I mean, Pamela. I've been a gobshite and I apologise unreservedly. We both want the same thing here."

Butch leaned back against the closed door and cocked her head to one side. "Prove it. What the hell is going on?"

Bunny scratched his head. "Honestly, I haven't got a fecking clue. Rosie rang me last night, told me she reckoned somebody had broken into her apartment but, aside from some things on the counter being in a slightly different position and a couple of DVDs being swapped around, there was no evidence. I thought maybe she was just freaking out because of the anxiety over her boyfriend disappearing. I also asked what someone might be after and she genuinely didn't seem to have a clue. I was in the process of going over it with her again, given what's just happened, when you interrupted us."

"Sorry if my official investigation is getting in the way of whatever the hell you're doing."

"Come on now, Butch. You know I didn't mean it like that."

Butch jutted her chin, not quite willing to concede the point. "Anyway, what's going on with this boyfriend?"

"I don't know that either. I'll tell you what, though – you should take another look at his apartment."

"As it happens, I was on my way there when I got the call about this." Butch looked down at her shoes. "I'm not officially asking this question, because officially, I definitely don't want to know the answer, but ... I take it you've already had a look?"

"We both know Tape Tierney would have done feck all ..."

Butch waved the point away. "Hypothetically, what did you find?"

"There's evidence of a struggle and it wasn't some drunk bloke smashing up his own place. There's a bloodstain on the outside of the bedroom window, which means that somebody left in an awful hurry, and whatever they were running from was scarier than a three-storey drop. Also, there's a bottle of vodka on top of a bloodstain in the front room, only none of the blood has transferred to the bottle. Like it was put there after the blood dried. Whole thing feels as if it's been staged."

Butch thought for a second then nodded. "But you've no idea who would attack this guy, where he now is – assuming he's alive – or why somebody's breaking into his girlfriend's office, and possibly her apartment, too?"

"No clue," confirmed Bunny. "And if that wasn't enough, you've probably seen from Tape's file that the name Rosie knew him by isn't the same as the one that appears on the lease. And he lied to her about what he did for a living."

"For Christ's sake," said Butch, puffing out her cheeks. "This thing is a mess."

Just then her phone rang and she pulled it out of her inside jacket pocket. "Great, it's O'Rourke." She put her finger to her lips and looked pointedly at Bunny before answering. "Hello, sir ... Yes, Forensics are just going over the office looking for fingerprints and I've got Carson liaising with campus security to get CCTV. I'm just about to speak to Ms Flint again. Could I give you a ring back in fifteen minutes with a more comprehensive update?"

Butch listened for a few seconds then yes sir-ed a couple more times before terminating the call. She looked at Bunny. "He's now very interested, which I can only imagine means the Commissioner is too. I've got the awful feeling I've been given a poisoned chalice here."

"There's nobody I'd trust with it more."

Butch rolled her eyes. "That's a rather transparent attempt to get back into my good books."

"Is it working?"

She smirked. "Like so many women before me, I find myself helpless when confronted with the legendary McGarry charm."

"You think that's good," said Bunny, holding up his carrier bag, "I've got a breakfast burrito here that'll make you believe in God."

"I already believe in God."

"But now you'll believe he's Mexican."

Despite herself, Butch laughed.

Bunny lowered the bag. "Look, no messing, I'm sorry for suggesting anything. I've not slept in the best part of a week. I'm cranky and I'm not thinking straight."

Butch pushed herself away from the door and stood upright again. "So, why not do us all a favour and go home and get some sleep. I'm on this now, not Tape Tierney. Let me get on with my job without having to worry about you throwing any spanners in the works. This is a high-profile investigation – the last thing it needs is you barging in with an actual or metaphorical flaming hurley."

Bunny rubbed the back of his neck. "Look, Rosie's an old friend and I kind of owe her one. I can't just walk away. I promise I won't get in the way."

"Ah, for fuck's sake," said Butch, reaching for the door handle.

Bunny got up quickly to block her path. "Honestly, this is a good thing. I'll work it from my end, you work it from your end. You won't even know I'm about."

"Yeah, because you're so legendarily subtle."

"C'mon, you know I can be when I want to be, and I'd never do anything to make you look bad."

Butch raised an eyebrow at this.

"Trust me, Butch. Hand on heart, Scout's honour. Anything I find out, you'll be the first to know."

"No secrets?"

"No secrets," confirmed Bunny.

She thought for a moment then sighed. "Alright. Fine. But keep your head down."

"As the bishop said to the actress, just keep doing what you're doing and you won't even know I'm here."

Butch nodded towards the door. "I don't suppose you could have a word with your friend. She seems positively antagonistic towards the gardaí."

"I'm afraid that isn't an easy fix. Do you know the history?"

"I do," said Butch with a shake of her head. "Despite her mother going to the police repeatedly, the poor woman was killed by Rosie's father."

"Actually, the man wasn't Rosie's dad. He died when she was only a baby."

"Christ," said Butch. "This girl has had plenty of luck, all of it bad."

"You're not wrong. That's why I want to help her if I can."

"While keeping out of my way."

"While keeping out of your way," agreed Bunny.

"Alright. You can start by getting the hell out of my sight," said Butch. "I'll ring you later and we can compare notes."

"Will do. Thanks, Butch. You won't regret this."

"Famous last words," she retorted, opening the door.

Out in the hallway, Butch stopped and held out her hand to Bunny. He considered it then went in for the anticipated handshake, which she slapped away.

"Guess again."

Bunny was momentarily confused before the realisation dawned on him. He grabbed one of the breakfast burritos from his bag and placed it in her expectant hand. Butch brought it up to her nose and took a long deep sniff.

"Jesus, that does smell incredible, alright."

Chapter Fifteen

TERRY HODGES IS NOT THE MOST HIGHLY PAID COURTESAN IN IRELAND

Bunny eventually found his way out of Trinity College. The folk there could be as smart as they liked, but as far as he was concerned, the place's lack of quality signage both inside and out was shocking. While attempting to make his way onto Nassau Street, he'd managed to pass the geography department twice. The irony had not been lost on him.

What he needed was time to think. A proper sit-down where he could seriously analyse the facts of the case. He needed to ruminate, cogitate and, quite possibly, contemplate. In other words, he was extremely keen to get himself to O'Hagan's for some much-needed libations while he tried to figure out his next move.

While he was sincere in his stated desire to keep out of the way of Butch's investigation, both he and Butch knew that, as an independent contractor, there were things he could do that she couldn't. He just needed to figure out what those things were.

As he skirted around the slow-moving crowds of tourists on Nassau Street pointing at maps, pointing at things, and taking pictures of each other doing both, Bunny became aware of a presence. To his right, a silver Mercedes-Benz was driving alongside him, matching his pace. A muscular man in a chauffeur's cap was behind the steering wheel. As Bunny looked across, the car moved ahead of him slightly and the tinted rear window buzzed down. A woman in expensive-looking sunglasses gave Bunny a dazzling smile.

"Mr McGarry," she said, in a soft French accent, "I was wondering if I might buy you lunch?"

"No, thank you," said Bunny. "I've still got a couple of breakfast burritos left." He held up his carrier bag and enjoyed catching the woman's confused facial expression out of the corner of his eye as he strode on purposefully.

After about thirty seconds, the car pulled up in front of him again, and this time, the woman leaned out of the window. "Perhaps we might just give you a lift somewhere?"

"No, thanks again. My mammy was always very clear about the dangers of getting into a car with strangers."

This elicited the kind of tinkling laugh that would probably have other men salivating like Pavlov's dogs at a bellringing contest. "I promise you, Detective – you are completely safe."

"You're not wrong," responded Bunny, as he continued to walk down the footpath. "Because I'm not getting in your car."

This time, as the car pulled in ahead of him, the woman opened the back door and got out. She was undeniably stunning. She could stop traffic. In fact, thanks to where her car had parked, that was exactly what she was doing. It's one thing to stop traffic, but the fact that nobody was honking and swearing was even more impressive.

If this had been a Hollywood movie, the scene would have played out in slow-mo and Bunny would have been left gawping like a dog in heat as the woman swished her hair to a backing track of some soppy song from the seventies. Thankfully, it wasn't, and Bunny was able to act like a grown-up when confronted with a sexually attractive member of the opposite sex. Besides, he had long ago realised that he was capable of only a certain amount of excitement on any given day, and he'd already used up most of today's quota on Mexican food.

Bunny had every intention of keeping up his steady pace and walking on by, but he stopped as a male voice drifted down from the scaffolding on the far side of the street.

"Alright, gorgeous – fancy a shag?"

Bunny jabbed a finger in the direction of the rather rotund builder in a hard hat, who was already being congratulated by his colleagues on his display of witty repartee. Bunny had a limited supply of excitement, but rage, on the other hand ...

"Oi, you, lardy bollocks. Women are entitled to walk up and down the street without having to be subjected to your misogynistic outbursts. If I ever hear you trying that bullshit again, I'll shove one of those scaffolding poles so far up ye, you'll have an arse like the flag of Japan."

"What's it to you?"

"As it happens, I'm a member of the Garda Síochána. Although they probably won't let me keep that job once I come up there, spank your bottom and make you run naked through St Stephen's Green so that everybody can see exactly what a big man you aren't. Have I made myself clear?"

The shellshocked builder mumbled something, but nobody was close enough to hear it now that his cheering section had fled the area rapidly.

"What was that?" Bunny challenged.

"Nothing," came the sullen reply.

"Yeah, that's what I thought. Now ... apologise."

"Sorry, guard."

"Not to me, ye winky-waving dunder-headed gobshite." Bunny pointed at the woman. "To the lady."

"Sorry. Sorry about that."

She nodded and gave Bunny a bemused smile as he walked towards her. "You certainly come as advertised, Mr McGarry."

"I have a bit of a thing about manners."

"I can see that. Now, perhaps we ..." The woman hesitated as Bunny walked straight past her. "Please, Mr McGarry ..."

He spoke without looking back. "Still not getting in your car, though. If you'd like to have a chat, I'll be in O'Hagan's pub in about six minutes. Make it eight – I want to get a pint in first. I'm gasping."

———

True to his word, eight minutes later, Bunny was sitting in the snug in O'Hagan's, throwing unashamedly lustful glances. Not at the lady seated opposite him, but at the pint of Guinness and burrito laid out on the table in front of him.

The woman extended a perfectly manicured hand. "Let us begin again. My name is Sabine."

Bunny shook it without looking up. "Bunny McGarry, but you knew that. I'd offer you a breakfast burrito, but I've only got one more left and I'm saving it for somebody."

He eventually shifted his focus to Sabine, who was favouring him with a warm smile. In his periphery, Bunny noticed the chauffeur sitting at a table on the far side of the bar, doing a bad job of pretending to read a newspaper.

"Thank you," Sabine said, "but that is quite alright." She consulted the Cartier watch on her wrist. "Besides, it is now after 2pm and far too late for breakfast."

"Fair point." Bunny re-wrapped the breakfast burrito and took it off the table. He then pointed at his own wristwatch. "Oh, lunchtime." He placed the burrito back on the table and started to unwrap it again. "Luckily, I got myself a lunch burrito."

Sabine laughed heartily. "I do enjoy you. I can see why Rosie speaks so highly of you. I—"

Bunny's phone started to ring.

"Sorry," he said. "I'll just …" He recognised the area code. "Ara, for feck's sake. Apologies, I'm going to have to take this."

Sabine waved her hand. "Of course."

"Declan," said Bunny, answering the phone. "Now is not a great time."

"You're not wrong, boss. You're not wrong. It's a terrible time. That's why you've got to get me out of here."

Bunny sighed. "I'm almost afraid to ask, but what happened now?"

"They've got us playing hurling."

"Sure, that's great. You love hurling."

"I do and I don't, boss."

"What are ye talking about? You're the assistant fecking manager of a hurling team."

"Exactly. I'm management. I don't actually play. Remember what that doctor said? I'm allergic to my own sweat."

Sabine gave Bunny the kind of smile that an advertising exec would see and think, "Holy crap, we're going to sell a lot of something." He tried to ignore it.

"Remember we talked about that," he told Declan patiently. "He was being sarcastic."

"And I'll tell you now what I told you then, boss. Doctors aren't allowed to be sarcastic. It goes against the hippocrapping oath."

"That's not ... D'ye know what – never mind." Bunny was all set to hang up when an unpleasant thought assailed him. "Hold up, if you're supposed to be out playing hurling, how're ye ringing me?"

"I got sent to the headmaster's office for no reason at all."

Bunny's stomach sank. "Deccie, by any chance did you use one of your tactical ideas?"

"They're only banned in Dublin."

"No, Declan. They're banned everywhere. They go against the laws of the game, the laws of the country, or they go against the basic principles of common decency."

"Says you."

"Yes, says me. And, judging by your current location, the referee agreed with me. I'm almost afraid to ask, but which 'tactic' did you use?"

"Wasp attack."

Bunny glanced across the table at Sabine's curious expression then put his free hand over his eyes and exhaled loudly. "And how many other players did you take out by waving your hurl about while you were being attacked by an in no way imaginary wasp?"

"Three." The hint of pride in Deccie's voice was unmistakable.

"Right. And, to be clear – while this is definitely not the point –

out of morbid curiosity, how many of them were supposedly on your side?"

"As it happens, two of them, but one of them was pure shite. He didn't obey any of my instructions. Do you know what his problem is?"

"I have a very good idea."

"He has no appreciation of the fundamentals of the game."

Bunny sat back and raised his eyes to the ceiling, as if praying for divine intervention. "Right, Declan – you're going to apologise to everybody. And then, for the love of God and your granny, try and learn some Irish. Can I have a quick word with the headmaster?"

Bunny sensed that the situation was going to require some finessing to get the staff on board in any way with the acquired taste that was Deccie Fadden.

"What?" responded Deccie. "Nah, he's not here."

"And you're in his office, using his phone?"

"They said to go to his office. I followed that instruction to the letter."

"Did doing so involve picking a lock?"

"It might have done."

Bunny bit his own knuckle in frustration. "Get back outside now, lock the door, then sit there quietly and wait. Do not touch anything."

"What'll that achieve?"

"Nothing, which is a big improvement on what you've achieved so far. Goodbye, Declan."

"But, boss—"

Bunny missed the rest of the objection as he hung up.

"Sorry about that," he said, turning to Sabine. "The assistant manager of my hurling team."

"Is everything alright?"

Bunny picked up his burrito. "Nothing a team of child psychologists and a possible stint in prison won't fix." He took a large bite and chewed enthusiastically before speaking again. "So, how do you know Rosie?"

"I have been a supporter of her work for several years now. I believe it is fair to say that I am the main backer of SWIT."

Bunny swallowed. "Is that right?" he managed, before coughing. "Excuse me." He took a sip of his Guinness then smacked his lips. "Ah, that's the stuff." Only then did he look back across the table at Sabine. "And can I ask, what exactly is your interest in Rosie's work?"

"I am – although I do not love the phrase – a sex worker."

"Really?" said Bunny, raising his eyebrows. "I'm going to take a wild stab in the dark and guess that you are at the ... I suppose we could call it the higher end of the market?"

The woman pursed her lips then nodded. "While I would normally tend towards modesty, I am currently pitching an autobiography, and the hook is that Ireland's most highly paid courtesan is spilling the beans, as it were."

"Sounds like a cracking little stocking filler for Christmas."

"That's what we're hoping," she said with a smile. "I don't mean to brag, but as we speak there is quite the bidding war going on."

"Good for you."

They were interrupted by O'Hagan's assistant manager, Tara Flynn, bringing over a coffee and placing it in front of Sabine. "Your coffee, *madame*."

"Thank you," replied Sabine.

"Cheers, Tara," chimed Bunny. "Sorry – where are my manners?" Bunny pointed back and forth between the two women. "Tara, this is Sabine; Sabine – Tara." They shook hands and smiled. "Tara is the assistant manager of this fine establishment. Sabine is the highest paid courtesan in Ireland."

"Is that right?" said Tara, trying to sound casual. "Terry Hodges was claiming that honour last week. I knew he was full of bullshit."

If Sabine was thrown by the conversation, she did a superb job of hiding it. "This is a very nice establishment you have here, Tara," she offered, then nodded in Bunny's direction. "However, I thought public houses typically frowned upon patrons bringing in their own food?"

"Oh, we do, but Bunny here is a special case. He gets favourable treatment as he's the master of ceremonies for our monthly table quiz. You should come along – it's tonight."

"It's tonight?" Bunny spluttered, earning him a glare from Tara. "I mean, it's tonight," he repeated, trying to sound like somebody who hadn't forgotten that very fact.

"Don't you dare back out on me, Bunny McGarry. You'll lose a lot more than your burrito-eating privileges if you do."

"I haven't forgotten."

"Speaking of which," said Tara, as she reached across and slapped him on the back of the head.

"What was that for?" he protested.

"You know what. You rang up Hamster yesterday and told him you've got an idea for a special round, after I expressly told you to stop doing stuff like that. The lad gets very sensitive about his questions."

"Ara, he loves a challenge. That big brain of his."

"Exactly. I've got one of the smartest men in Ireland putting together quiz questions in exchange for a couple of pints. Don't go upsetting him." Tara's eyes flicked towards Sabine. "Anyway, I should leave you two to … whatever the hell this is. Fair warning, Sabine – if you give him a tab, he'll never clear it."

"Slander!" objected Bunny. "I hope you're willing to back up that assertion in court."

"I dunno," said Tara with a smile. "Good legal representation is very expensive these days. The only way this place could afford that kind of expenditure is if you actually paid off your tab. Nice to meet you, Sabine."

And with that, she left.

Sabine took a sip of her coffee. "She seems nice."

"She is," agreed Bunny. "Anyway, I'm not trying to be rude, or to be sort of weirdly nationalistic here, but is it not a bit odd that the highest paid escort in Ireland is a Frenchwoman?"

Sabine set down her coffee cup. "No, not at all. If you think about it, it is the least surprising thing in the world. I mean, a man of your experience – I'm sure you know the sign outside of most lap-dancing clubs in this country?"

Bunny nodded and gave a sheepish grin. "Guaranteed: no Irish girls. I see your point."

"Precisely." Sabine waved a hand up and down her person. "I am the exotic. The mysterious. The other."

"And you're very unlikely to have gone to school with somebody's sister, or be in a yoga class with their wife."

"Exactly."

During the lull in the conversation, Sabine gave Bunny an assessing look and he took another drag on his pint.

"I'm still trying to figure you out, Detective McGarry."

"If anything," he said, "I'm even simpler than I appear."

"No," she said, with a dismissive flick of her hand. "That really is nonsense. You want to pretend to be this abrupt and gruff man, but that's not what you are. You use it to your own end. When approached by somebody you don't know, you want to hold the meeting on your turf" – she pointed at the table – "and here we are."

"Rosie really does speak extremely highly of you, and she is not easily impressed. I've done some digging of my own, too. You have a well-documented problem with authority, but from what I can see, it stems mainly from the fact that you don't like how the world works and, unlike most people, you are not prepared to sit back and do nothing."

Bunny took another bite of his burrito. "Are you a psychiatrist as well as everything else? Or do you just turn your hand to anything that involves the client lying down?"

Sabine shot him a look.

"Sorry, that sounded less dickish in my head."

"I'm sure. Still, it does rather confirm a sense I'm getting. Would I be wrong to suggest that while you don't disapprove of what I do, you do disapprove of me?"

Bunny sat back in the leather booth and finally gave Sabine his undivided attention. "Since you ask, I really couldn't give a shit what two consenting adults do of their own free will, and if there's money involved ..." He shrugged. "Worse things happen at sea. And the argument Rosie makes – or rather SWIT, which is basically Rosie, albeit with your money behind her, apparently – about how decriminalising prostitution would help protect the men and women who engage in it, while helping prevent others from being forced into doing it, makes sense. Quite aside from anything else, it's worthy of an intellectual discussion, and Rosie is smarter than anyone else I've ever met. The one thing she isn't, though, is a political animal."

Sabine gave a slight nod. "I see."

"Yeah," said Bunny, all joviality having disappeared from his voice. "She goes on national TV and slaps a government minister around the place – who, to be clear, had it coming. Still, as I read the newspaper reports about it, which I dug out this morning, I was reminded of the phrase she regularly uses: 'I am good when well prepared'. She was very well prepared for this, wasn't she?"

Sabine said nothing.

"That's what I thought," said Bunny. "I'd lay good money on the fact that the information she used came from you, and I don't like the idea of my friend being used as a Trojan horse."

Sabine ran a finger along the edge of the table before raising her gaze and staring Bunny dead in the eye. "You are correct. I knew that information – not from the man in question, but powerful men do so love to talk as, otherwise, how would you know they are powerful men? I disagree with your assessment, though. My friend was going into a fight in which she was considerably outmatched – I just gave her a little something to even the odds. She has helped me with things in the past. I was merely returning the favour."

Bunny folded his arms. "And what really is your interest here?"

"Do you know, Detective McGarry, what the difference is between me and the girls you will find standing on the street corners of this city any given night of the week?"

He shook his head.

"That's because there isn't one. There are the superficial things – I do what I do in nicer, and mostly, safer spaces. I get very well paid for it, too. I enjoy it – for the most part. And when I say for the most part,

I'd suggest I enjoy my job more than ninety percent of people enjoy theirs, at a conservative estimate. I am not ashamed of what I do. It is my body; I believe I can do with it as I see fit. Many people may disagree with that, but it is still my body. I'm not asking anybody to share my morals, merely to respect what I believe are my rights. As you said, consenting adults et cetera.

"If somebody enjoys the job, then great. If somebody is forced into the work, then, as with any other job, the people doing the forcing should be arrested and locked up, and the people under duress should be protected. If poverty forces someone to work in the industry when they don't want to, then we need to fix whatever is wrong in our society that means some people cannot survive without doing so."

"So, you're just trying to help?" asked Bunny.

"In my way, yes. But more than anything, the thing that has been really getting to me for the last few years – the reason I have decided to support Rosie in any way I can – is that I am sick to death of the sheer hypocrisy of it. Watching politicians bleat publicly about morality while living their lives to a whole other standard in private. Berating women on street corners while screwing women in penthouses."

"That's all admirable," countered Bunny, "but there's more here. Whatever's going on with Rosie, I'm guessing you know something about it. So why don't we skip to that part?"

For the first time during their conversation, Sabine looked unsure. She glanced around before deciding to continue. "I honestly don't know anything about Mark's disappearance. I met the man only once. He seemed nice. He and Rosie appeared to be very much in love. I'm sure you would expect a woman in my position to be cynical about such things – and maybe I am, a little – but not enough not to be heartened by the sight of two people who are truly besotted. Maybe I'm wrong about that, but I consider myself a good judge of character. To get where I am in my career, you really have to be."

"Noted," said Bunny. "That's not the bit that has you worried, though, is it?"

"No," admitted Sabine. "The book, *my* book – its tell-all nature is why publishers are fighting over it. It's also why I'm guessing it has quite a lot of people feeling nervous."

"Ah."

"Yes. I am not setting out to embarrass people for the sake of it. Those who engage in rank hypocrisy, though, or those who, shall we say, cross certain lines – they are the only people who need to be worried."

"I bet they're not the only ones who are, though."

Sabine shrugged.

"How many people have read your book so far?" asked Bunny.

She leaned in. "Here's a secret, Mr McGarry, that I have not shared with anyone else – I haven't written it yet. My agents are telling everyone I have, but that it is being kept under lock and key to prevent leaks. We are essentially selling it sight unseen, with merely hints of what is to come." A smile crossed her face. "If there's one thing I've learned, it's how to tease. It hasn't even got a name yet. As a working title, my agent is using *The Book of Revelations*."

Bunny laughed. "I imagine that'll go down a bomb with the Catholic Church."

Her smile turned wry. "Between you and me, that might not be the main reason the book will upset the Church."

"As the actress said to the bishop ..."

Sabine crinkled her perfect brow. "I don't understand?"

"Don't worry about it. Just a silly phrase. So, lots of people are getting wound up about this book."

"So it would seem," she agreed. "And, as you say, the word is out. Despite the whole thing only existing" – she tapped a fingernail to her forehead – "up here. That way, nobody can take legal action either, as you cannot sue for something someone has not yet written."

Bunny nodded. "Clever. But I take it we're guessing that somebody somewhere thinks that Rosie might have a copy?"

Sabine sighed. "Unfortunately, I think they may well do. To be clear, I've never even discussed it with her, but when I wrote a couple of articles last year – one for a French magazine and another for a US publication – Rosie was kind enough to read through them for me before I submitted. If someone has been snooping and reading emails and so on, they may have reached the mistaken conclusion that she has also read the book."

"The one that doesn't exist."

"Yet," clarified Sabine. "Yes. I'm afraid she's an unintended participant in this game and I deeply regret her being dragged into it. This is why I am here. I wanted you to know the facts and I wanted to offer any assistance I can. Regardless of what you think of me, I think the world of Rosie, and we both want her to be safe."

Bunny worked his jaw for couple of seconds. "Well, I suppose that might explain at least a bit of this shitshow. And by the way, I will be sharing this information with the Garda Síochána."

Sabine nodded. "Whatever you think is best."

"Do you have any idea who could be sniffing around?"

She shook her head. "Honestly, no. I've been racking my brains, trying to think who in particular might be this upset, but no names spring to mind. Certainly, I can see no benefit in anyone involving Mark Smith in this."

"Not that it's any of my business, but if whoever's coming after Rosie ..."

Sabine caught Bunny's drift and bobbed her head in the direction of the chauffeur. "I have Henry. We're pretty sure our house was broken into a couple of weeks ago. As I said, there is nothing to be found, but since then, Henry has upped our security considerably."

"That doesn't mean you're not in danger."

"Why, Mr McGarry, I didn't know you cared."

"I'm not a big fan of anybody dying. Keep that to yourself, though – I'd hate to ruin my hard-man image."

"Your secret is safe with me, Detective. You need not worry. Henry is a man who has, shall we say, certain skills from his former life – driving is only one of them. And besides, he and I are on a plane out of here tomorrow evening. Within a day, nobody will know where we are."

Having dropped this bombshell, Sabine got to her feet.

"Hang on a sec," said Bunny, putting out a hand. "I might have more questions."

"I have thought this through in great detail before I came to meet you, Detective. I believe I've given you all the information I can. If anything else comes up, Rosie will know how to contact me. Thank you for your time."

With that, Sabine turned and walked out of the pub, with Henry the chauffeur following in her wake.

Bunny was still staring at the door two minutes later when Tara came over.

"Was she really ... y'know?" she asked, waggling her eyebrows.

"Yes," said Bunny.

"Are you and her ..." Tara left the sentence hanging.

Bunny huffed. "Would you give over. Course not. No money has changed hands."

"Right," said Tara. "Well, it's about to."

"What?"

"She never paid for that coffee. Cough up."

Chapter Sixteen

PREPARE TO LOSE ALL RESPECT FOR OTTERS

Detective Pamela "Butch" Cassidy pushed through the doors to O'Hagan's and was confronted by the unexpected sight of a packed pub on a Wednesday night. Even more unusually, there wasn't a match on the telly. Instead, people were four to a table and listening intently to a familiar voice over the PA.

"And now," Bunny announced, "the answers to round five – the weird world of animals round. This was my idea and, as always, if you would like to query any of the answers, I will be only delighted to hear it."

Bunny's invitation was met with a sarcastic cheer.

Butch moved past some of the drinkers waiting to be served. Bunny was on the far side of the horseshoe, sitting at the bar, on his throne, with a pint of Guinness in one hand and a mic in the other. A nervous-looking guy with a thick bush of brown hair and an equally immense beard was seated to his right. Even having never met him before, Butch knew that this individual was the fella nicknamed Hamster.

As Butch caught sight of Bunny, he noticed her too, and a wide grin spread across his face.

"But before we get to the answers, ladies and gentlemen," he said into the mic, "we are delighted to be joined by Detective Pamela Cassidy from the serious crime task force. Let's give a warm round of applause to one of our brave boys and girls in blue."

Butch could feel herself turning beetroot red as the pub's patrons applauded enthusiastically while simultaneously enjoying her obvious discomfort. She gave an embarrassed wave then flicked the Vs at Bunny, which raised another cheer.

As Butch began to work her way round the bar, Bunny started to reveal the answers to round five.

"Question one: a group of rhinos is known as what? The answer is ... a crash."

Up went a mixture of groans and one table's worth of cheers.

"And the team Up the Dubs is fined yet another ten points for giving the answer as 'a hen-do from Cork'."

More cheers.

"I believe that now puts their score at" – Hamster whispered something to Bunny – "minus twenty-seven."

More cheers.

"You're in serious danger of breaking the record you set last month, lads. Moving on. Question two: what shape is wombat shite? It is cubed. Cubed."

"Like fuck it is," came a shout from the back of the room.

Bunny stood up on his stool. "Who said that?"

Butch noted the pointed absence of any response.

"That's what I thought," said Bunny, sitting back down. "Just to reiterate – what is the number-one rule of quiz night?" Nobody answered, so Bunny pointed at the young man sitting at the table nearest to him. "Ciaran Marsh?"

Ciaran looked panicked. "Ehm ... Take your empties back to the bar?"

"No, that's not it," said Bunny with a shake of his head.

Tara Flynn's head popped out from behind the bar. "Yes, it bleeding well is."

Bunny gave an exasperated sigh. "Alright, what's the second rule, then?"

"No questions about cricket," shouted a voice.

Bunny gave a begrudging nod. "Okay what's the third rule, then?"

From the far corner came the roar, "You do not talk about Fight Club."

"Right, that's another ten points off Up the Dubs. One more penalty, lads, and you're buying everybody a drink."

Bunny's pronouncement was met with the most enthusiastic cheer of all.

"The third rule," continued Bunny, pointing at his assistant, "is that nobody ever, *ever* questions Hamster."

There was a chorus of grumbling from some corners and Bunny gave the room a disapproving look. "He does a brilliant job for us and we're not continuing until everybody repeats the rule."

A couple of people half-heartedly echoed the third rule. Bunny slammed his fist down on the counter, which caused the background hubbub of continuing conversations round the room to die out almost instantly. He took the time to eyeball the crowd in front of him.

"On the count of three, what is the third rule of quiz night? One ... two ... three ..."

"Nobody ever, *ever* questions Hamster," repeated the room in near-perfect unison.

Bunny nodded. "That's better. Now, on to question three: true or false, cows produce more milk when listening to heavy metal? That is false – cows actually produce more milk when listening to slow jams. There's also a lesson there, to all the lads, on the subtle art of seduction."

The cheer on this occasion was decidedly female.

"The answer to the question can otters accurately be described as murderous necrophiliac interspecies sex offenders is ... true!"

A mix of cheers and boos again.

"Incidentally, Murderous Necrophiliac Interspecies Sex Offenders is also the name of Hamster's and my new punk band. Look out for the gig posters! We are terrible. Question five: during what four-month period does the seventy-two-hour window in which the female panda becomes sexually excited occur? The answer is February to May."

"So who did I shag last night, then?" came a shout from the corner again.

"That," responded Bunny, "would have been a skunk. To be honest, Dinny, I can't help but think the skunk could have done better for herself."

Bunny's jibe was met with a lot of catcalling and laughter.

"And the final question in this round: what animal has a penis eight times the length of his body? The answer is ... the barnacle." Bunny placed his arm around his assistant's shoulder. "Although, ladies, I will also accept Hamster as an answer."

More cheers.

"We shall now have a short intermission to allow for libation, urination and flirtation."

————

"This place is rammed," shouted Butch over the din.

"Sure, of course it is," responded Bunny. "I'm quite the draw."

"And so modest."

Hamster, who had now been roped into helping out behind the bar, set a fresh pint of Guinness in front of Bunny, and a lime and soda in front of Butch.

"Would you look at that," exclaimed Bunny. "Is there nothing this man can't do? Remember, Hamster, if that whole Geography thing doesn't work out, people will always need booze."

With a tip of his imaginary cap, Hamster moved off to continue serving the thirsty quizzers. Butch received the definite impression that the lad was revelling in the reflected glory of being Bunny's sidekick. She picked up her drink and took a sip.

"So," said Bunny, "how's work?"

Butch rolled her eyes. "Subtle."

"Well, the next round starts in a couple of minutes, so I can't treat you to as much foreplay as I'd normally give a lady."

Butch pulled a gagging face. "Well, that's me having lost my appetite for pretty much everything."

She'd actually been intending to grab something quick to eat once she left the pub. She also felt very uncomfortable being there in the first place. A couple of hours ago, DI O'Rourke had pulled her to one side when he dropped in to see the Mark Smith – or Daniel Poole – apartment for himself.

"Do you know why I put you on this case, Pamela?"

"Is it because I'm an excellent detective and you respect my abilities, sir?"

"Actually, it is."

It showed the esteem in which she held O'Rourke that her only response had been a raised eyebrow.

"Seriously," he'd protested, "it is. This job is a lot more than simply analysing information, and you've always known that. You're not on this case just because you're Bunny's friend. And for the record, you're here because I consider myself to be Bunny's friend, even if he's a little circumspect on that fact. He needs protecting, and so does the Garda Síochána, because whatever the hell we're dealing with here, it carries the very real prospect of turning into some kind of PR disaster."

"Thanks again for the assignment."

He'd nodded. "I understand you hate it, but one day you'll find yourself in my position, and you'll see it from a very different angle. Incidentally, if I can stop being your boss for a moment – you don't get ahead in this job by avoiding the awkward situations; you get ahead by handling them."

"Unless you're the nephew of the Minister for Justice."

O'Rourke had straightened his already-straight tie. "Yes, but last time I checked neither you nor I had that distinction. Look, handled right, this could be a very good thing for you. The Commissioner himself has eyes on it."

Butch had nodded. "And just so I know – what are the rules of engagement here, regarding Bunny?"

"We need to know what he knows."

"And how am I supposed to manage that? I mean, I think it's safe to assume he's going to want to know what we know."

"And that's fine," O'Rourke had assured her. "I trust you to manage the situation." Translation – I have deniability. "Look," he'd continued, lowering his voice slightly, "I know you admire him, but just remember, Bunny McGarry's greatest strength and his greatest weakness is that when he sinks his teeth into something, he never ever lets go, and he pays no attention to who he hurts in the process."

As Butch stood at the bar with Bunny, O'Rourke's words were still at the forefront of her mind. In fact, they'd been eating away at her ever since.

She placed her drink on the bar. "Can I just remind you that we agreed that information sharing would be a two-way street?"

"Absolutely," said Bunny.

"I'm deadly serious. Don't you dare mess me around, Bunny. There are a lot of eyes on this."

"I gave you my word. In fact, I think I have a rather juicy titbit that will be of significant help in your investigation – inasmuch as it pertains to the breaking and entering side of it."

"How so?"

"This afternoon, I had lunch with the most highly paid courtesan in Ireland."

Butch furrowed her brow. "Is it your birthday and I've forgotten? And to be clear, if 'lunch' is a euphemism here, I really, *really* do not want to know."

Bunny proceeded to recount his meeting with Sabine. As he finished, Butch held her hand to her forehead and closed her eyes.

"Great," she said. "Just great. This case now involves every high-powered and horny dick in Ireland. Literally."

"I'm afraid so."

She opened her eyes and looked at Bunny again. "It would have been handy to know this a few hours ago."

"Well," began Bunny. "First, I waited to get hold of Rosie to confirm what Sabine had told me, because I've been around the block enough not to just take as gospel the word of any attractive lady who propositions me on the street. I confirmed it all – including Rosie having no idea about this book – and then I did try and ring you."

Butch grimaced then nodded. He had. She had four missed calls from him before she'd texted to say she'd meet him later. "Fair enough," she conceded.

"So, any chance of quid pro quo?"

"There's not that much to tell – at least not in terms of actionable evidence. Duncan, Rosie's teaching assistant, has a bit of concussion and a nasty bump, but nothing too serious. Assuming this break-in wasn't random – which seemed the case even before your revelations about this bloody book – the perpetrator knew Rosie's schedule and that the office should have been empty, which implies a certain degree of research. Duncan and Rosie describe the guy as about six foot two, short brown hair. We've got a photofit that could easily be six different blokes in this pub alone. What says more is that when he was disturbed, he didn't say a word – just took down poor Duncan with minimal fuss then calmly made good his escape. We've got him on CCTV entering and exiting the building, but he's wearing a baseball cap throughout and clearly knows where the cameras are."

Bunny had been listening while taking a long sip of his pint. He set the glass down on the bar. "So a professional," he concluded.

Butch nodded in agreement. "We've fingerprinted the office, but it's a safe bet we get Rosie, Duncan, a couple of random students, and whatever cleaning staff go in and out. There's more chance of you actually becoming Ireland's most highly paid courtesan than us getting an actionable print."

Tara Flynn, all business, appeared in front of them on the other side of the counter. She gave Butch a quick nod before addressing Bunny. "Two minutes, quizmaster."

"No problem," Bunny replied. As Tara rushed off, he turned back to Butch. "So what did you make of Mark Smith's – or whatever-his-name-really-is's – apartment?"

"Your theory holds water. Bloodstain outside the window and the absence of one on the vodka bottle. I've got four uniforms down there now, canvassing all the apartments we didn't get an answer from earlier on, but we already found somebody across the courtyard, who reckons they saw somebody jump out of a window."

"Really?"

"Judging by the smell coming from the lad's apartment, I'd bet he was stoned when it happened, but he said he noticed something falling. By the time he made it to his window, he only saw a guy walking away – reasonably fast, possibly with a limp."

"Did he—" started Bunny.

"Happen to notice anybody hanging out the window waving a machete or a gun? No. Having said that, I'm not at all confident he'd have noticed them even if they *had* been there. The lad was, what we would call in the business, a low-quality eyewitness. We'll see what else turns up. What's more interesting is what we *can't* find."

"How's that?"

"The apartment," said Butch. "I've got Tinker digging around, as this is his area of expertise, but the company that rented it seems to be a shell company owned by a shell company, and so on. We can't find any kind of contact."

"Building companies might be dodgy on occasion, but that sounds like the wrong kind of dodgy."

Butch pursed her lips, unsure if she wanted to share anything further.

"What?" asked Bunny, sensing her apprehension.

"It might be nothing," said Butch, "but it isn't unprecedented for governments or police forces to stick undercover operatives into organisations they think might be problematic."

"I've been thinking the same thing," agreed Bunny, "but I can't really make it fit. SWIT is, at best, an organisation that could bring up a few questions that might not sit well with the powers that be, but it's hardly CND, Greenpeace, Republican Sinn Féin, or whatever pack of right-wing Nazi fucknuggets are the current flavour of the month. It's far too much effort to go to."

"Yeah, that's what I thought too," concluded Butch. "Still, something stinks to high heaven here, doesn't it?"

Tara Flynn reappeared behind the bar. "Alright, let's crack on. We're already running ridiculously late."

"Such a taskmaster," muttered Bunny.

Butch slapped him on the back. "Alright, I'm gonna get out of here and see if the canvassing teams have had any luck."

"Right so. Don't be a stranger, Pamela."

"Yes, Bernard. And, you – don't make a nuisance of yourself."

He feigned a hurt expression. "When have I ever done that?"

"Are you serious?" she responded. "Tell that to Tape Tierney's bludgeoned bollocks."

"Trampled testes," responded Bunny.

"Napalmed nuts."

"Pulverised penis."

"Demolished dick."

"Whipped winkie."

"Flabbergasted phallus."

"Got ye!" said Bunny pointing triumphantly. "You lose. Phallus starts with a 'p'."

"Wait, what game were we playing?"

"Later, gator."

Tara returned, completely exasperated by this point. "Bunny?"

"Alright, woman. Keep your hair on. Speaking of hair, where has Hamster disappeared to?"

"I've no idea," replied Tara.

As Butch started to push her way around the still-heaving bar towards the exit, Bunny's voice came over the PA. "Alright, folks. Everybody back to your seats. Now, has anyone seen my Hamster?"

"He's snogging the face off Yvonne Burke," shouted a female voice from one corner.

"No, he's not," came a male voice from the other corner. "He's having a piss."

"He's a very intelligent lad," said Bunny. "There's every chance he's doing both at the same time."

The hoots and hollers this drew from the crowd were still going strong by the time Butch pushed her way out the door.

Chapter Seventeen

THE PROBLEM IS A PROBLEM

Almost exactly twenty-four hours after the Spider and Furkser had last met, the Spider found himself in exactly the same car park, his and Furkser's cars in exactly the same formation, and the exact same infuriatingly stoic expression on Furkser's face. Even the same light from the distant lighthouse periodically washed across the dunes from left to right. Not *everything* was the same, though – the weather was worse; a steady downpour angling from right to left in the beams from the cars' headlights, whipped by the strengthening wind blowing in off the sea. The Spider's mood had also grown significantly worse.

"How on earth did this happen?"

Furkser went to speak but the Spider cut him off. "And so help me, if you come back with, 'it happened', then I will not be responsible for my actions."

The vein above Furkser's temple seemed to throb as he worked his jaw for a moment before answering. "Buchanan went in to search the office in the middle of the day, as I determined it would be less conspicuous than night-time entry and would also get it done quicker – as you requested." Just the slightest hint of emphasis on the word "you". "The subject and her assistant came back unexpectedly. They were both supposed to be in a lecture. It was pure bad luck."

The Spider dug his nails into the leather of the steering wheel. "There's that word again – 'luck'. Perhaps it's the rose-tinted glasses of reminiscence, but I do not recall luck being such a prominent factor when we worked together in the past. It's beginning to feel like your luck is running out."

This earned the Spider a sideways look that made him pause for a moment. When dealing with men such as Furkser, the trick was to know how hard to push. The Spider reckoned he was very close to the red line of no return.

"I take it before being disturbed, he didn't find any evidence of the manuscript?"

Furkser shook his head.

"Very well," said the Spider. "What's done is done. It appears that even prior to this ... Unfortunate incident, the gardaí had already decided to pay matters more attention."

"Subject five has also enlisted the help of some copper who's off on sick leave. McGarry."

"Is he a concern?"

"He's sniffing about." Furkser paused for a moment. "He was also approached by subject nine after he left Trinity College today."

The Spider's head snapped to the right. "What? Why am I only hearing about this now?"

"Because, as per your instructions, we keep the discussion of operational concerns to a minimum over phone lines. They appear to have had a relatively brief meeting in a pub."

"Do we know what was discussed?"

Furkser wrinkled his brow. "No. As per instructions, we were doing loose surveillance."

"Very well. The gardaí are also investigating the company that rented your former friend's apartment. Luckily, that was the only involvement of that company, and besides, they can dig as much as they want – they won't find anything. That being said, the fact that they're looking is in itself bad news."

He drummed his fingers on the steering wheel. He'd all but made his decision prior to the meeting, and nothing he'd heard from Furkser had swayed him from it. Sticking to a plan when circumstances had altered significantly was a recipe for disaster. Sometimes, the only way out is to regain the advantage by any means necessary.

He reached down into the car's centre console, picked up his packet of cigarettes and lit one. After a couple of puffs he spoke again. "We have lost containment. The only option open to us now is to clean house and hope the situation is still salvageable once the dust has settled."

"To be clear, do you mean—"

"Both of them. Tomorrow. Will that be a problem?"

Furkser considered this for a moment then shook his head. "No problem."

The Spider tossed his half-finished cigarette into the rain-soaked night. "It'd better not be – for all of our sakes."

Before Furkser could say anything else, the Spider gunned his car's engine and drove off into the night.

Chapter Eighteen

THE BEST COMPANY MONEY CAN BUY

That morning, DI O'Rourke did not have an appointment with the Commissioner. Instead, he'd received a voicemail at 6:22am from Ferguson himself, instructing him to "Get here now!" So, fifty-seven minutes later, O'Rourke found himself once again standing in the outer office of the highest-ranking police officer in Ireland.

He looked around, wondering if there was enough space for a single bed so that he could sleep there, given that being called to the office first thing in the morning had swiftly become the new normal. O'Rourke couldn't remember the last time he'd had a decent night's sleep. Neither could his wife, as she had made very clear while he'd hurriedly got dressed.

Before O'Rourke's fist could make contact with the imposing door into the inner office and knock, the equally imposing voice of Commissioner Ferguson roared from behind it, "Come in."

O'Rourke duly did as instructed, entering to find the Commissioner sitting behind his desk, looking incongruous in a tracksuit, while Carol reeled off the names of some of the finest restaurants in Dublin.

"Brannigan's?"

"Too red meat-y."

"Brasserie Monique?"

"Too French."

"The Red Dragon?"

"Too Chinese."

"Mario's?"

"Too currently under investigation for tax fraud."

"Jolie Kitchen?"

"Too I got the shits last time we ate there."

"Tramps?"

The Commissioner shook his head. "The food is superb, but I made a joke at that thing ..."

Carol nodded. "I did warn you."

O'Rourke couldn't help but notice that the only person he had ever seen chastise Commissioner Ferguson and live to tell the tale was Carol.

Ferguson looked positively sheepish. "Yes, I remember. There must be somewhere?" he said in a pleading voice. "My beloved is very picky when it comes to food. As she likes to remind us, she was studying at the School of Culinary Arts in town before I whisked her off her feet."

Carol closed her notepad and dropped it onto the desk.

Ferguson gave her a confused look. "What?"

"The School of Culinary Arts."

"Don't tell me you went there as well?"

"No, Commissioner. But I have been there to enjoy one of their taster menus ..."

"Do you mean ..."

"It's worth asking. And, more importantly—"

Ferguson slapped the desk, excitement writ large across his face. "Using it as a venue looks like I'm being thoughtful."

"Celebrating her life. One of her great passions," continued Carol.

"And she does love telling people about her time there. Do you think they could pull something together at short notice?"

"I've no idea, but it's worth a shot." Carol looked at her watch. "It'll be a couple of hours before I can get anybody on the phone ..."

"Carol," said the Commissioner in an ominous whisper. "Look at my face ..."

She nodded. "I'll get a home number and wake somebody up."

Commissioner Ferguson clapped his hands together and rubbed them with glee. "Excellent. Excellent."

Carol got to her feet and rushed back to her desk, giving O'Rourke the briefest of nods as she hurried by.

Ferguson motioned towards the chair Carol had just vacated, and O'Rourke moved forward to sit down.

"Forgive the ludicrous attire," said the Commissioner. "Circumstances required me to get out of the house early this morning, so I needed to roll out a little white lie to my wife about a sudden urge to follow doctor's advice and actually go to the gym."

"If I might ask, sir – I thought the catering for your wife's birthday party was being covered by a certain TV chef?"

Ferguson's face moulded itself into a scowl, as if he'd just swallowed the most bitter of pills. "Yes, it was supposed to be. However, the individual in question decided to leverage the situation, and rang me last night in order to request that I 'fix' some speeding-ticket issues he is experiencing."

"Oh dear."

"Yes. Oh dear, indeed."

Commissioner Gareth Ferguson was renowned for several things, but two of the brightest stars in that particular firmament were one, his loathing of anyone attempting to peddle influence to circumvent the law, and two, his ability to bear a grudge. O'Rourke had once heard it expressed that given the choice between crossing Ferguson and crossing the M50 motorway blindfolded, you should take the blindfold every time and hope for the best.

Ferguson turned to face the window and watched the treetops swaying in the morning breeze. "Not only shall laughing boy's speeding problem be dealt with in full by the courts, but I've made some calls, and he should probably install a revolving door at his establishment, seeing as the health inspectors will be visiting it with metronomic frequency from now on."

O'Rourke nodded. Ferguson never needed to break the law – not when he could think of so many, *many* ways of using it to his advantage.

"So," continued Ferguson, turning back, "now that we've covered the bonhomie section of proceedings, let us get to the elephant in the room – the one that has just laid a monumental turd on my recently cleaned carpets."

"I take it you received my update on the Rosie Flint case?" asked O'Rourke.

"No, Fintan. I called you in as I find myself increasingly attracted to you, and I long to look across this desk into those deep soulful eyes of yours."

O'Rourke obviously knew his boss was joking, but for the life of him, he still couldn't come up with any kind of riposte.

"Yes," the Commissioner went on, "I have brought you here to discuss that particular monumental balls-up. How are we being blindsided by this?"

"I'm not sure what you mean, sir. Respectfully, at your instruction, Detective Cassidy from my team became the primary point of contact on this case only yesterday morning. Since then, while there have been developments with the breaking and entering, and the assault, she has done all she can to get up to speed with proceedings."

"Yes, yes, yes. I am primarily referring to the involvement of one Sabine LeFèvre." The Commissioner looked down and pulled irritably at the zip on his tracksuit top. "What mentally deficient nincompoop came up with the idea for such a ghastly garment?"

O'Rourke paused for a moment, thrown by the non sequitur, before stating, "I believe the tracksuit was invented just before the Second World War by Le Coq Sportif, but only really surged in popularity in the late sixties when Adidas released one in collaboration with the German great Franz Beckenbauer. Although ..." He trailed off as he noticed Ferguson's raised eyebrow. "Sorry, sir. I now see that was clearly a rhetorical question."

"No, no, Fintan. A detailed history of the tracksuit was exactly why I called you in here at this ungodly hour."

O'Rourke gave a thin smile. "Happy to oblige."

"Indeed. While I am loathe to drag you back to the small matter of policing, have you come across Ms LeFèvre before?"

"No, sir, but it's been a while since I worked any vice cases."

"Vice?" Ferguson scoffed. "Do you think she's standing on street corners, Fintan? Asking passing motorists if they're looking for a good time? As it happens, I have met the lady in question several times."

O'Rourke did an extremely bad job of hiding his surprise. "I'm sorry, sir?"

"I didn't know who she was on the first couple of occasions. If memory serves, my beloved tipped me the wink, as it were, having picked it up from somebody else. As I recall, Ms LeFèvre was on the arm of a foreign diplomat at one event and an obscenely wealthy tech entrepreneur at another. It became obvious only when she was introduced to us as the niece of a papal envoy."

"Fuck off!" said O'Rourke, before remembering himself. "Apologies, sir – I meant—"

"Yes, I think we can take it as read that you meant to say 'fuck off, sir'," the Commissioner cut in, with a wiggle of his substantial eyebrows. "To continue my point, I am reliably informed the woman in question is the most highly paid, shall we say, lady of negotiable virtue, on this fair and noble isle."

"And her clients introduced her to you, sir, the most senior police officer in the country?"

"Not all of them, I assume. But don't be naive, Fintan. Have you met the so-called great and powerful? You think such men care? They undoubtedly got a kick out of it. Even once I knew who she was, while I avoided photo opportunities, obviously, I bore the woman no ill will. As my wife rightly commented, she is exceedingly good company. Believe me, anyone who can make the Belgian ambassador tolerable is worth every penny. She even gave the wife a tip about her golf swing that, to this day, she swears shaved a good four strokes off her handicap."

Again, O'Rourke found himself at quite a loss as to how to respond to this.

Ferguson smirked. "Welcome to what life is like when you become one of the seat-stuffers required to attend government bashes. More money does not make people more moral – quite the opposite, in fact. The only difference between the individuals who spent the night in one of our cells and those who spent it at a state dinner, is that one group can afford to be better dressed. Not that they necessarily are."

"Are you aware," asked O'Rourke, "that the lady in question is writing a book?"

Ferguson barked a bitter laugh. "Am I aware? Am I aware?" He drummed his fingers on the desk. "Officially? Needless to say, Fintan, let us consider this entire chat as being just between us."

"Of course, sir."

"Well then," he said, leaning back in his chair. "I have been aware of the book for the last couple of months. Interested parties are ... 'interested' doesn't really do it justice. Shitting themselves? It turns out rather a lot of people were under the false impression that they were buying companionship and discretion. As far as I'm aware, nobody is complaining about the quality of the former, but it seems the latter was never as guaranteed as they assumed. Let's just say that on several occasions, friends of friends of friends have brought up this book with me. I have made it very clear to one and all that somebody writing a book full of the truth cannot be accused of blackmail, given that she has not asked anybody for any money. Having said that, judging by my wife's reaction alone, I believe publishers are right to assume this thing will be a bestseller. It is not our job to protect the reputations of fools and adulterers."

"Understood, sir."

Ferguson cracked his knuckles. "However, if the lady in question and, apparently, the bloody book have now become centrepieces in one of our investigations, then that does concern me. Greatly."

"Do you have any idea who might be trying to steal a copy of it?"

"Ha. If you can find me somebody who *wouldn't* want to read it, do let me know. As for who might be particularly worried about its contents, well, if you were to start with a copy of *Who's Who* and cross off anybody who doesn't have a penis, that wouldn't be a bad starting point."

"Should we put surveillance on Ms LeFèvre and Ms Flint?"

The Commissioner worked his tongue around his mouth. "But that opens up a whole other can of worms, doesn't it? Then we can be accused of surveilling enemies of the state, as it were."

"That is a problem," agreed O'Rourke.

"That it is."

The two men looked at each other across the desk for a long drawn-out moment.

"I take it you're not going to direct me in this matter?" asked O'Rourke.

The Commissioner shook his head slowly. "As always, should you officially request it, the entire hierarchy of the Garda Síochána is here to assist you in any way it can." He followed up his words with a smile that contained very little warmth.

O'Rourke nodded. Essentially, it was his job to make this go away while also making it seem it had never been there in the first place.

"Also," continued the Commissioner, absentmindedly pulling his tracksuit zip up and down, "our friend Mr McGarry is already involved – albeit not in any official capacity. Perhaps, for once, that could work in our favour? And by 'our' here, I mean 'your'."

"Understood, sir."

"And whatever the hell you do, do try to keep it out of the papers. We do not want to put our heads above the parapet – not when the political classes are all set for their little battle royale to decide who will be beckoned forth to lead."

"I hear it might be—"

"The Arsehole? Or the Minister for Foreign Affairs, to give him his official title. With emphasis on the word 'affairs'."

Both men paused.

"You don't think ..." started O'Rourke.

"No, and neither do you. The man might be a notorious shagger, but he famously doesn't pay for his meals, so I can't see him paying for anything else."

"Yes, sir."

"That'll be all, Fintan. And as Napoleon said, I'd rather have a general who was lucky than one who was good. Try to be both."

O'Rourke nodded as he got to his feet and headed for the door.

"Oh, and Fintan ..." The detective turned to look back at the Commissioner. "Unofficially, if you do find a copy of the book, it would make an excellent birthday present."

Chapter Nineteen

WHAT'S MORE ANONYMOUS THAN ANONYMOUS?

Bunny had been relieved to receive the phone call from Ivan Retton –
not least because his paltry supply of leads had all but dried up.
Truth be told, he didn't consider himself to be any great shakes as a
detective. Sherlock Holmes he was not, although he had spent the
morning and a large part of yesterday taking an idea he'd lifted from
221B Baker Street's most famous occupant and adapting it for his
purposes. The McGarry mind might not have been the finest
deductive engine of its generation, but it had its own kind of feral
cunning that, when applied, could be pretty effective in most
situations. Also, on the upside, Bunny didn't need to be off his face on
morphine and coke in order to kick it into gear.

Bunny met Ivan as arranged outside St Stephen's Green Shopping
Centre, and they headed off together down towards Chatham Street.
Ivan was on his day off and so the suit he was wearing was neither
gold nor adorned with pigeons. They made awkward small talk as
they walked. Bunny asked about Ivan's now-grown children and his
wife, and Ivan responded with understandable pride, his humble
nature battling with his obvious delight at his daughter's impending
qualification as a paediatrics doctor. Bunny had less news to share –

no wife, no kids, just a career he was currently taking a break from, and which he wasn't entirely sure he wanted to resume.

It wasn't as if Ivan had come to terms with his drink problem and then the two of them had stopped being friends. It was rather that drinking together had been their activity of choice whenever they met up. It worried Bunny what it said about his lifestyle that somebody quitting booze meant he and they lost touch. He'd been thinking about it, and he honestly couldn't say who had stopped ringing whom. Ivan had always been excellent company, and surprisingly gregarious for a man who stood stock-still and silent for a living. Bunny guessed that he simply had been part of a life that Ivan had decided to leave behind for good reasons. He was honestly happy for his friend – not least because it was clear that Ivan was a lot happier in himself. None of this made their meeting any less awkward, and it felt a lot more so when they took a right turn down Clarendon Street and stopped outside a pub.

"This is the place," announced Ivan.

"A pub?" responded Bunny in surprise. "Would it not be better to meet him somewhere more ... less ... I mean ..."

Ivan squinted and gave his companion a look Bunny remembered all too well. One that said the man thought you were talking absolute nonsense. "We must meet here. He is manager."

Bunny shut his mouth and followed Ivan inside.

It was a nice place. As it was just before 3pm, the lunch rush had long since subsided and the post-work crowd was still a couple of hours away, so business was understandably slow. There was the odd book-reader and laptop-tapper interspersed with a few duos chatting over coffee or a pint. Bunny and Ivan took the corner booth.

A thin man who was edging towards gaunt, about fifty years of age with tightly cropped white hair and a matching thick brush moustache, nodded at them from behind the bar. He fussed over a few things, spoke quietly to the woman working beside him, then came over to join the two men. He offered Bunny a firm handshake and introduced himself as Paddy Butler. He had a strong Dublin accent and a surprisingly soft voice. It seemed as if he consciously had to push it in order to raise it above its natural whisper.

"Thanks very much for agreeing to speak to me," said Bunny.

Paddy gave a nervous nod and picked at one of the beer mats in front of him. "I've known Ivan here for years and he vouched for ye, so, y'know."

"He tells me you were Mark Smith's sponsor."

"I was, only I didn't know him by that name."

"What did you know him as?"

Paddy glanced at Ivan, who gave him an encouraging nod.

"Before we get into that," said Paddy, "can we just clarify exactly what's going on here?"

"No problem."

Paddy scanned the pub, then leaned in and lowered his voice even further. "It's just that ... Look, the 'anonymous' part of Alcoholics Anonymous is pretty important. Having said that, these obviously aren't ordinary circumstances. I haven't heard from John" – Paddy raised a finger – "that's who I knew him as – John Myrtle – in a few days. That's unusual, and everything else aside, I was already concerned before Ivan dropped round. John's not been answering his phone. So, I spoke to a couple of people, and we agreed it made sense that I help you as much as I can. I don't want to betray any confidences, though, so I guess I'm going to have to tread a fine line here."

Bunny nodded. "I completely understand. I wouldn't want you to. I'll be honest with you, this is new ground for me too, but I think first and foremost we both want to make sure the guy's okay."

Paddy sat back on his stool, looking slightly reassured by Bunny's words. "Okay, then. If you wouldn't mind, maybe you could start by telling me what you know?"

It wasn't how Bunny usually would have started an interview, but given the circumstances, it didn't seem like an unreasonable request. As Ivan and Paddy listened, Bunny brought them up to speed, more or less, with the events of the last couple of days. He left out any mention of Sabine or her book, as he was unsure whether it played any part in this. When Bunny had finished, Paddy, who'd been staring at the table as he listened intently, raised his head and licked his lips.

"Yeah. To be honest, and odd as this is to say, it didn't feel like John Myrtle was really his name. Not that I'm saying Mark Smith or … what was the other one?"

"The apartment is in the name Daniel Poole."

"I mean, any or none of those names could be his real one. You occasionally get people at AA who want to use a pseudonym, but nobody makes a big deal out of it."

"So how long has he been attending meetings?"

"I met him about six months ago, and he'd just moved to town at that point. Or, at least, that's what he told me." Paddy gave a soft laugh. "God, you've got me questioning everything now."

"And you're his sponsor?"

"That's right. He asked me after a couple of months. I'd only done it once before and" – Paddy averted his eyes, winced, and Bunny sensed a pain pass through the man – "let's just say it didn't go great. But me and him got on well, so I thought it was about time to try again. I've been twelve years sober now."

"Congratulations." Bunny wasn't sure if that was the right thing to say but he couldn't think of anything else. "How long had John been sober?"

"He said two years. I'd believe him on that point." He looked to Ivan for support.

Ivan nodded. "I agree. That's not something anybody who attends meetings would lie about."

"And had he any relapses in that time?"

"Not really," said Paddy. "Everybody has those bad days and long nights. They're all part of the process, really, but he'd come through them. He attended meetings three times a week, and up until this week he'd never missed one. Not one."

"So," said Bunny, "him falling off the wagon at this point would come as a big surprise?"

Paddy paused, looked to Ivan again for a long moment, then ran a couple of fingers over his moustache. "I ... Let me put it this way – there's a reason that every time one of us stands up to speak, we acknowledge that we are an alcoholic. It doesn't matter how long it's been, it's not something you were, it's something that you are. In that regard, if anybody has a relapse, it doesn't come as a surprise. That's not the way we think about it."

"I see what you're saying." A thought struck Bunny. "If this isn't a stupid question, did John ever say what his drink of choice was?"

"Now that you mention it, he only ever referred to beer and wine."

"So not vodka?"

Paddy shrugged. "Look, an alcoholic is an alcoholic. You'll take what's there."

Bunny bit his lip. "Did he say what he did for a living?"

Paddy shook his head. "Not really. I think he referred to himself as a consultant a couple of times, but honestly, it was pretty clear he wanted to avoid talking about it. I do know he used to be in the military."

"Really?" said Bunny, thinking back to the fastidiously folded clothes he'd seen in the wardrobe at the apartment, and the perfectly made bed. "British Army, I assume?"

"Initially, but it sounded like he, ehm ... What would you call it? Went freelance at some point. He didn't give specifics, but I think it's fair to say that coping with what he'd seen and done was a big factor when it came to the drinking."

Bunny nodded. "But he didn't say what he was doing in Dublin?"

"Nothing that sounded terribly believable. Again, being honest with you, I assumed it was probably something a bit dodgy, but it's not my place to judge or pry. AA is all about helping you live your life and not judging what that life is."

"And did he ever mention a lady called Rosie Flint?"

Paddy took a deep breath and nodded. "Never mentioned her second name but Rosie was someone we talked about a lot."

Paddy started to drum his fingers on the table. Bunny could tell he was weighing up what he was going to say next, and he didn't want to say anything to make the man feel as if he were being put under pressure.

Eventually, Paddy looked back up and jutted his chin, as if he'd come to a decision. "Alright. Seeing as the guy's disappeared, this might be important." He looked at Bunny directly. "He has strong feelings for the girl. Says he loves her. He was struggling. We had several discussions – he'd lied to her and he wanted to come clean, desperately, but he didn't think she'd understand."

"Did he say what these lies were?" asked Bunny.

Paddy shook his head. "Just that he hadn't told her the truth. He wanted to spend the rest of his life with her." Paddy pointed across the table at Bunny. "I remember him using those exact words. He said he'd never felt about anyone the way he felt about her. I told him that if she loved him, she'd hopefully understand. More importantly, a big part of what we talk about at AA is being honest with others and ourselves. I did worry that if he came clean and she rejected him, that could have been a trigger, but from what you've told me, that didn't happen?"

"No," said Bunny. "Rosie has no idea where he's gone. As far as she's concerned, he just disappeared."

Paddy ran the tip of his tongue over his lips, brushing against the underside of his moustache. "Here's the thing ... Whatever was going on with John, the more we talked about it, the less I thought it was something like him having a wife tucked away somewhere. I mean ... Look – I was always aware he was" – Paddy swayed his head from side to side – "being economical with the truth, and that's before I knew all this stuff about the different names and him saying he worked at that building site when he clearly didn't. But the one thing I really believe" – he looked first at Ivan and then across at Bunny – "I'd bet my life he was truly in love with that girl."

For the next few minutes, Bunny asked any questions he could think of – people or places John or Mark or whatever you wanted to call him might have mentioned, any friends, anyone else from the meetings who might know anything. Any clues as to what kind of work he was doing. It soon became clear that Paddy had given up all the useful information he had. Bunny thanked him for his time, and thanked Ivan for the introduction, before leaving the two men alone.

As he pushed open the pub's main door and walked out into the afternoon drizzle, Bunny ran through all he'd heard, again and again. It felt like the more pieces of the puzzle he got, the less clear the picture became. The John fella seemingly had had a lot to hide, but despite the lies, his feelings for Rosie might have been genuine after all. None of which explained why he might have disappeared or who might have gone to such lengths to make it appear as if he hadn't.

Bunny had the horrible feeling that something was coming that would clarify the situation, and whatever it was, it wasn't going to be good news.

Chapter Twenty

THE BEST-LAID PLANS

Sabine LeFèvre looked down at the contents of the small suitcase laid out on the bed in front of her and tutted. In happier moments she liked to think she had many fine qualities; however, an ability to travel light had never been one of them. Packing for a short trip was challenging enough, but nowhere near as bad as packing for a supposedly short trip that, in reality, would be considerably longer. She and Henry were scheduled to fly to Paris in a few hours, to catch a connecting flight to Moscow. Their return flights were scheduled for three days later.

The whole idea was to make it look as if Sabine were taking one of her regular trips abroad. Over the years, she'd accompanied clients to many different cities. She sincerely loved Dublin, but when all was said and done, it remained a small town at heart, where it felt as if everyone knew everyone else's business. Accompanying a client to a conference, real or imaginary, followed by a couple of days of sightseeing, was usually a refreshing break from the norm. Such a service was only offered to regulars, of course, and, needless to say, it did not come cheap.

That was not what was happening on this occasion. Most of those flight bookings were for the benefit of anybody who might be unduly interested. The reality was that in Paris, she and Henry would be catching a taxi from the airport, which would take them to Saint-Cloud, where a car would be waiting that could not be traced back to them. They would then drive through the night to a tiny village outside Bilbao, to a house that could not be traced back to them either. Hence Sabine was leaving her home of over a decade with nothing more than a small suitcase. She corrected herself – now was not the time for melodrama. It wasn't as if she were leaving it for ever; it was merely a temporary solution to an unexpected situation.

When she had spoken to the enjoyably eccentric Bunny McGarry the day before, she had played things down, as she had been doing to Henry for a considerably longer period, but the reality was she was becoming more and more concerned.

Sabine was not naive – she knew there were people who would be very upset to hear she was writing a book, and she had known that as soon as she engaged an agent and feelers were sent out it was inevitable that the word would spread. It had been just three months since she and Henry had shared a bottle of wine on the beach and she'd informed him that she was retiring. From that moment on, their unconventional relationship had begun to mould itself into a more familiar configuration.

She had come to know Henry during his time as her friend's driver. Monica had been "in the business" before leaving it in an unusual manner. She'd married a client and they'd moved to Australia for a fresh start. It happens. Not as often as some customers might think, but it does. They were happy too. Every year, Sabine received a Christmas card from them, with a picture of their growing brood.

She'd employed Henry to fill the same role. At first, he'd been taciturn and overbearing, treating everyone she met as if they were a potential threat. At the time, she'd been younger than she let on, and more naive than she'd realised. Then, one night, trouble – real trouble – came her way, and before she'd had time to realise just how much of it she was in, Henry had been there. A couple of Dutch bankers were left with a permanent reminder of the importance of manners, and she begrudgingly agreed to listen to Henry a little more.

Over a considerable amount of time, things started to change between them.

While they'd grown closer without realising it, the nature of Sabine's work meant that there still had to be a certain distance. He was her security – a lover's jealousy was impossible baggage to carry in such a role. He'd always appeared to appreciate that, and yet men were men. She never understood that lazy joke about them not being able to multitask, but in her experience, most of them were incredibly bad at being able to compartmentalise. The two of them had left a lot unsaid until the time was right, and then, that night on the beach, they had finally said it all.

Over the last couple of months, though, something hadn't been right. Not between her and Henry – that had been going wonderfully well – but between them and the world around them. It had taken them both a couple of weeks to verbalise it, but somehow it had been both frightening and reassuring when they'd realised they'd been sensing the same thing. It was hard to put your finger on – an uneasy feeling; the sensation of being watched; that glimpse of something out of the corner of your eye that was not quite right and gone when you tried to give it your full attention.

At first it had just been suspicions – spotting vehicles driving by a little too slowly, the eyes of strangers lingering a little too long. It wasn't as if she hadn't been followed before – jealous wives, a couple of clients who'd mistakenly believed they were more than clients, at least one tabloid hack trying to get a story. This was different, though. Her retirement, which was common knowledge among her regulars, did rather limit the reasons for someone being interested in her. It also simply didn't feel right.

Just before her discreetly acquired agent had started pitching to publishers, Sabine had spent a couple of days making phone calls. She considered most of her regular clients to be old friends, and she took the time to assure them that the time they had spent together would remain strictly private. Equally, even though they hadn't enjoyed a similarly close relationship, a certain organised-crime figure was reassured that neither he nor his wife would be getting a mention.

When considering the idea for the book, which she had been for quite some time, Sabine had agreed a set of ground rules with herself. No one who hadn't done anything to deserve it would be named or referred to in a way that would identify them. Only those who had either behaved in a truly unacceptable manner or were guilty of rank hypocrisy had anything to fear.

Sabine's support for Rosie Flint and SWIT remained sincere. She had no time for those who paid lip service to one set of beliefs while living by a very different code in private. These parameters still left her with plenty of material for a book; in fact, while she actually hadn't started writing anything yet, she had a sneaking suspicion it could stretch to two or even three volumes.

Still, that creeping feeling of being watched, Henry's belief that his emails had been hacked, and Sabine's house being broken into, followed by Rosie Flint's apartment and office – whatever this was, it was escalating. The whole thing felt like an overreaction. She'd received entreaties from a couple of people to keep their names out of the book – one of which she'd agreed to for, it had to be said, a substantial fee. Sadly, the individual in question had significantly overestimated the level of interest in him. Simply put, there was nothing about him that was worthy of being printed. Still, she'd given half of the money to a dog shelter she was particularly fond of. Karma might be a bitch, but at least that bitch would now have a warm bed for the night.

She'd made a list of those who might have reason to be worried about the book's publication, and none of them had the resources or the temperament to mount this kind of offensive. She was missing something, she had no idea what it was, and that was beginning to terrify her.

The disappearance of the mysterious Mark Smith made even less sense to her. Maybe it wasn't related, but it was too big a coincidence to brush aside. So no, for better or worse, she and Henry were getting out of here, and doing so in such a way as to make it as difficult as possible to track them down. She knew too much to ignore that icy feeling at the back of her neck, warning her that something wasn't right.

The doorbell rang. She glanced up and then over at the clock on the wall.

Henry's head appeared around the bedroom door and he smiled at her. "The car is a little early, so you still have three minutes to stare mournfully into that suitcase before you actually have to close it."

She stuck out her tongue but couldn't resist laughing. "You have no appreciation for how hard this is."

He grinned back. "All I need is you, my love."

"You say that, *monsieur*. You haven't seen what this looks like without access to hair straighteners and a full complement of serums and moisturisers."

It was Henry's turn to stick out his tongue before departing and pointing at the clock as he did so. "Two minutes."

The doorbell rang again.

"Alright," she heard him call as he headed down the hall. "I'm coming. I'm coming."

Sabine took one last look at the contents of the suitcase as she heard the front door open. She could always buy a hairdryer when she got there – that would free up a little more space.

She was dimly aware of the murmuring of voices as Henry spoke to the driver. She only looked up when she heard the thumping noise.

"Henry? Is everything alright?"

No response. She felt that icy feeling on the back of her neck again.

"Henry?" she repeated.

It didn't feel right.

It didn't feel right.

It didn't feel—

Then, as she had somehow known it would, the figure appeared in the doorway. And now, it was too late to get out.

Chapter Twenty-One

AN EVENING'S STROLL

Bunny pulled down his flat cap closer to his eyes and strode on purposefully. He wasn't normally a fan of headwear but he was attempting to travel incognito. This was no casual evening stroll. Looming ahead of him in the distance was his goal – the construction site of yet another new and no doubt shiny building as the Irish economy strode boldly into the twenty-first century. He noticed buildings came with mission statements these days. It really knocked you back on your arse to realise that inanimate structures had their lives more together than you did.

He was on Charlemont Place, with the tree-lined Grand Canal to his left and the Grand Parade on the other side of the water. The light rain was enough to discourage the normal plethora of love-struck couples walking hand in hand along the waterside. The last bloom from the setting sun, trapped unromantically behind cock-blocking cloud cover, mingled with the streetlights as they came on, lighting the way for weary commuters trying to get from A to B as quickly as possible, and dog walkers attempting to get from door to dump at a similar speed.

Bunny felt his phone vibrate in his pocket. He took it out and recognised the number. Part of him was tempted not to answer, but he was still a few minutes away from his destination and morbid curiosity got the better of him.

"Deccie, long time no hear."

"I rang you yesterday and the day before, boss."

"Yes, I remember now. How are things?"

"I'll tell you how things are, boss. I'll tell you. Diabolical."

"Well," responded Bunny, "while I am, of course, very sorry to hear that, can I just say that it truly warms my heart to hear you making use of that word-of-the-day calendar I got you for Christmas."

"Seriously, boss. I don't have time to engage in our normal witty repartee."

"Again, well done."

"Can you get here in the next fifteen minutes?"

"Leaving aside the fact that I have no reason to do so, and the other fact that I'm kind of in the middle of something – no, Deccie. No, I cannot make the normally four-hour drive to Kerry in the next quarter of an hour."

"Alright, I reckon if I try and hide behind some of those bushes they've got round here, I could probably stretch it to half an hour."

"I'm afraid it's still going to be a very definite no, Declan."

"Ah, boss! What's the point of you owning that sports car if you're not going to get some use out of it?"

Bunny was both proud and sensitive when it came to his 1980s Porsche 928 S LHD. He'd bought it from an insurance company who were writing it off, and had then persuaded some mechanics to restore it for him. It had been fraught with problems since he'd owned it, and that was before it had taken a regrettable, if necessary, dip in the sea.

"It's a Porsche, Deccie, not a time machine. Concord couldn't get to you that fast."

"It's in the garage again, isn't it, boss?"

"No, as it happens." It was, but Bunny was picking it up in the morning. "Anyway, while I know I'm going to regret asking, what has brought about this latest crisis?"

"Dancing!"

Bunny moved nimbly around a poodle and its owner, as one of the pair did their utmost to take a dump on the pavement while the other tried to pretend it wasn't happening. "Declan, if I can give you some serious advice, one man to another – the women go mad for a man who can dance."

"Sure, don't I know that."

Bunny was taken aback. "So what's the problem?"

"I'll tell you what the problem is. They have some very strict – what I would call overly restrictive – definitions of what is and isn't Irish dancing."

"Ah, right. And what would be your definition?"

"I am Irish, ergo any dancing I do is Irish dancing."

Bunny considered this for a second. "I mean, I can see what you're saying, Deccie, but I'm guessing others disagree with that viewpoint."

"You could say that. They brought us to this kelly thing."

"Céilí, I'd imagine, but go on."

"It's wall to wall with babes."

"Some things we probably don't need to share."

"So I'm, like – hold back, lads, I'll handle this."

"Loving the confidence."

"And the DJ drops a track—"

"That seems unlikely."

"I give it a couple of seconds, let myself feel the groove, and then I move into the centre of the dance floor and *bam*! It's Deccie o'clock."

"Excuse me?"

"I am popping, locking and dropping. I'm talking the robot, the running man, the cha-cha slide—"

"You're losing me here, Declan."

Deccie continued regardless, the excitement growing in his voice. "And, as if I need to make this clear, the place is going mental. Whooping, cheering, clapping. Women want me, men want to be me."

"Easy there, Travolta."

"I'm going into my big finale – the electric worm ..."

"I thought it was just called the worm?"

"Not how I do it."

"Let me guess," interjected Bunny, "you had an allergic reaction to your own sweat?"

"No, don't be daft. This teacher, 'Bollocks Breath' Byrne—"

"Please tell me you didn't come up with the nickname?"

"He comes in, grabs me, drags me off the floor and says he's going to batter the head off me."

Bunny stopped in his tracks and the playful tone dropped from his voice. "And did he?"

"No. Ms Wainwright intervenes and sends me to the headmaster's office."

Bunny resumed walking. "Alright. Well, this one seems like a simple misunderstanding."

"That wouldn't surprise me," admitted Deccie. "I've not understood a bleeding thing since I've been here. They keep insisting on talking Irish at ye. It's like they're trying to be awkward."

"You think that's bad, wait until you visit France. Nothing but French."

Deccie gasped, genuinely scandalised. "People just love being difficult, don't they?"

"And the French doubly so."

"Anyway, what I was thinking was, maybe you could come get me and tell them that you need me for some important police business?"

"See, the problem with that, Deccie, is it would be a lie. And what have we said about telling lies?"

"That it's a necessary evil."

"That is not what we've said."

"It's what you said when you flooded that toilet while we were on that tour of Croke Park."

"That was entirely different."

"It's exactly the same," protested Deccie. "Yet again, I'm up to my knees in shite."

Bunny was coming up to the building site now, and a familiar figure was standing on the corner, waving at him.

"Anyway," he said to Deccie, preparing to tie up the call, "I have every confidence that you'll figure it out. You are, after all, a real people person."

"But, boss—"

Bunny hung up.

Marco was standing under an awning, his small backpack in one hand and a sleeping bag in the other. His shoulders were rounded in a way that made him look like he was always preparing to duck. It was as if life had taught him to expect the unexpected, and that the unexpected would never be pleasant. Bunny stepped out of the rain and joined him under the canopy.

"I was starting to worry you'd not got the message," said Marco.

"No worries on that score. I got here as soon as I could. This is brilliant work, Marco. Well done."

A flush of pride touched the other man's face and he stood a little straighter. "It was a team effort. Jimmy, Tanya, Bryn, Noel – they all helped out."

"Well, I owe you all big for this, and I won't forget it." Bunny reached his hand into his coat and pulled out his wallet, but Marco waved it away.

"No, no, no. No need for that."

Bunny felt awkward. "Are you sure?"

"You helped out Micky and got those two pyromaniac arseholes off the streets. Let's call it even."

"Ara, let me give you something for all your trouble?"

Marco shook his head. "No need. It was nice to feel useful, y'know?"

Bunny put his wallet away. "If you ever need anything ..."

"Yeah. Likewise."

Bunny nodded towards the building site, where scaffolding stretched around the bare bones of the building-to-be. "He's up the top?"

Marco nodded. "Yeah. He snuck past the security guard, which isn't hard to do, to be fair. Lazy sod hasn't got out of that cabin since it started raining." He pointed down the path. "There's a gap in the fencing just over there."

"Thanks again," said Bunny.

He watched as Marco moved away, then he squeezed through the gap in the fence and found the stairs that led up to the roof. He passed through floors of bare concrete on his way up, where the only movement was blue tarpaulin coverings flapping in the breeze.

He reached the roof through a doorway with no door. Near the building's edge, a figure stood silhouetted against the night, staring intently at the street below.

Bunny cleared his throat to get the man's attention. As the figure turned around, he didn't look particularly surprised to see his visitor.

Bunny gave a tip of his cap. "Dr Livingstone, I presume?"

Chapter Twenty-Two

THE INVISIBLE MAN

Bunny had been looking for the man for several days, but now that he'd found him, he was at a bit of a loss as to what to say. As Rosie Flint had known him, this was Mark Smith. He was wearing a brown leather jacket and blue jeans, and despite sporting several days' stubble, he was unmistakably the man from the photo. He seemed disinclined towards conversation; instead, he chose to focus intently on the Grand Parade.

Bunny took a few steps forward and the two men stood there watching the relatively light amount of traffic as it passed on the other side of the canal. It wasn't that Bunny was afraid of heights, but the other man standing mere inches from the edge of the roof was making him nervous.

"So," Bunny began. "What should I call you? John or Daniel?"

The man rewarded him with a look over his shoulder. Then, after a moment, he nodded, almost approvingly. "You found Paddy?"

"I did," replied Bunny. "I don't know the history, but he seemed a bit concerned that his second stint as a sponsor hadn't gone well. You could probably do with giving him a call. Let him know you're alright."

This earned Bunny a shake of the head. "Too risky. If you can find him, so can somebody else. By the way, my name is actually Mark Smith."

"Really? Ironically, I think that's the one everybody's dismissing as the obvious fake."

"Not that you'll find anything if you go looking for somebody by that name. At least, you won't find me."

"Let me guess – you've got those kind of military records that they set on fire then bury underground?"

"Something like that."

Bunny noted that the guy had an accent you might vaguely place as English but no more exact than that. "Sorry, I just realised I'm being rude." Bunny extended his hand. "I've not introduced myself ..."

Smith looked at the hand but didn't take it. "I know who you are, Mr McGarry. Rosie told me all about you. I figured it would be you she'd call, given her attitude towards the police in general." He nodded at Bunny's hand. "No offence, but no, thank you. Don't come any closer, either, if you please."

Bunny drew his hand away and took a step back. "No problem. I don't suppose I could interest you in coming away from the edge there, could I? You're making me nervous."

Smith looked down at his feet then back at Bunny. "I'm not ... That's not what I'm here for."

"Oh, I know that. You're trying to watch over her."

Smith gave the briefest dip of his head as his only acknowledgement. "Can I ask – how did you find me?"

"It wasn't actually me," admitted Bunny. "I have to give most of the credit to Sir Arthur Conan Doyle."

At this, Smith turned and looked directly at Bunny. This time, Bunny noticed the dark rings around the man's bloodshot eyes. At a guess, he wasn't drinking again, but he wasn't sleeping either.

"I basically stole old Arthur's idea, the Baker Street Irregulars. I figured you might try and get in contact with herself, or somebody else might be sniffing around, so I enlisted some homeless friends of mine. Rosie being Rosie, I imagined she follows a pretty set routine that consists mainly of going back and forth between her office and her apartment. I asked them to cover as much of the route as possible, keeping both an eye on her and an eye out for you. As we've all become very good at ignoring homeless people ..."

"... nobody would think they were being used for surveillance," finished Smith. "Very clever."

"Well, that Arthur Conan Doyle was one smart cookie. He was, quite literally, away with the fairies near the end there, but we all have our little eccentricities, don't we? Speaking of which, don't you think it's about time you explain to me what the hell is going on?"

Smith rubbed a hand over the patch of angry red skin on his neck. He left a long enough pause that Bunny was beginning to wonder if he was going to speak again, but when he did, all he said was, "It's complicated."

"Now, that I can definitely believe. In the last few days, I've gone from thinking you might be off on the mother of all benders, to back home in Blighty somewhere with your none-the-wiser wife, to reckoning there was a reasonable chance you might be dead."

"And what do you think now?"

Bunny took a moment to consider this. "To be honest with you, as I'm always telling people, I'm really not much of a detective."

Smith held out his hands. "You seem to be doing okay."

Bunny pulled his coat a little tighter around himself. "Jesus, you can really feel the wind up here, can't you?"

His remark elicited no response at all.

"You've got that strong and silent thing down. Fair play. I'd guess Rosie has a type."

From his side-on view Bunny couldn't be sure, but he thought he picked up a slight twitch of irritation in Smith at that last remark. "Okay, so ... I'll hypothesise and you tell me whether I'm hot or cold." Bunny took Smith's slightly raised eyebrow as all the agreement he was going to get. "You're a professional. You were sent here to do a job. However, I'm guessing you've gone off the reservation – or would it be more correct to say you've gone *on* the reservation in this scenario? I probably shouldn't use cowboy metaphors – a couple of Clint

Eastwood films aside, I'm a bit out of my element. There's one thing I'm not sure of, though – given your less-than-chatty nature, you strike me as an unlikely honeypot. I'm going to guess you were never supposed to actually meet Rosie?"

Smith gave a slight shake of his head. When he spoke his voice came out softer. "No. That wasn't supposed to happen. That ... was an accident."

"Good," said Bunny. "Because at the moment, I find myself inclined to consider liking you. Now, I'm aware there will be elements of recent events that may give me cause to reconsider, but I'm currently not planning to boot you off this roof for so casually messing with her heart."

With the wind nipping at him, Bunny reached instinctively for the metal flask he kept in his inside pocket, but thought better of it just in time and stopped himself. When dealing with a recovering alcoholic standing on the edge of a rooftop, helping oneself to a swift whiskey against the cold might look a tad insensitive. "So, she was just collateral?"

At this, Smith turned around fully to face Bunny, an expression of honest confusion across his face. "What?"

"I presume your primary interests here were Sabine and her book?"

"No," Smith replied firmly, before turning back to the rooftop edge and resuming his vigil. "Look, a friend of mine – a guy I served with – came to me and told me he had some work. Basic surveillance on a few people. One of the main ones was ..."

Bunny noted how Smith looked down and his otherwise straight posture sagged slightly. "Rosie," he supplied.

"I'm afraid I don't have the answers you're looking for about what's going on," Smith continued, "but I can tell you they only became interested in Sabine after she and Rosie got close. I wasn't supposed to ..." He trailed off. When he turned his attention to Bunny again, Bunny was shocked to see tears in the man's eyes. "I was never supposed to talk to her. I swear – it happened by accident. But it happened. And then, I got to know her and one thing led to another." He bit his lip. "I should have come clean. I know that. But if I had, she wouldn't have wanted anything to do with me."

Smith sat down abruptly, still inches from the rooftop edge, his legs crossed beneath him. Bunny almost leaped forward to grab him.

"I'm a useless piece of shit and I've done some terrible things in my life, but when I was with her I felt ... different." The tears rolling down his cheeks mingled with the soft drizzle from the night sky. "I guess I saw myself a little bit as she saw me, and for the first time in a long time it felt nice. I felt ... worthy."

Bunny considered placing his hand on Smith's shoulder but decided against it. "Yeah," he offered instead. "The love of a good woman will do that to a man."

"I thought that maybe if I gave it up, she'd never have to know that I lied. I told Furkser I wanted out. He's an old friend – at least, he was supposed to be. I thought he might understand."

"Let me guess – it'd be him that you had a violent confrontation with in your flat?"

Smith wiped his eyes and nodded.

"By the way, your mate tried to pass it off as you being an alcoholic who fell off the wagon."

"With friends like him ..." started Smith. To emphasise his point, he shrugged down the right shoulder of his leather jacket and pulled up his T-shirt sleeve to reveal a bandage. "Stuck a knife through my shoulder. He'd been aiming higher. I was lucky to get out alive." He pulled the jacket back on. "Seriously, Furkser is bad news. If you see him coming, head the other way."

"Thanks for the tip," said Bunny. "Is that why you're up here? Because the same people following Rosie are now looking for you too?"

Smith didn't say anything to this. Bunny moved forward slightly in an attempt to meet the other man's eye. "Look, Mark – how about you and me go and talk to a few friends of mine in the gardaí?"

Smith shook his head firmly. "No police."

"But—"

"I said no police," he snapped. "They can't be trusted."

Something in Smith's tone made Bunny think this wasn't your normal bog-standard wariness of the police.

"Why do you—"

Smith raised his hand for silence and pointed across the canal. "There she is."

He followed Smith's direction to where the unmistakable figure of Rosie Flint was striding down the footpath, bag on her hip, earphones in and no doubt blaring some seventies punk rock.

Bunny watched Smith bite his nails nervously as he watched her. When Smith spoke, it was as much to himself as it was to Bunny. "If they were ever going to do something, it would be here. Fewer people. Less traffic. Multiple exits."

"Listen to me. I can help you, if you just ..."

Bunny jumped back as Smith turned and ran past him without a word, heading straight for the stairs. Bunny looked back across the canal to where a man was walking about thirty yards behind Rosie. Bunny noticed the guy raise his hand and touch his ear.

He bolted down the stairs as fast as he could after Mark Smith, hoping against hope that it wasn't already too late.

Chapter Twenty-Three

FRIENDS REUNITED

By the time Bunny was near the bottom of the stairs that ran through the shell of the building, Mark Smith was already outside, pulling himself over the chainlink gates in one smooth movement, like a gymnast working a pommel horse. He wasn't running away, he was running to something, and Bunny wasn't chasing after him but rather heading for the same location.

A portly security guard emerged from his cabin and started to wave his arms ineffectually in Smith's wake. "Whoa, whoa, whoa!"

Bunny stumbled as he jumped down the last few steps, and the security guard turned to confront him. "Stall the —"

Bunny shoulder-charged him to the ground without breaking stride. There was no time for niceties or explanations.

Furkser kept his pace steady. It was all a matter of timing.

Rosie Flint was about fifteen yards ahead of him on the pavement. He just needed to maintain his speed and his longer stride would allow him to catch up with her without him looking as if he was trying to do so.

Luckily, the weather was crappy, which worked to their advantage by keeping the pedestrian traffic to a minimum. Luck hadn't exactly been on their side over the last couple of days. His mind flashed back to his most recent conversation with the Spider and a knot of anger twisted in his gut. The worst thing was that the condescending arse had been right – this was a situation of Furkser's own making.

It had been an uncharacteristic bout of sentimentality that had led to him giving Mark Smith the gig. The guy might be a washed-up drunk trying to get his life back on track, but back in the day he'd been something else. He'd also saved Furkser's life by dragging him out of a firefight in an African hellhole that, officially, they'd never been in.

That had been the point at which Furkser had decided that government work was too much hassle for too little money. He'd paid his debt to Queen and country, and then some. A part of him must have felt that he still owed Smith something, but that bit was now dead. Smith had lied to him repeatedly, and then had the gall to tell him he was quitting mid-mission, and also wanted to shack up with the woman he was supposed to be keeping tabs on.

The woman in question, Rosie Flint, was now ten yards in front of him. Furkser glanced over his shoulder and confirmed that the van was on the move. He'd given them the exact spot to aim for. Buchanan was driving and clearly keen to make up for the previous day's screw-up attempting to search Flint's office.

It wasn't as if Furkser could go pointing the finger at anybody; not only had he messed up by bringing in Smith but he'd also all but told the Spider that Smith was dead. He should be. Again, Furkser had allowed a moment of sentimental weakness to slow his hand enough for the chance to pass him by. If the man had any sense he'd be long gone, possibly drowning himself at the bottom of a bottle. He'd better pray that he never crossed Furkser's path again, as Furkser was now well and truly over his trip down memory lane. The past was the past, and he would enjoy making Smith part of it permanently.

Five yards now. While logic dictated that he couldn't hold Rosie Flint responsible for Smith's appalling lapse in judgement, a part of him was going to enjoy doing precisely that. The reason this was a snatch instead of a kill was that they needed to find out definitively what she knew and, more importantly, who she had told. Nobody was ever going to hear from Rosie Flint again, but an awful lot hinged on whether or not the problem she represented had been contained. Fortunately, he'd had the operational sense to keep Smith in the dark, so at least they were airtight at their end. He'd spend the night making sure they knew all that she knew, and then ... Marshall had already found a spot in the middle of nowhere to bury a body where it would never be found.

The van passed him on the right-hand side. Dammit, Buchanan – too soon! Furkser felt for the syringe in his left-hand pocket as he quickened his pace slightly. Ahead of him, he noticed Flint's body language shift, as some instinct kicked in belatedly and she sensed danger. She pulled out her earphones and looked at the van pulling up beside her.

One yard. Furkser withdrew the syringe and uncapped it with his left hand as he reached out for her with his right, just as the side door of the van began to open. Faster than he anticipated, she spun round and threw a right into his unguarded face. He drew back as the metal dug into the skin just below his eye. The bitch had her keys clenched between her fingers.

Instinctively, he fired a right-handed jab into her face and she stumbled backwards. Before she could fall to the ground, Marshall hopped out of the van and grabbed her. He threw one arm around her waist, pinning her arms by her side, and snaked the other around her neck, pulling her into a tight chokehold.

He yelped as she kicked him hard in the shins, but he maintained his grip as he flopped back into the van and dragged her with him. He wrapped his legs around her as Furkser glanced up and down the road to double check they hadn't been observed. Satisfied, Furkser slipped into the van and slammed the door shut behind them. He watched the terror in Flint's eyes begin to fade as she lost consciousness.

"Okay," said Furkser, prompting Marshall to pull away his hand and give him access to Flint's neck. With practised efficiency he located the carotid artery and injected the etorphine. "She should be completely out in a minute." He slammed his fist into the van's metal roof then felt the vehicle start to pull off.

He looked down at the unconscious form of Rosie Flint and raised his free hand to his eye. He pulled it away to see blood on his fingers. "Stupid cow."

Still, at least something had finally gone right.

As he went to sit down, he tumbled forward as the van veered to the left, rocked violently then screeched to a halt, accompanied by the sound of shattering glass.

"Shit. Watch her!"

———

As he'd pulled away from the kerb, Buchanan's attention had been focused on the passenger-side wing mirror. An elderly man a few doors down from where they'd snatched Rosie Flint had stepped out onto the footpath and was staring at the van, as if trying to figure out whether he'd seen something or not. The old man's interest was why Marshall had only spotted the flurry of movement coming from his right at the last second.

He looked round just in time to register Mark Smith sprinting towards the van, raising his arm and hurling himself at the driver-side door. Smith's elbow came crashing through the window, showering safety glass around Buchanan and forcing him to take his hands off the wheel to shield his face. The van crunched into a parked car to the left and came to a halt. Smith grabbed a fistful of Buchanan's jacket with his left hand and unleashed a messy but ferocious barrage of blows through the window with his right. Buchanan tried to fend off the attack, but Smith was like a man possessed. Both of Smith's hands grabbed him around the neck and slammed his head into the steering wheel. Once ... twice ...

Before Buchanan could be bludgeoned a third time, the hands released him. As woozy as he was, he managed to pull himself away from the window, glancing back just in time to see the unmistakable figure of Furkser come crashing into Smith, sending them both tumbling to the ground.

———

Bunny's lungs felt as if they were about to burst. He'd followed Mark Smith as the slightly younger and considerably fitter man had sprinted across the Ranelagh Road bridge towards the van that had taken Rosie Flint. Despite Bunny going flat out, the other man had only added to his lead. Bunny had no choice but to watch as Smith recklessly hurled himself into the side of the van, managing to bring it to a halt all the same.

While Smith was busy laying into the driver, Bunny had the presence of mind to pull out his phone and dial 999. "Detective Bernard McGarry, Summerhill ... attempted kidnapping in progress, intersection of Ranelagh Road and Grand Parade, suspects armed."

He hung up before the person on the other end could say anything. A tall man appeared out of the back of the van and tackled Smith to the ground. The two of them started to roll around, tearing at each other like wild animals. Bunny ran past them.

He reached the side door of the van just as it slid open. Its progress was halted as Bunny grabbed the far end and, with all his might, slammed it into the blond man who was trying to climb out. The blond looked understandably startled, a state of being that was intensified as the heavy metal door crashed into his head. He tried to scuttle back inside but didn't move fast enough – Bunny drew back the door and slammed it once more, this time catching the man's left arm and eliciting a sickening crack of bone closely followed by a scream.

Bunny opened the door again then threw himself to the ground as a hail of bullets erupted from inside.

Only when he heard the gun dry-click did he hop back to his feet and take in the scene in the back of the van. The blond man was scrabbling about in his jacket, no doubt looking for the spare clip to his gun. Beside him lay the comatose form of Rosie Flint.

"Toss the gun," ordered Bunny, prompting a swear-word-laden response from the blond guy.

Bunny grabbed the man's shattered arm firmly with both hands then repeated his request. This time the man did as he was told. Without another word, Bunny grabbed Rosie Flint and pulled her into a fireman's lift.

First things first – he needed to get her the hell out of the way. He turned and ran in the opposite direction to the one from which he'd arrived. He could get Rosie to safety and then figure out how to deal with her attackers, assuming a helpful armed-response unit didn't show up in the meantime.

Maybe his subconscious heard something, or perhaps some survival instinct kicked in, but Bunny dived into the driveway of one of the canalside houses just as shots rang out behind him.

Unable to use his hands to brace himself, he and Rosie landed in a messy pile – Bunny scraped his knees on the concrete and unconscious Rosie hit the bumper of the Opel Astra parked in the driveway.

Bunny checked his friend was still breathing then scrabbled over to the concrete pillar that marked the end of the drive. He leaned against it as he struggled to draw breath, his lungs heaving with the effort.

He darted his head out from behind the pillar just long enough to see the van's driver standing by the passenger-side door, his gun still raised. Bunny looked around in an attempt to locate anything he could use as a weapon, but nothing presented itself. Wheelie bins might be better for the environment, but what he would have given at that moment for a good old-fashioned metal bin lid. Slamming somebody's face into one of those could ruin their whole day.

In the absence of anything like that, Bunny was going to have to rely on his wits. He didn't fancy the odds. Last he'd seen, Mark Smith had his hands full dealing with one man, which left the other two as Bunny's problem. On the upside, the-fella-from-the-back-of-the-van's career in juggling was going to be put on hold for a while. The driver, on the other hand, while bloodied, was clearly armed and, safe to assume, pissed off. Bunny had ridden the element of surprise further than he could have reasonably expected it to take him, but he was now all out of that.

He eased himself back onto his feet and crouched down, waiting for somebody to come around the corner. Then, in the distance, he heard the blissful sound of sirens. It was possible they weren't heading here, but these men couldn't be sure of that any more than he could.

He risked another quick glance around the pillar and spotted the tall man who'd been fighting Smith bleeding heavily from the mouth as he shoved the driver back into the van. A couple of seconds later he heard the unmistakable sound of the engine roaring into life and the crunch of bodywork as the van pulled itself free of the parked car and sped off down the road.

Bunny stood and, panting heavily, risked a longer look. Relief washed over him as the van disappeared into the distance.

Any elation felt by Bunny fell away when he noticed the figure lying at the side of the road. He hurried back across the street and fell to his knees beside the supine form of Mark Smith. Smith's hands were clasped to his belly but they couldn't hold back the blood gushing forth from the wound. He looked up at Bunny with wide eyes. More blood sputtered from his mouth before he managed to speak in a hoarse whisper. "Rosie?"

"She's safe," answered Bunny, and Smith's head sagged back with relief.

Bunny gently raised Smith up and patted his face firmly. "Come on, stay with me. Hang in there, soldier."

In lieu of a response, Smith coughed up more blood. Bunny watched helplessly as, with obvious agony, Smith took his right hand away from his wound and pushed it into the pocket of his jeans. With his last ounce of energy he shoved something into Bunny's hand. A key on a keyring featuring a pair of green and gold boxing gloves.

Smith gurgled then grabbed a fistful of Bunny's jacket and pulled him closer. "Don't ... trust ... police."

And then, with a last rasping gasp, he died.

Chapter Twenty-Four

BY THE LIGHT OF BURNING BRIDGES

Bunny leaned back in his chair and studied his hands. There was blood under the fingernails of the left one – a dead man's blood. He clenched it into a fist. Instinctively, he reached for the Styrofoam cup in front of him, then thought better of it.

He was sitting in the same interview room in Pearse Street Garda Station that he had occupied a few days ago. The room was unchanged – the unplaceable musty stench was the same, it was quite possible that the cup of tea and/or coffee in front of him was the exact same one, and from the one mouthful he'd already taken, he couldn't rule out the possibility that it had already passed through at least one other person. The biggest difference between today and Tuesday morning was his mood, which could best be described as dark, verging on belligerent.

The door opened and, with a crushing predictability, the same man walked in. "Detective Inspector Fintan O'Rourke," said Bunny. "What a massive non-surprise."

Another difference was that today, as O'Rourke walked across the room to take the seat opposite Bunny, Butch slipped in the door behind him and stood against the far wall. Judging by their identical facial expressions, this was going to be one fun little meeting.

O'Rourke tossed his coat onto the table and sat down. "Jesus Christ, Bunny." He held up his thumb and forefinger about half an inch apart. "You are this close to finding yourself locked up in a cell, so do not even attempt to piss me about."

"And what exactly would the charge be?"

O'Rourke's nostrils flared. "I'm pretty sure interfering with a police investigation is something the courts still frown upon, but I'm no expert. Oh no, wait – I am."

Bunny scoffed and folded his arms. "Ara, feck off. Interfering? I've been helping."

O'Rourke sat forward. "Helping? Really? That's right, I forgot" – he jabbed a thumb over his shoulder in Butch's direction – "you and Detective Cassidy back there are sharing information." Without turning around, he raised his voice. "Detective Cassidy, when was the last time you spoke to Mr McGarry?"

"Last night," supplied Butch sullenly as she looked at her feet.

"And did he happen to mention one Mark Smith in conversation?"

"Only that he had no idea of his whereabouts, sir."

Bunny looked directly at Butch. "And at the time, that was correct."

"'At the time'," repeated O'Rourke, "clearly being the operative words, given that –what? – less than twenty-four hours later, you and Mr Smith are involved in a shootout in South Central Dublin with person, or persons, unknown. This being South Central Dublin, mind you, and not South Central LA. Although, increasingly, you seem to be treating it like they are one and the same."

"It wasn't a shootout," snapped Bunny. "For a start, the phrase 'shootout' implies that there was more than one side doing the shooting. We were attempting to prevent the kidnapping and God knows what else of poor Rosie Flint. How is she, by the way? I've been asking, but nobody has given me an update."

"We'll get to that later," said O'Rourke.

Bunny leaned forward. "You'll get to it now."

The two men proceeded to glare at each other across the table.

Their staring contest was broken only by Butch sighing loudly. "Oh, for fuck's sake, she's fine, all things considered. Got some bruising on her face and they'd injected her with some kind of tranquilliser, but there's no lasting effect."

"Does she know about ..."

"Smith?" finished Butch. "Yes," she added in a lower voice.

Bunny thought about asking how his friend had taken the news, but it felt like a pointless question. He could already guess – not that he wanted to think about it.

"Thank you, Detective Cassidy," said O'Rourke. "See how easy it is to exchange information, Bunny? Now, seeing as you've played her for a mug, do you not think Detective Cassidy deserves an explanation as to how you and Mr Smith came to team up?"

"Feck off, Rigger. It's not how you're making it sound." Bunny looked at Butch again over O'Rourke's shoulder. "I got a tip as to where he might be – with the emphasis on the word 'might', and I was following it up."

"Where did this tip come from?"

"Where tips come from." Bunny waved his hand round. "I passed the man's picture around some acquaintances of mine in the homeless community, somebody recognised him."

"Bit of a coincidence," said O'Rourke.

"Not really. I did it along the route Rosie takes to and from work. I figured if Smith was still hanging around, he might be trying to keep an eye on her."

"And is there any reason why, when you did find him, you forgot to inform your friends and former colleagues in the gardaí?"

"You're starting to piss me off, Rigger."

"Stop calling me that and, in case it wasn't clear, you started pissing me off quite some time ago, *Bernard*. So, to repeat the question – why didn't you call us?"

"There was no time. I got the tip, checked it out and found Smith standing on top of this building site, watching over the Grand Parade because he knew Rosie walked home that way every night. We had a chat for a couple of minutes then, out of nowhere, he took off at a run. I'm guessing he recognised the lads who were about to snatch Rosie off the street." Bunny looked down and noticed the blood under his fingernails again. "He sprinted over there like a man possessed and threw himself at a moving vehicle to stop the bloody thing. Then he got into a scrap with one of the boys."

"And what were you doing while all of this was going on?"

Bunny sat back in his chair. "Initially, I was trying to catch up with the guy. Then I made it my priority to protect the civilian and get Rosie the hell out of there. Which I did."

"And do you have any idea who or what these men are?"

"Dead, if I get my hands on any of them."

O'Rourke rolled his eyes.

Butch cleared her throat. "Sorry, sir, but ... What did you and Mr Smith discuss before all of this happened?"

Bunny gave a brief summary of all he could remember from the conversation. Namely that Smith, whose real name really was Smith, had been brought over here by an ex-army buddy called Furkser to do some surveillance work, and that he, in his own words, had accidentally fallen in love with the person he was supposed to be watching. He didn't know why he was supposed to be doing it – all he knew was that his former colleague had tried to kill him when he attempted to quit because of the aforementioned conflict of interest.

When Bunny had finished, O'Rourke and Butch said nothing for a few seconds, then the DI cleared his throat. "Did he mention Sabine LeFèvre?"

Bunny closed his eyes for a few seconds in order to cast his mind back. Then he opened them again and pointed across the table at O'Rourke. "He did. I said something about them watching Rosie because of her association with Sabine, and he said it was the other way round." He looked at O'Rourke and Butch in turn. "I meant to ask more about it, but I never got the chance. What do you think that means?"

The two detectives averted their eyes. Bunny started to experience a horrible sinking feeling in his stomach. "What are you not telling me?"

O'Rourke started to inspect the cufflinks on his shirt sleeves. "We are not at liberty to—"

Bunny slammed his fist on the desk. "Fintan, I've just told you everything Smith said to me. Has Sabine been taken?"

O'Rourke kept his eyes cast downwards for a second, then returned his gaze to Bunny sitting across from him. "An hour ago, the bodies of Sabine LeFèvre and her associate Henry Ballard were found in her home out in Bray. They were both dead, having been shot multiple times. Twice in the chest, once in the head."

Bunny's mouth went dry. "Oh my God." He blessed himself. "What the hell is going on?"

O'Rourke's tone was softer now. "We were rather hoping you might be able to give us an idea on that front?"

"It doesn't make any sense."

"No," agreed O'Rourke. "It doesn't. This started out as a fairly simple missing-person case, now three people are dead, and it appears we have sophisticated and brutal professional hit squads running round the city."

"Whatever's going on," said Bunny, "Smith said he'd been brought here over six months ago to start doing surveillance. From what she told me, Sabine LeFèvre hadn't even thought about writing a book at that point."

Butch spoke from her position leaning against the back wall. "Also, why try to kidnap Rosie but just go for the straight kill on the other two?"

Bunny considered this. "They did try and kidnap her, but when I was getting her out of there, they seemed happy enough to shoot indiscriminately in her direction. It had a ... I guess you'd call it a dead-or-alive feel."

A heavy silence descended on the room. Nobody had any answers to give.

Eventually, O'Rourke stood up and pushed his plastic chair under the table before leaning lightly on the back of it. "Right, Bunny. This shouldn't need to be said, but seeing as it's you, the powers that be would like me to officially inform you that you are to stay the hell away from everything to do with this case, and a failure to do so will result in expulsion from the force and arrest. Is that clear?"

Bunny looked up at the DI. "Rosie Flint asked for my help, and if she still thinks she needs it, she's going to get it."

O'Rourke swore under his breath and Butch turned to face the wall, shaking her head and muttering.

"I'm not trying to get in anybody's way, but I made a promise."

At this, Butch spun round and strode towards him, anger blazing in her eyes. "You made me a promise too, remember?"

"I know what it looks like, Butch, but I haven't—"

"Oh, please," she snapped. "Spare me!"

"Hang on ..." Before Bunny could say anything else, Butch stormed out of the interview room and slammed the door behind her. He looked back at O'Rourke. "Thanks very much for that, Fintan."

"Give me a break. If you'd been honest with her in the first place, then you wouldn't have made her look like a bloody fool."

"For the last time – I told you everything I knew. I met Smith, like, five minutes before the poor man died in my arms. I'm not messing anybody about – this is too important. I want the same thing you do – Rosie Flint to be safe and to figure out whatever the hell this shit storm is."

"Fine. Then how about you leave it to the authorities to sort out? She asked for your help with a missing-person case. Unfortunately for the poor bastard, Mark Smith has been located and he isn't going anywhere soon. So now you can leave it alone."

Bunny said nothing.

O'Rourke gave a humourless laugh. "But you won't." He shook his head. "This is so you. And to be clear, that's not a compliment."

"Again, Fintan – seeing as we're repeating ourselves – I've told you everything I know." Technically, Bunny thought, that was true. Technically.

"So," countered O'Rourke, "in this new spirit of cooperation, and to be crystal clear, there's nothing else here you're not telling us?"

Bunny thought of the key in his pocket – the one with the boxing-gloves keyring attached to it. Then he thought of Mark Smith dying in his arms and his last words as he thrust it into Bunny's hand. 'Don't trust the police.'

Bunny cleared his throat. "That's right."

O'Rourke turned to leave. "You're a terrible liar." He left the door of the interview room open as he walked out of it and called back over his shoulder, "Get the hell out of this police station. And for your sake, I'd better not see you again for quite some time."

Chapter Twenty-Five

DISCO INFERNO

The Spider sat at the corner table of the bar cum nightclub in Temple Bar as the godawful music attempted to bore into his skull through volume intensity alone. He considered the pint of gaseous beer in front of him that he had bought with zero intention of drinking it. He did so to avoid looking around the venue. Apparently, Thursday was "nurses get in free" night. The fact that many of the people surrounding him were, apparently, medical professionals was truly terrifying.

In particular, he was trying not to look at the mass of writhing limbs that was the couple at the next table over. The woman was attempting to fit the man's entire face into her mouth while he was gyrating his hips towards any part of her considerable anatomy he could get them near. If the pair moved any closer to him, the Spider was going to become an unwilling participant in a threesome. Not that he would allow that to happen, of course. He'd already decided that if anyone in this place touched him, he'd kill them.

It wasn't that hard to do. The only upside of being in a room full of horny inebriated cattle rubbing up against one another is that he knew from experience that it was the easiest, most convenient crowded room imaginable in which to kill someone. One well-placed blow and you could simply pop your victim down into a chair with an "Oh, somebody has had a bit too much." Not only would people not realise what you had done, but there was also a very high chance they would cheer. Then it would end up being some bouncer's problem as he tried to herd out the cattle at closing time.

God, he hated people.

Furkser sat down opposite him.

The Spider raised his voice. He wasn't concerned about being overheard or noticed. The rest of the room was far too busy doing its own thing, given that in the last couple of minutes alone, he'd witnessed two drug deals, a blazing row and a probable conception. "Why are we meeting here?"

"We have a problem," replied Furkser.

"I know. Still, why are we meeting here?"

Furkser looked around nervously, which drew the Spider's attention. Furkser checking out his surroundings was, of course, normal, but looking nervous while doing so ...

"The French problem has been dealt with—" he started.

"But you screwed up the other half," the Spider interrupted. "Did you think I didn't know that? Passers-by intervened? Really?"

Furkser licked his lips. "They weren't passers-by. One was that McGarry bloke ... and the other was Smith."

The Spider raised his eyebrows. "Smith?"

Furkser bobbed his head briefly.

Now it all made sense. "Hence why we're meeting in the most public place available at this time of night." The Spider scanned the room again. This time he noticed the other two members of Furkser's team attempting to blend into the crowd. "I see Mr Marshall has his hand in a cast and Mr Buchanan looks like his face has been tenderised."

"We realise we fucked up."

"In your defence, it appears you were attacked by a ghost. You told me Smith was dead."

Furkser winced. "I never actually used the word 'dead'."

"Really?" responded the Spider archly. "You lie to me,

jeopardising years of work and vast amounts of money, not to mention my hard-won reputation, and you choose to defend yourself with semantics?"

Furkser said nothing. Instead, he chose to study the sticky floor while rubbing his bruised knuckles.

The Spider tried to calm himself. Allowing emotion to cloud his judgement was a luxury he could not afford. Furkser clearly realised that a screw-up of this magnitude was a termination-worthy offence with the termination in question coming not with a golden handshake so much as an unmarked grave. Furkser more than anyone understood this, given that he'd carried out a similar instruction on the Spider's behalf in the past. It was why Marshall and Buchanan were also there. They'd guessed correctly that for better or for worse they were all in the same boat.

"Okay," said the Spider. "What's done is done."

Furkser crinkled his brow in disbelief, while the song in the background changed from one energetic dollop of dross to another.

"To be clear, I will never work with any of you again after this, and you can consider all bonus payments forfeited, but the reality is we need each other. We're at the finish line. Your screw-up has managed to raise the Flint woman's profile even further. Do whatever it takes, and obviously, discretion is no longer a consideration."

Furkser nodded.

The Spider went to get up, but thought twice. "And what about Mr Smith?"

"He is now dead," confirmed Furkser.

"You'll understand if I seek out a second opinion on that."

As he got to his feet, the thrusting man from the next table, surprisingly still in possession of a face, unlocked himself from the no doubt love of his life whose name he definitely knew, and lurched towards the bathrooms. The Spider was nimble enough to avoid colliding with the man himself, but nobody was fast enough to evade the jet of rancid vomit that spewed forth from the guy, and which covered a large section of the floor, not to mention the Spider's shoes and left trouser leg.

"Sorry, buddy," said the chucker, giving the Spider a hapless look as puke dribbled down his chin.

Over the man's left shoulder, the lady from whom he had so recently decoupled was fleeing the scene, while over his right, a bouncer with a face like thunder was hurtling towards them.

As the bouncer reached them, the Spider adopted a slur and waved a hand. "Sorry, sorry."

The bouncer grabbed the unwell lothario by the shoulder and directed him firmly towards the door. "Out. Now."

The Spider followed in their wake. It had been a long week, and he decided he deserved a treat. He slapped the drunken man on the back jovially. "Come on. Let's get you outside and take care of you."

Chapter Twenty-Six

WHO KNEW AN EXPLOSION COULD GO WRONG?

Commissioner Ferguson sat staring sullenly at the top of his desk. Both hands were propping up his chin, his dicky bow hung loose around his neck, and the cummerbund of his tuxedo lay discarded on the table as O'Rourke finished his report.

"... We caught the licence plate of the van used by the three men on a camera at the junction. The vehicle was stolen out in Tallaght last night."

"And I look forward to you telling me first thing in the morning that it has been located somewhere, burnt out, and with zero possibility of any usable forensics. Whoever these bastards are, I'm getting the very strong feeling this isn't their first rodeo."

O'Rourke made no attempt to disagree.

"Have we any leads on the mysterious Mark Smith?"

"His prints have come back clean from Interpol. We're going through the protocol to ask the British government whether they have any record of the individual in question being a member of their Armed Forces."

"And, again, the very best of luck with that wild-goose chase. How exactly did McGarry find the man?"

"Seemingly he had friends of his in the homeless community

staking out Ms Flint's route home, on the assumption that Mr Smith might be keeping an eye on her."

"Couldn't we have thought of something similar?"

"I'd remind you, respectfully, sir, that until a few hours ago, this was a missing-person case, with a possibly connected B and E."

"Yes, yes," said Ferguson, batting the suggestion away with a wave of his hand. "And technically, the missing person has now been located, poor bastard. It does say something when somehow McGarry has more resources than we do. I must remember to bring that up at the next budget meeting. Have Miss LeFèvre's and Mr ..."

"Ballard."

"... Ballard's," continued the Commissioner, "next of kin been informed?"

"We're working with the French authorities to identify them, sir. We believe LeFèvre may not be the lady in question's original second name."

"No, I can't imagine it is." Ferguson sat back and pressed his fingers on the top of the desk absent-mindedly. "This is a very fine mess indeed, is it not?" He indicated the chair opposite. "For God's sake, sit down, Fintan."

O'Rourke did as instructed.

"Needless to say," the Commissioner went on, "whatever this thing is, it's now your number-one priority."

"Yes, sir. As it happens, we rolled up the Gerrard brothers investigation this evening with nine arrests, and the DPP is happy we've got a strong case."

Ferguson nodded. "And I look forward to reading coverage of that on page eight, once I've waded through the seven pages of sensationalist handwringing that this debacle will receive once the press realise the identities of the individuals involved. Where are we on that, by the way?"

"Currently, we're running with the line that they're separate incidents, and that the deceased can't be named until next of kin are informed."

"And let me guess, our friends in the fourth estate are happy to toe the line and stay out of the way of our investigations?"

O'Rourke shrugged. "The usual suspects are sniffing around. Right now, they're all running with double murder and shootout on the Grand Parade with a fatality. Best guess, by mid-morning the lead dogs will have caught the scent on who Sabine LeFèvre was and that Rosie Flint is involved ..."

"And then," said the Commissioner grimly, "strap in, because the ride's going to get terribly bumpy."

"I'm not sure even the rise of the grannies will pull the focus from this story."

"Excuse me?" said Ferguson, looking genuinely perplexed.

"Sorry, sir. You may've been too distracted with other things. Catherine Royce gave a speech at the party conference. Came out swinging. She took the whole grandmother thing and ran with it. Basically saying how nobody cared about things more than the grannies of Ireland do because they worry about the grandkids getting jobs, the environment, owning a house. They remember the bad times, the good times, the fifty-percent-income-tax times. I'm not doing it justice, but rest assured, the press and the public ate it up. Suddenly, she's got a bit of momentum in the leadership race."

"Really? That *is* good news. I assume it's still going to be ..."

"The Arsehole? Yes, sir. Seems fairly certain, but Royce might get a much bigger role. Deputy leader seems a real possibility."

Ferguson nodded approvingly. "Have you ever met her?"

"No, sir."

"Smart woman. It probably speaks very badly of the party and the country that she's not held a more prominent position before now. Especially when you consider the other contenders. The Arsehole aside, there's that grinning idiot from Bantry and Clueless of Cavan."

"Clueless has formally dropped out."

"There's a loss."

O'Rourke nodded in agreement. "Fingers crossed it'll all take a bit of the press attention away from this."

Ferguson barked a bitter laugh. "Some chance. Not even that ongoing metaphorical bloodbath is any match for an actual one involving hookers and those who are hooker-adjacent." He pulled a packet of cigars from his desk drawer and nodded towards the window. "Do an old man a favour, Fintan – open that window there like a good chap."

"I thought none of the windows in this building opened?"

"They don't," said Ferguson, "but I'm a man of massive power and influence."

O'Rourke got up and opened the window.

"Much obliged," said the Commissioner, puffing his cigar into life. "Let's assume I've already offered you one and you've turned it down with the minimum amount of healthy-living piety owing to me being your boss." Ferguson kicked off his shoes and placed his socked feet upon the desk.

"I meant to ask, sir – how did your wife's birthday go?"

O'Rourke's enquiry was met with the kind of heavy sigh only a man of Gareth Ferguson's impressive girth could pull off. "Let me put it this way – the only upside to the horrific events previously discussed is that they temporarily took my mind off that disaster."

"Oh dear. Sorry."

Ferguson grunted the apology away and leaned further back in the triumph of engineering that was his chair.

A long pause laid itself out and, despite not wanting to, O'Rourke could not resist filling it. "Was it the guest list?"

"No. No. I mean, there's every possibility that at a later date that particular bill is going to be due, but circumstances did rather outpace it."

"The catering?"

"Again, no. That was nothing short of a triumph. Either the culinary school is producing a generation of genius-level talent or else – as I have long suspected – many of the supposed gastronomic virtuosos with whom we are currently blessed are actually overhyped and undercooked charlatans."

O'Rourke nodded. "Did your wife just not like the surprise?"

"Strike three, Fintan. Loved it. Absolutely loved it. Beamed from ear to ear the entire evening, even while crying tears of joy. Quite possibly the happiest I've ever seen her."

"Right. I see ... Actually, sir, I don't see it at all. How exactly was it a disaster?"

Ferguson shot O'Rourke a look from under hooded eyelids then gazed forlornly at the ceiling. "Do you enjoy fireworks, Fintan?"

"As much as the next person, I guess."

"Not if the next person is my beloved. The woman absolutely adores them. Bit too flashy-flashy bang-bang for my taste, if I'm honest. However, she has sat by my side through more than enough dreary Heineken Cup rugby games for me to be happy to suck it up and make all the appropriate *ooh*ing and *ahh*ing noises. And, trust me, no expense was spared on that front. I got the very best organised fireworks display company in the land to put on a big show right there in our back garden, to dazzle and mesmerise our guests. Not to resort to lazy racial stereotyping, but the company in question had not one, not two, but three Chinese gentlemen working for them. That's how you know you're getting the good stuff. The Chinese are to fireworks what we Irish are to excessive drinking and grudge-holding."

"Ah," said O'Rourke. "Did they not go off?"

"How dare you, Detective Inspector? Three Chinese men!" He held up the corresponding number of fingers to emphasise his point. "Three! It was spectacular. My wife loved it. My guests loved it. I loved it – because of the first two things rather than for any newfound delight in pyrotechnics I'd acquired. I'll tell you who didn't love it, though – Kevin."

"Your dog?"

Ferguson gave a single slow nod. "I mean, yes, technically, he is my dog – our dog, really – but while I have come to tolerate him, of myself and my beloved, only one of us has ever described him as the most beautiful soul they've ever met."

"I see."

"Yes," said Ferguson, with an odd air of grim joviality. "Poor Kevin lost his tiny little mind. He broke through a door – a wooden door, mind you – and ran screaming across the lawn. Did you know dogs could scream, Fintan? Because they can. Screaming across the lawn, sprinting, while shitting himself all the way – again, something I didn't know was physiologically possible for a dog, or indeed anyone, to do – but, again, they can. And while making his escape, he took down, in no particular order ... a large buffet table; the lady captain of the golf club; and a really pretty good, if phenomenally overpriced, Frank Sinatra impersonator, before speeding off into the night. His current location is unknown, although, given his speed and trajectory, we can't rule out that he's just about reached New York."

"'Oh dear' doesn't really seem to cover it," said O'Rourke.

"No, Fintan, it doesn't. Before I received this particular joyous phone call, I and many of my guests were out trawling Seapoint and the surrounding areas in a so-far-fruitless search for the aforementioned traumatised Labradoodle. Once I leave here, I will be rejoining the search, and indeed continuing it throughout the night until poor Kevin is found, or I die in the attempt. To be clear – those are my only two options. Let's not even pretend the poor woman likes me anywhere near as much as she does the damn dog."

O'Rourke looked round the room, at a loss for the appropriate remark to make in the circumstances. In the end he settled for, "I'm sure he'll turn up."

"Really?" the Commissioner shot back. "Because that is most definitely not the kind of week I'm having. Anyway, back to the reason we're here – the appalling slaughter of Sabine LeFèvre and Henry Ballard, plus the perplexing Mark Smith, and the attempt to kidnap the blighted Rosie Flint. Seeing as this is likely going to be the last moment of quiet before the storm, and I won't hold you to this, but have you the first idea what the hell is going on? Big picture, I mean."

"Honestly, sir, I don't. From what McGarry has reported Smith saying, it now appears that this thing centres around Rosie Flint, and not Sabine LeFèvre as we initially suspected. However, Ms Flint is either lying through her teeth, and is a talented actress to boot, or she has no idea why that is. What doesn't help is that she isn't exactly a massive fan of the Garda Síochána."

Commissioner Ferguson blew a smoke ring at the ceiling. "On that point, at least she and I are in agreement. I've had to suspend two gardaí from Wexford today for – I shit you not – stopping two black gentlemen in a car, seemingly on the grounds of driving whilst black, and then proceeding to try to implicate them as suspects in every crime they could remember happening in the last six months."

"Permission to swear freely, sir?"

"Granted."

"Dickheads!" blurted O'Rourke.

The Commissioner shrugged. "Bit vanilla, Fintan. I would have gone with knuckle-dragging, pea-brained, limp-pricked disgraces – not just to the uniform or the country, but to the actual human race. The worst part of my job isn't knowing those kind of peanut-brained buffoons exist, it's the fact that I have to suspend them pending a thorough investigation, rather than my preferred option of putting them in stocks outside my office so that I can flay them alive on my lunch breaks."

"That is a very vivid image, Commissioner."

"Oh, believe me, what you just got was the greatly toned-down version. Sorry," he apologised as he flicked some ash into a vaguely cylindrical award for something, "I got distracted. What were we talking about?"

"Rosie Flint's distrust of the gardaí, which I'm assuming is a result of her family history."

Ferguson nodded. "I'm going to guess that'll end up being on page five. Not that I can blame the woman. That case was an appalling indictment, and I don't care that some toothless committee said otherwise. It was before my time, I assure you. God knows, I'd like to believe that such situations would be handled a lot better these days, but hand on heart, I can't guarantee it. Big ships such as this one take an infuriatingly long time to turn around."

Ferguson fired another couple of smoke rings into the air, then rolled the cigar around his mouth in contemplation.

"To go back to my original question – whatever the hell this thing is, it must involve a lot of money. This man, Smith, was apparently on it for the best part of the year, and he was clearly just one of the grunts. Add in the one, possibly two teams of professionals involved in today's bloody business, and it adds up to somebody going to a whole lot of expense. Given the axiom about having to spend money to make money, they must be expecting to make a whole lot in return. The kind of money we're talking about isn't made by ripping off a bank or blackmailing somebody."

The Commissioner had more or less summed up the question that had been running around O'Rourke's head all evening. "I agree. That's what has me so confused. Where do you make that kind of money?"

Ferguson turned and gave O'Rourke a long look. "This is the thing that worries me most. Only one place, Fintan, and one place only – politics."

Chapter Twenty-Seven

THE APPLIANCE OF SWEET SCIENCE

Bunny stood across the road from the squat two-storey building just off Sheriff Street. It didn't look like much; certainly, its reputation dwarfed its physical reality. Reardon's Boxing Gym was a Dublin institution. It wasn't the gym where your kids went to learn how to box, it was the gym they went to when nobody at the other place was willing to get in the ring with them any more. Reardon's produced champions, but that was really a by-product of its main achievement, which was churning out hard bastard after hard bastard. Bunny had seen pictures in the newspaper of Reardon's alumni holding aloft gold medals and belts. He'd also put more than a few of those fellas behind bars. Mountjoy would have one hell of a boxing team if anybody outside of a Hollywood movie was actually stupid enough to give a prison a boxing team.

He pulled out the key Mark Smith had shoved into his hand right before he died and studied it again. The distinctive green and gold boxing gloves of the keyring matched those on the sign above the front door to Reardon's. In fact, the sign was the only indication of what was inside the building – it wasn't a place you walked into by accident. The key attached to the keyring had the number 28 cut into it. For a locker, obviously. Bunny jiggled it between his fingers and puffed out his cheeks.

The problems here were twofold: first, if he were to do this, there was no way around it – he would be actively withholding information from a Garda investigation into a triple murder with attempted kidnapping, burglary and assault thrown in for good measure. Never mind getting himself thrown off the force, he could – and would – see jail time if this went south. Despite being utterly exhausted, he'd gone home yesterday and had another terrible night's sleep. The thing that he was contemplating doing felt like crossing a line – one that couldn't be uncrossed. Still, the pleading look on Mark Smith's face as he'd uttered the words "Don't trust the police" kept coming back to him again and again. Even if Bunny were to leave aside whatever unwritten rule he thought there was that said you had to honour a dying man's last wish, he needed to know why Smith was so certain that the gardaí couldn't be trusted. Nothing about this case made any sense, and Bunny was now thoroughly, gut-wrenchingly sick of it.

His second problem was that, in practical terms, he needed to go into Reardon's gym to retrieve the contents of the locker. For several reasons, including his contribution to bolstering numbers in the hypothetical Mountjoy boxing team, he didn't think he'd be very welcome.

The owner, Brian Reardon, was now well into his seventies and had always been scrupulous in keeping his gym away from any associations with criminal activity. Not as the result of having any great morals, it was just that the man lived for boxing. He was smart enough to know that the strict rule had to be that whatever the men who used his gym got up to away from the gym, it had to stay outside, otherwise the place would inevitably get dragged into something that would destroy it.

Reardon's was neutral ground and everybody understood that. A few years ago, one gangland wannabe had felt differently and decided to seek his revenge in a feud by shooting a rival as he was leaving the gym. If the rumours were to be believed, the man in question was delivered personally to Brian Reardon by the top man in the gunman's own organisation. The man's body had never been found. Brian Reardon was no angel himself, it was just that boxing was his religion and not even heaven could help anyone who broke his golden rule.

Bunny shoved the keyring back into his pocket. "Feck it. Might as well be hanged for a sheep as a lamb."

———

Bunny slipped through the front door and tried to look inconspicuous. In his experience, the trick was never to stop moving. People who didn't belong stood round gawping at things, so he walked into the gym and turned immediately to his left.

The place reeked of old sweat and sawdust. There wasn't much that would tell you the twenty-first century was trundling along outside the front door. Everything about the place was old school. In the boxing ring to the right, two men were sparring while another shouted instructions. Seven or eight more men were dotted around the room – one working the speed bag; a couple pummelling heavy bags; the rest skipping, talking, taping their hands or doing work with a medicine ball. Bunny noted with approval the minimal number of weights in evidence, except for a few racks of barbells in one corner. People had become obsessed with building muscle for the sake of it, but in his experience of fighting, all most muscle was good for was giving your opponent something extra to hit.

One of the bods working the heavy bag – a ginger middleweight – stopped and looked at Bunny. Bunny gave him a broad smile and a nod. Keep moving. Just keep moving. As he scanned the room, he noticed a battered red swing door over in the far-left corner, which looked like the most likely location for the changing rooms. While trying to appear as if he were in no particular hurry, Bunny skirted the edge of the room and headed towards it.

As he pushed through the door, he could hear showers running somewhere out of view. The stench of deodorant was so overwhelming that it nearly made your eyes water. On the benches along one side of the room, a short guy with a back in desperate need of a shave and, possibly a mow, was getting dressed after his shower; on the other benches along the other side, a massive fella with a long ponytail was changing into his workout gear. And there, at the end of the room, was a bank of lockers. Bunny headed straight for them. At least here there wasn't any need to make conversation – men did not talk to other men they did not know while in various stages of undress.

Locker 28 was close to the floor. Bunny hunched down, dug the key out of his pocket, and inserted it into the lock. After a bit of wiggling, the door opened with a brief, teeth-jarring screech of metal.

"Sorry," said Bunny, without looking up.

He wasn't sure what he'd been expecting to find, but inside the locker was a battered-looking plastic carrier bag. A quick glance revealed it to contain an inch-thick manila folder. He resisted the urge to look at its contents. Instead, he grabbed the bag, left the locker open with the key still resting in it, and headed back the way he came.

The short guy, in a voice he vaguely recognised, said, "Here, aren't you—"

"Howerya," muttered Bunny, neither pausing nor looking round.

He pushed through the swing door leading back into the main gym and stopped dead. Three men were standing there waiting for him. On the left was the ginger middleweight Bunny had seen working the heavy bag. He pointed at Bunny. "Are you sure this is him?"

The little fella on the right of the trio sneered at Bunny. This guy Bunny did recognise. Jason Potts.

"One hundred percent," Potts confirmed, jabbing a finger in Bunny's face. "Bunny fucking McGarry."

"Actually," said Bunny, "you've got me confused with somebody else. Fucking isn't my middle name – it's Philomena, actually. Weird family tradition. Bit embarrassing, really. Still, was lovely chatting."

The immense fella in the middle, who looked as if he were

designed more for sumo wrestling than for boxing, placed a meaty paw on Bunny's shoulder. His face was pock-marked and he spoke in a voice that sounded like somebody moving heavy furniture. "The man tells me you're the one who jumped Gary Kearney."

Bunny shook his head. "That doesn't ring any bells."

"Bullshit," spat Potts. "I was there. You jumped him from behind round the back of O'Hagan's up on Baggot Street. He never even had a chance to get a shot off."

"Ah," said Bunny. "Sorry, I'm with you now. I was thrown because you didn't use his full name. I know him as Gary 'Hits Defenceless Women and Children' Kearney."

"He's a friend of mine," said the big fella.

"Well," said Bunny, "we've all made mistakes. I'm not one to judge. Now, if you'll excuse me, lads – I've got important Garda business to get back to."

"I heard you were suspended."

The source of this interjection was revealed when the ginger fella moved to one side to reveal a sprightly figure with long, flowing, slicked-back white hair. The man's bright, dancing eyes belied his seventy plus years.

"Howerya, Brian," said Bunny. "It's been a while. I love what you've done with the place."

"Thanks. Glad to see you're keeping busy now that you're suspended from the guards."

"Actually, I'm on sabbatical."

"You don't look Jewish," rumbled the big fella.

Bunny gave Brian Reardon a pointed look.

The older man shrugged. "I'm not training teams for *University Challenge*."

"Fair enough," chirped Bunny, trying to sound cheerful. "Well, it was great catching up, but I need to get going."

Bunny tried to extricate himself but the big fella tightened his grip on his shoulder.

"You see," began Reardon, "if you're not here on police business –

and you definitely aren't – then I'm afraid the rules that apply are the rules of my gym. In particular ..."

Bunny followed Reardon's eyes as he looked up at a string of words painted on the far wall – *If you're here, you're here to fight.*

"Thanks, but no thanks, Brian."

Reardon laughed. "Fair enough. No harm in asking. You can go."

The big fella looked round at Reardon, confusion all over his massive face.

"Okay," said Bunny quickly.

The friendly smile dropped from Reardon's face. "But whatever's in that bag you didn't have with you when you walked in here two minutes ago stays here."

"But—"

"Stays. Here."

Bunny nodded. He looked down at the carrier bag in his right hand then back up at Brian Reardon. "I don't suppose I can choose who I fight?"

"Would you believe I'll choose your opponent at random?" asked Reardon with a laugh.

"No."

"Good instincts."

"By any chance," countered Bunny, "were you Gary Kearney's manager as well as his trainer?"

Reardon nodded. "You cost me a lot of money. That boy was an earner."

"He had several less appealing attributes as well."

The older man shrugged. "I don't care what they do outside of the gym."

"How convenient for you."

"To be clear," continued Reardon, "the deal is, you last three minutes in the ring with Marty here" – he pointed at the big fella who was grinning like a cat who'd just inherited a dairy – "and you can walk, or at least crawl, out of here with whatever's in that bag. No questions asked. Or, you leave here right now, empty handed."

Bunny bobbed his head. "Just so we're clear, the Marquess of Queensberry rules?"

"If you like."

"I don't."

"Fine," said Reardon. "Anything goes."

"And not a second over three minutes?"

"If it even lasts that long. Marty here put his last opponent in a coma in under a minute."

Bunny nodded. "I can see that. He's not exactly a dazzling conversationalist."

"I'll conversationalist you in a minute," rumbled Marty.

"Thanks for proving my point." Bunny turned his attention back to Brian Reardon. "Three minutes as soon as we step into the ring. Anything goes." Bunny looked around at the other occupants of the gym, all of whom had stopped to watch. He raised his voice. "Don't want people to see you're not a man of your word, Brian."

"Are we doing this or not?" asked Brian.

Bunny clapped his hands together. "Let's get ready to rumble."

———

Bunny sat on a bench with a rack of various-sized dumbbells in front of him. He reached inside his jacket pocket and took a swig from his flask of whiskey. The carrier bag containing the manila folder lay at his feet. Not by coincidence, pretty much every man in the gym was standing between him and the front door. At the far side of the hall, Jason Potts was tying up Marty's gloves while the big fella grinned in Bunny's direction. Bunny held up the flask in a mock toast and took another drink.

Brian Reardon made his way over to Bunny with the red-headed guy in his wake. "Are you sure you don't want gear to change into?"

"No thanks, Brian. I'm in a bit of a hurry, so I'll go as is."

"Fair enough. Darren here will put gloves on you, and we've even got you a brand-new gumshield."

"I'm touched, but none of that is necessary."

Reardon wrinkled his brow. "If you're sure. I'll be in there as referee and timekeeper."

"Referee?"

"I don't want him to actually kill you, Bunny. It'll mean me having to fill out all kinds of health and safety forms."

Bunny nodded. "Those can be a bugger, alright."

———

Two minutes later and Marty was shadowboxing in one corner of the ring while staring at Bunny. Brian Reardon stood in the centre of the canvas. "So, Bunny, are you coming in or not?"

Bunny screwed the top back on his flask and shoved it into his inside pocket. "Finally," he said with a slight slur as he got up from the weight-training bench and began to stride towards the ring. He made his way to the corner where Marty was warming up and, plastic bag in hand, climbed the first couple of steps. Bunny pointed at the ropes. "D'ye mind?"

Marty considered his opponent's request then put one foot on the bottom rope and pulled up the others with his gloved hand.

"Thanks very much," said Bunny. "Such a gentleman." He then proceeded to climb between the ropes and, despite Marty's assistance, got himself into a tangle. In the background, little Jason Potts was sniggering away. As Bunny fell and landed inelegantly on the canvas he heard a voice cry, "He's pissed!" He gave a hapless wave while attempting to drag himself to his feet and stumbled against Marty as he did so.

"For Christ's sake," Brian Reardon muttered behind him.

In a flash, Bunny bounced up and stepped nimbly towards the far corner, tossing down the plastic bag. "Right, Brian," he announced, looking at his watch. "Three minutes, starting now. Ding-ding!"

Reardon turned to Marty as the big man howled in frustration and spat out his mouth guard.

"What the hell?" Marty roared. He attempted to hold up his right hand but it was handcuffed to the middle rope.

Reardon walked over to look more closely, then turned back to Bunny. "Very funny. Give me the key."

"Key? Do those things come with keys?" He consulted his watch pointedly. "I make it two minutes forty left. Tick-tock."

Reardon glared at him.

Bunny leaned back in the far corner. "Rules are rules, Brian, and you're a man of your word."

Reardon pointed at Potts. "There's a hacksaw up in the toolbox. Go get it."

As Potts ran off, Marty started to pull at his right hand, trying to free it through force alone.

"Don't be an idiot," snapped Reardon. "You'll break your wrist."

Bunny scanned the room and noticed that several of the boxers were doing their best not to be seen laughing. He felt the phone in his pocket vibrate. When he pulled it out the number was what he'd expected it to be. He held up the handset. "While we're waiting, does anybody mind if I take this?"

His request was met with a stream of invectives from Marty.

"Thanks," said Bunny. "I'm going to take that as a 'work away'." He consulted his watch again. "Two minutes, by the way." Bunny answered the call. "Declan, *conas atá tú*?"

"What?" asked Deccie.

"That means 'how's it going', but seeing as you still don't know that, it sort of answers itself."

"I haven't got that much time. And who is that in the background screaming dog's abuse at you?"

"Don't worry about it. Although, to be honest, now isn't a great time for me either."

Jason Potts came stumbling back from the office, a rusty-looking hacksaw in his hand.

"Seriously, boss," Deccie continued. "You can't let somebody disrespect you like that. You'd want to give him a slap."

"I'm hoping that will not be necessary."

Marty was now holding out his hand while Jason Potts attempted to saw through the handcuffs.

"Hang on a sec," Bunny told Deccie, placing his hand over the mouthpiece. "Careful there, lads. We don't want anybody getting injured." He returned to the phone, glancing at his watch as he did so. "I can give you eighty-seven seconds, Deccie. What's up? Go."

"I was awake last night at 3am – it doesn't matter why. Anyway, we're beside the sea and I saw these lights out on the ocean." Brian Reardon had now shoved Jason Potts aside angrily and was trying to cut through the handcuffs himself. "Long story short," continued Deccie, "I am ninety-five percent certain that the teachers at this school are using it as a front for international drug-running."

"Right," said Bunny. "Well, things have taken an unexpectedly Nancy Drew turn, haven't they?"

"What I'm saying is, you better get down here now, boss, arrest the teachers, bust me out, and then you and me need to get to McDonald's because I've not had any chips for nearly a week. It's barbaric."

"Okay, Declan. You keep gathering intel while pretending to be somebody who is actually trying to learn some Irish, while I assemble a strike team."

"You're not taking me seriously, are you, boss?"

Bunny peeked at his watch again. "No, I'm not. To be clear, Declan, I am never ever coming to get you and I do not need you for important police business. Start learning some Irish." Bunny ended the call before Deccie could respond.

He took a couple of steps so that he was standing in the middle of the ring and spoke loudly. "I make that ... three ... two ... one ... and we are done." Marty made yet another futile attempt to lunge at Bunny. "I'd shake hands, but I can see you're busy," Bunny quipped.

Brian Reardon dropped the saw. "Very clever," he said through gritted teeth. "Well done."

With a quick bob of his head, Bunny picked up the shopping bag, climbed out of the far side of the ring and headed for the door.

Jason Potts, his face a livid red, appeared in front of him and blocked his way. "No way. You cheated! Again! Get back in the ring."

"Let him go," snarled Reardon.

"No, it's not fair," Potts squealed. "He didn't even have to throw a punch."

Bunny shrugged. "If you insist."

Three seconds later, Bunny stepped over the freshly unconscious form of Jason Potts and rubbed his knuckles. As he reached the front door, he patted his pockets and pulled out a small metal object.

"Would you look at that? I *do* have the key for those handcuffs."

Bunny tossed the small key in the air, caught it and put it back in his pocket before exiting with a jaunty tip of a cap he wasn't wearing.

Chapter Twenty-Eight

THIS IS YOUR LIFE

Bunny took a deep breath and knocked on the door. There is simply no way to prepare for some things. This was one such thing.

"Who is it?" came Rosie's worn and weary-sounding voice from inside the apartment.

"It's Bunny."

"Are you alone?"

"I am."

It wasn't as if he wasn't expecting it, but the look on Rosie's face when she opened the door still made his breath catch in his throat. Dressed in a paint-splattered hoodie and sweatpants, she blinked several times and studied his shoulder, as if trying to find words where there were none. She had that wrung-out look, as if she'd cried every last tear there was to cry. It was the look of someone from whom the world had taken everything.

She poked her head into the hallway and looked up and down the length of it. "I've had gardaí calling me, knocking on the door. They were standing in the hallway until I told them to get the hell out." Her face hardened into an accusing stare. "Is sending you round their next trick?"

"I'm here to see you as a friend. I'm not here on anybody else's instruction. I promise."

Her face softened instantly and she put her hand to her mouth. "I know. I'm sorry. I didn't mean to …"

"Don't worry about it. Jesus, what you've been through." He shifted his weight awkwardly. "Can I come in?"

She stepped to one side. "Sorry. Yes. Of course."

Bunny moved past her and made his way down the hall. Rosie's instincts hadn't been wrong. This morning alone he'd received two phone calls from O'Rourke. The gardaí were beside themselves that a woman who had narrowly avoided being kidnapped the day before by people who clearly were not in the least bit concerned about leaving bodies in their wake, had checked herself out of hospital and point-blank turned down all Garda protection.

As much as he wished she'd take the protection, Bunny hadn't come to try to convince her otherwise. He knew better than anybody how hardwired and justified Rosie's distrust of the police was. He was also more than aware that what he was about to tell her wasn't going to help on that score.

Rosie sat on the sofa and pulled up her legs. She hugged her knees to her chest and began to rock gently back and forth. Bunny took a seat in the armchair opposite.

In stark contrast to his last visit, the apartment was an absolute mess. It looked as if she'd started to scramble eggs at some point then simply left them sitting in the pan. A cardboard carton sat open on the counter, and an egg that had been dropped on the kitchen floor remained where it had fallen, congealing on the tiles, fragments of its shell scattered hither and thither.

"Are the police still outside?" she asked as she stared at the floor.

"They are," he confirmed.

While Rosie had turned down personal protection, it didn't mean the gardaí couldn't provide elements of it anyway. On his way here Bunny had clocked a significant uptick in uniformed patrols in the area, and there was at least one van parked across the road that didn't look as if it was going to be making any deliveries any time soon. Any burglar that was unlucky enough to try anything on this street over the next few days was going to be in for a nasty surprise.

"I can't stand it," Rosie said. "It feels like everybody thinks they have a right to every part of my life." She waved a hand in the air. "They came in here, the gardaí, while I was in hospital. They said they found bugs. My phone was tapped."

"Really?"

She scratched compulsively at her forehead while nodding repeatedly. "That Detective Cassidy woman said they reckon they were only put in in the last couple of days, but they can't be sure. And seeing as everybody's playing me for an idiot these days, I'd be the last to know."

Bunny tried to think of the right thing to say. Rosie was overflowing with grief, anger, and God knows what else, and he couldn't blame her for any of it. She was in some nightmare where not only had the man she thought she loved horribly betrayed her, he'd also then gone and died while trying to save her. Good luck getting a handle on all that.

She turned her head and looked out the window. "They told me you spoke to him?" Her voice came out soft and brittle.

Bunny tilted his head. "I did."

She tried to summon defiance but couldn't quite pull it off. "So, he was sent here to spy on me?"

"He was. For what it's worth, he hated himself for lying about it. He was trying to make it right, or at least he was trying to get out of doing it, then all this kicked off. I found him because he was trying to watch over you. Because he knew you were in trouble. He also charged in there like a man possessed to save you." Bunny looked down at the carpet for a moment, then back up at Rosie. "God knows he lied about a lot, but for whatever it means, I don't think he lied about loving you."

Rosie ran the sleeve of her hoodie across her eyes. "Does that make all of this better or worse?"

Bunny sagged back into the armchair. "I'm afraid you'll probably spend quite a few long fruitless nights trying to find an answer to that question."

She nodded. "Why are Sabine and" – she clenched her eyes shut – "I don't even know his name. I should know the man's name."

"Henry," said Bunny softly.

"Henry," she repeated. "Why are they dead?"

Bunny shook his head. "I don't know. I'm sorry."

Rosie leaped off the sofa abruptly. "I'm making you a cup of tea."

"Great."

She proceeded to enter the kitchen and started opening and closing cupboards, seemingly at random. After a couple of minutes she gave up and leaned against the counter. "It appears I have no tea."

"Don't worry about it," said Bunny. "I'm trying to cut back. I found it's beginning to interfere with my drinking. If you like, I can nip out and get you some?"

She shook her head. "Don't bother. I'm getting out of here tonight."

"Right," said Bunny warily. "Can I ask – where are you going?"

"I don't know. Anywhere." She hugged her arms to herself. "Anywhere that isn't here." She looked round the room. "This place has been ... soiled. I don't think I'll ever sleep a wink here again."

Bunny heaved himself out of the armchair and moved to the far side of the counter. "I get it. I really do, but Rosie, given the circumstances ... We still don't know who these people are and why they're interested in you."

"'Interested'? That's a funny way of putting it."

"Still. I know it isn't ideal, but for the moment, why not just let the gardaí protect you?"

"No," she said firmly. "No. No way. Never."

"I understand, but—"

"No," she snapped. "No, you don't. The police were supposed to protect my mother and they didn't. She asked repeatedly."

"I know. I know. And that was awful," agreed Bunny. "Appalling. I'm not saying otherwise, but it was a long time ago now. A lot has changed. Pamela Cassidy – I'd trust her with my life."

Rosie pointed angrily at the door. "Then off you go and let her protect you. This is none of your or anybody else's business. My mind is made up."

He held up his hands and took a step back. "Okay, Rosie. Okay. Whatever you say. I'm just here trying to be a friend."

Bunny looked back at the armchair where the plastic bag he'd brought with him was still sitting. He didn't want to do this, but the woman had a right to know. He closed his eyes for a second then opened them again. "There is something else."

"What?"

"Before he died, Mark directed me to where to find a file."

Rosie sounded suspicious. "What was in this file?"

"You'd better sit down."

She placed the drawstring from her hoodie in her mouth and chewed on it absentmindedly as she moved her weight from foot to foot, unsure what to do.

"Please," said Bunny.

Her eyes flitted up to meet his for the briefest moment, then she looked away and nodded.

Once seated, Bunny took the file out of the bag and held it up. "I found this about an hour ago. He didn't tell me where he got it but it's about you."

Rosie put out her hand. "Show me."

"I will – in just a second. Let me prepare you for it, though ..." Bunny shifted nervously in the chair. "This doesn't just go back a few months ..."

Rosie lowered her hand and folded her arms. "How far back does it go, exactly?"

"More or less ... your whole life."

She gawped at him. "My whole life?" she repeated, a look of bewilderment on her face.

"Not ... not like it's been for the last few months. But somebody, someone ... somebody was checking up, regularly."

Rosie got to her feet and put out her hand again. "Give it to me."

He did as he was told. She took the file, put it down on the counter and opened it. For several minutes Bunny sat there in silence, save for the sound of pages being turned slowly, and the occasional gasp.

Eventually, Rosie turned back to him and pointed down at the file. "There are ... copies of my school reports in here. Reports on my foster parents. There's ... everything in here that happened to me after my mother died. *Everything*."

Bunny nodded. "It's ..." He was at a loss for words. He'd been thinking about the contents of the file ever since he'd opened it an hour ago and nothing had come to him.

Rosie held up a couple of sheets, tears in her eyes again. "You're in here too, Bunny."

"I know what it looks like, but let me explain. Just give me sixty seconds. Please?"

He looked directly into her eyes and saw the anger and pain swirling in them. She bit her lip and nodded.

"I swear this is the truth. When I first met you, I was genuinely interested in the work you were doing, and I did want to help. The bit you don't know, and I'm sorry for not telling you the complete truth, was that I didn't get involved by accident. A senior guard told me you were in college with his daughter. He asked me to keep an eye on you because they were worried about you being out on your own in dangerous places at night."

Rosie's voice cracked as she tried to speak. "And you— And you wrote reports?"

Bunny shook his head. "No, I didn't. I just rang the guy and told him what was going on."

Rosie slammed the two pages onto the counter and glared at them. "So who wrote them, then?"

"I'm assuming he did."

"And who did he give them to?"

"That," Bunny said, "is what I'm going to find out as soon as I leave here. If you give me a chance, I'll try and figure out what the hell is going on."

"Good," she snapped, before shoving the file across the counter until its contents spilled onto the floor. "Because I want to know who the hell has been stalking me my entire life." She pointed accusatorily at the papers. "With the help, apparently, of the Garda Síochána. Including you." She lowered her head, tears streaming down her face now. "Including you," she repeated.

Bunny got to his feet and went to move towards her. She took a step back and threw out her hands. "Don't you come near me."

He mirrored her movements but held up his hands in surrender. "I'm sorry. I'm sorry for ... Christ, everything. I swear I never thought I was part of something like whatever the feck this is. Just give me a couple of days, stay here, and let me find out what's going on and who the hell these people are."

"No. You do whatever you want," said Rosie, "but I'm packing a bag and getting the hell out of here. Now."

"Where are you going to go?" pleaded Bunny.

"I don't care."

"That isn't going to work, Rosie. You need ..." He trailed off. Really, he should have thought of it sooner.

"What?" she asked.

"I know somebody," he said. "Somebody who can protect you while we figure out what's going on." Rosie went to speak but he held out a hand to stall her. "Not the police. Nobody like that."

"Who, then?"

"As hard as this might be to believe – nuns."

Chapter Twenty-Nine

WITH FRIENDS LIKE THESE, WHO NEEDS ENEMAS?

Bunny rang the doorbell of the redbrick Georgian house in Rathmines and took a couple of steps back. Experience had taught him that this was a front door to which you paid some respect – mainly because you were never entirely sure what lay behind it, and finding out was unlikely to be a pleasant experience. He'd just come from Rosie Flint's apartment via the garage where he'd picked up his recently repaired car. It looked as good as new – as it should, seeing as he'd now spent enough to buy it fresh off the factory line at least once.

He waited the amount of time the average person would typically wait before ringing the bell a second time, then left it unrung and waited some more. Another thing he'd learned was not to rush the individuals inside the house, because one of them in particular did not appreciate it.

Bunny knew little about how the rogue order of nuns known as the Sisters of the Saint worked, but he assumed it was safe to call this place their Dublin headquarters. Orders of nuns, by their nature, were not welcoming to male visitors but, as far as he was aware, the Sisters were the only order where arriving unannounced would get you introduced to the business end of a shotgun, and that was assuming they were in a good mood.

Eventually, the door opened and the wizened head of Sister Bernadette appeared. Bunny had first met her about seven months ago, and since then they'd had reason to help each other out on a few occasions. None of this was evident from either Bernadette's facial expression or her welcome. "What do you want?" she snapped.

"Ehm, it's me, Bernadette – Bunny."

"I am aware of that. I have neither gone blind nor senile since the last time we met, Detective McGarry. Now, at the risk of repeating myself, what do you want?"

"I ... I don't suppose I could come in for a minute?"

"Correctly supposed," she confirmed.

"Only ..."

"Spit it out, man. I'm in the middle of something. And for the love of God, take your hands out of your pockets and stand up straight."

Bunny did so and instantly felt like an idiot. He was a thirty-five-year-old man, not a schoolboy. "A woman I know needs your assistance."

"I'm afraid we're at full capacity at the minute."

"I wouldn't ask if it wasn't important."

"And I wouldn't say no if it wasn't impossible."

"Please – it's no exaggeration to say that it's life and death. You might have seen stories in the paper this morning – the attempted kidnapping up on the Grand Parade. It was her they were after."

"And how did she get away?"

"I suppose you could say thanks to the intervention of her boyfriend and me." Bunny shifted awkwardly. "It was him that died."

Bernadette pursed her lips. "Dare I say it, but couldn't the gardaí deal with this? They must have some use."

"She won't trust them. In fact, she wants to get as far away from them as possible."

"Which does beg the question – what are you doing involved in this, Detective McGarry?"

"I'm still on sabbatical, and besides, Rosie and I go back a long way."

Bernadette went to speak then stopped. Instead, she tilted her head to the right. "Rosie?"

"Rosie Flint," replied Bunny.

"The SWIT woman?"

"That's right."

"Dreadful name for an organisation. She does speak a lot of sense, though." Bernadette sighed and opened the door further. "I suppose you'd better come in."

Bunny closed the door behind him and followed Bernadette down the hallway, stepping carefully over the various car parts strewn across the newspaper-covered floor.

"Watch where you're standing," Bernadette warned. "Sister Assumpta got bored while I was out this morning and decided to take the engine of the car apart to see how it works."

As they passed the door on the left that led to the front room, he noticed the ancient Sister Margaret asleep in front of the horse-racing on the TV, while the aforementioned Assumpta sat on the carpet, staring intently at what Bunny thought might be a carburettor. Both of them ignored him entirely.

"Well," he offered, "the thirst for knowledge is a wonderful thing."

Sister Bernadette walked into the kitchen and scoffed. "Yes, the woman loves to pull things apart and see how they work. Now all we need to do is find somebody who is as keen to put things back together again afterwards." She took a seat at the table and indicated the pot in front of her. "I suppose you'll be wanting tea?"

Bunny didn't reply.

"Do you want tea or not?"

"Ehm ..." Bunny pointed at the man sitting in the corner of the room. The guy's wrists were bound with cable ties and he was wearing only a black bag over his head, a pair of Y-fronts and some shoes.

Bernadette waved her hand dismissively. "That's just Lev. Don't mind him."

"Right," said Bunny slowly. "Is he your … prisoner?"

"Not at all. He's going to be helping us to smash a certain people-trafficking ring. Isn't that right, Lev?"

"Absolutely," came Lev's voice from under the bag, in an Eastern European accent that Bunny couldn't place. "I will be absolutely thrilled to do so." He spoke in an excited and happy tone normally only heard from timeshare salesmen and children's TV presenters.

"Right," said Bunny again, any appropriate response to this revelation escaping him.

"I have seen the error of my ways and I am incredibly keen to become a better person," continued Lev.

Bunny looked at Bernadette, who, having given up on him, was busy pouring herself a cup of tea, then looked back at Lev. "What the fuck?"

Bernadette slammed the teapot on the table. "Language!"

"Sorry," apologised Bunny.

"The language that we use," chirped Lev, "is a reflection of the respect we have for ourselves and others."

Bernadette picked up a biscuit. "Well said, Lev." She turned her attention to Bunny. "About your friend – she can't come here if she has that much interest in her. We'll have to use a place we have down the country."

"Grand," said Bunny. "How will I get her there?"

"You won't," the nun replied firmly. "This is what we do. We don't need your help."

"Okay, only … She'll need to get away from the police surveillance on her, not to mention everything else."

Bernadette pulled a face. "Tell me something I don't know." She got to her feet, crossed the kitchen and opened a drawer in a dresser. She withdrew a sealed orange envelope and handed it to Bunny. "Give her this – unopened. Tell her to follow the instructions in it to the letter, at exactly 5pm this evening, and we will handle the rest."

Bunny looked at his watch. "That's only four hours away."

"Excuse me," said Bernadette archly, "I was under the impression this was an emergency? Or are the people you mentioned only thinking about killing her at some unspecified point in the future?"

Chastened, he shoved the envelope into his coat pocket. "You're right. Sorry. No time like the present. I'll head over there now and give her this."

"No," said Bernadette evenly, sitting back down at the kitchen table. "You'll do that in an hour or so. What you'll do now is bring your car around to the back door, shove Lev here into the boot, drive him around for a bit, and then let him out safe and sound somewhere discreet."

"The car doesn't have a very big boot."

"Luckily, Lev is not a very big man."

"I can't ..." started Bunny. He shut up when he noticed Bernadette's facial expression. "I mean, sure, no problem."

"Thank you very much," said Lev, still sounding unnervingly cheerful. "And can I say, thank you again for the wonderful guidance you have given me."

"You're welcome," said Bernadette, nibbling at a Rich Tea biscuit.

"If I may ..." continued Lev. "Would it now be possible for me to take out that thing ..."

"Yes," agreed Bernadette. "To be honest, I'd forgotten it was up there."

"An easy mistake to make," said Lev, before giving a jolly if slightly unhinged laugh.

Bernadette looked back up at Bunny. "Well? You have your instructions. What the hell are you still doing here?"

As Bunny was leaving to go and get the car, a squelching noise that would stay with him for the rest of his life reached his ears, closely followed by a near-ecstatic groan of relief.

Bernadette's voice followed him up the hallway. "Oh, Lev! You're going to have to clean that up before you leave."

Chapter Thirty

AN AULD ACQUAINTANCE

Bunny found himself reminiscing about his early days on the force under the protective wing of the giant that was DI Roger Plummer. He'd first come into contact with Plummer when he'd been only six months out of Templemore and still a wet-behind-the-ears country boy trying to figure out Dublin. It was unusual for someone like Plummer to take an interest in a guard still on probation, but the pair had been introduced in the pub and, Plummer being a Kerry man, they'd bonded over their respective counties' sporting war without end. Bunny was more of a hurling man than a football man, but Cork was one of the few counties that took a serious run at both, so he and Plummer talked mostly football. Kerry had a hurling team, but the last time they'd been contenders pre-dated the invention of the motor car.

That was something a lot of people didn't get about true sporting rivalries. You don't actually hate the so-called enemy; on the contrary, you need them. Victory is only victory and defeat is only defeat when there is something to hold it against. So it had been that he and Plummer had watched a few GAA games down the pub, and had even gone down to a Munster final in Páirc Uí Chaoimh, which Cork had duly lost in an absolute stinker of a display. It had been so bad that on the train back to Dublin, Plummer had let him off easy. Nothing was worse than the sympathy of a rival.

That was how Roger Plummer had become Bunny's mentor and friend. When Bunny got himself into a couple of scrapes during his early years on the force, Roger Plummer, always a charismatic and well-liked man, had smoothed things over for him. At the time, Plummer was one of the go-to guys for the big cases, although his reputation took a bit of a kicking when he was put in charge of the manhunt for Craig "the Rocket" McGuigan, the man even the most lunatic splinters of the IRA considered too batshit mental to have on the books. McGuigan had attempted to kidnap the head of a pharmaceutical company for ransom, only to end up killing the poor man, his wife and a co-conspirator. The inability of the guards to catch him, and the Rocket's ability to regularly ring in to radio shows to give interviews while on the lam, had become a running joke. There had been cartoons in the papers. Not particularly funny ones, but then they never really were. It didn't help that McGuigan was never arrested in the end – he managed to kill himself in a high-speed traffic accident while driving inebriated.

After that, Plummer and Bunny had started to see less of each other, as Plummer took a gig in the Special Detective Unit, which provided protection for government ministers, foreign dignitaries and the like. He also moved back down south in what he had all but told Bunny was a last-ditch effort to save his marriage to his wife, Claire. It hadn't worked.

The last time Bunny saw him had been a few years ago, at Plummer's retirement drinks back up in Dublin, where someone had told him that Roger and Claire had availed themselves of the recent constitutional change and got divorced. While they had done it discreetly, the story went that it had not been terribly amicable. You wouldn't have guessed any of this from the man himself, who had been the life and soul of the party as always.

Since the party, the two men had tried to connect a couple of times, but it had never quite worked out because of one thing or another. Plummer seemed to spend a lot of his retirement going abroad on golfing trips and living what he made sound like the life of Riley. Then there had been the cancer diagnosis. Bunny had rung Plummer as soon as he'd heard the news, and he'd visited his friend and colleague a couple of times, but not often enough. He felt guilty about that. He hadn't even known that Roger had been moved into a hospice until this morning, when Plummer's old right-hand man, Tom Draper, had eventually told Bunny. He'd said that Roger hadn't wanted people making a fuss, but still.

As Bunny entered the private room, his first reaction was that he was in the wrong one. Plummer was such a boisterous, large presence; it was hard to think that was the same man now lying asleep in the bed in front of him. He looked diminished in every way. His head of thick red hair was now white and thinning to the point that his scalp was visible. His face was so ravaged that you could see the jawbone move under the thin yellow skin as he shifted in his sleep. Tubes ran to and from him, and an oxygen mask lay nearby, to assist him with his breathing, if required. The day's *Irish Times* lay under his skeletal hands, unopened, as he slept. The nice Nigerian nurse at the desk had been very encouraging, saying how Roger would be delighted to see somebody. Bunny got the impression that a visit was a rare event.

He touched the man's cold hand and spoke his name softly. After a few moments, Plummer's eyes flickered open. Bunny could see the initial look of confusion in them.

"Rog, it's me – Bunny."

The man's eyes widened in recognition and the ghost of that gregarious smile put in an appearance. He spoke in a croaky voice. "Bunny!" The rest of what he tried to say was lost in a coughing fit.

A glass of water with a straw was sitting on the bedside table. Bunny picked it up and offered it to him. Roger, with effort, eased himself into a more upright position in the bed and took the drink. "Thank you. Sit yourself down there."

Bunny took the indicated seat beside the bed. "Sorry for waking you."

"Not at all. I sleep in the day as there's not much to be doing." He pointed at the TV up in one corner of the room. "I watch the quizzes and that in the evenings."

"So, how are you feeling?"

"Ah," Roger said with a shake of his head, "it is what it is." A glint flashed in his eye. "So, do you reckon your boys might be able to put up a bit of a fight this year?"

For a couple of minutes the two men proceeded to take a step back in time and traded quips about their respective teams, their chances for the next campaign and their failings in the last. For Bunny, it was like seeing the big man coming back to life.

"Hopefully," he said, "you'll at least reach the Munster final before we batter you."

"Fingers crossed," replied Roger, "I might just make it for that." His tone was jovial but it nevertheless broke the spell and reality came crashing down around them.

Bunny fidgeted for a few seconds then looked up. "How long are they giving you?"

"Well," Roger said with a sad smile, "better hope Kerry don't have many draws. I don't think I've got many replays left in me."

"Are you seeing much of the family?"

Roger turned his head slightly and looked out the window. "Not that much. Me and Claire didn't end well, and Deirdre and Yvette ... Well, sure, they were always their mother's daughters. It ended up a bit me and them. Besides, Deirdre is over in Scotland now, and Yvette is doing great things in the States. Very busy career women."

Bunny nodded. First thing this morning, when he'd looked in that file and realised he'd been lied to all those years ago, he'd felt angry. Now, faced with the man who had told those lies – or at least what was left of him – his anger burned away completely. He felt like a prize shit for having to bring it up, but he didn't have a choice. He owed Rosie that much.

He cleared his throat. "Speaking of your daughters, Rog – do you remember years ago, when you asked me to keep an eye on Rosie Flint?"

Plummer shifted in the bed, too weak to put much energy into selling the lie. "I don't ... That was a long time ago now." He laughed weakly. "I can barely remember last year's All Ireland. Just as well, really."

Bunny tried to smile in return, but knew even as he did so that he had to plough on. "At the time, you told me you just wanted to keep an eye on her because she was at college with Yvette. That wasn't true, though, was it?"

Roger went back to looking out the window. "Long time ago now," he repeated.

"Thing is," said Bunny, "I've seen the file, Rog."

At this, Plummer met Bunny's gaze then averted his eyes, ashamed. "It's not what it looks like. Somebody was just concerned about her. Asked me to check in. Make sure she was okay."

"I believe you," said Bunny. "The thing is, though – whoever your file got passed on to, things have changed. The people who had it? They tried to kidnap Rosie yesterday."

Plummer's eyes had grown wide and his lower lip started to wobble. "No, no. That ... That can't be. I just ... I just kept an eye on the girl. Made sure she was okay. They asked me. I ... made sure she was okay."

Bunny reached forward and patted his friend and colleague's hand. "Don't distress yourself, Rog. She's alright. I didn't mean to upset you. I just need to know who you gave the file to."

"I ... I don't know. It was last year. I'd not had my diagnosis long and we were trying the chemotherapy. Jesus, but that doesn't half take it out of you. Wouldn't wish it on my worst enemy. I got a call. This guy came round and I gave him the file. Hardly said a couple of words to me. I remember thinking he was a rude bugger."

"No name or anything?"

Plummer shook his head. "I wasn't at my best at the time."

"I understand," said Bunny softly. "The other thing I need to know—"

"Don't ask me that," Plummer cut him off. He pulled away his hand and folded his arms.

"I have to, Rog. I'm really sorry, but we need to know. I don't understand what's happening here, but I promise you, the girl is in danger."

"But ... But ... But ..." Spittle stuck to Plummer's lips and his whole face tensed.

"Is everything okay?" The nice Nigerian nurse was standing in the doorway, looking concerned. "Are you alright, Roger?"

"I'm ... Bunny here is just leaving."

The woman's eyes flitted between the two men, concern on her face. "Fine."

Bunny got to his feet. "On my way. Just give us one minute."

The nurse looked at Plummer, who gave a reluctant nod. She began to move back to her desk a few feet down the hall. "Just one minute," she added before leaving the room. "He does need his rest."

"Absolutely," agreed Bunny, before turning back to the bed. "I'm sorry to upset you, Rog. I know that whatever this was, you were doing what you thought was right, but it's something else now."

Plummer said nothing, turned towards the television that wasn't on and started to tap his finger on the newspaper.

Bunny waited for a moment but nothing more was said. "Please, Rog."

Plummer turned to face Bunny directly, his wet eyes full of anger. He tapped pointedly on the newspaper again.

"Just ..." Bunny held his tongue as the belated realisation dawned upon him. He took a step forward and examined the picture on the front page of the newspaper. In particular, he took a long hard look at the man on the left of the shot. You wouldn't notice it unless you looked carefully, but he had a very prominent jawline.

A strong jaw.

A jaw Bunny recognised.

"Holy shit!"

Plummer turned his head away again and tossed the paper to the floor.

Chapter Thirty-One

RETAIL THERAPY

Rosie hated shopping for many reasons – one of the biggest was that it was impossible to do without having to deal with strangers. She knew that she wasn't good at making eye contact, which made her look shifty. Knowing this made her nervous, which, in turn, made her look shiftier. While she liked the idea of second-hand clothing, she also couldn't get her head around the idea of wearing something that somebody else had worn, regardless of how many times it had been washed since. Sometimes it felt like she was in a permanent battle with her own brain. Her solution was to go shopping as infrequently as possible, and when she did so, she'd buy a bunch of clothes, alter those that fitted so that they were to her taste, and give the rest away to charity.

Adding to her normal retail anxiety was the fact that she was in Clerys, the venerable department store that had been a fixture on O'Connell Street for well over 150 years. It wasn't somewhere that someone of her age and tastes typically shopped. She knew this because she'd got hold of a retail report that one of her colleagues at Trinity College had written, and had memorised it. She found people difficult to work out, but she had always had an innate understanding of numbers.

At this time on a Friday afternoon, it seemed to be mostly full of elderly couples and women pushing prams, observations which correlated with the report. Rosie felt she stuck out like a sore thumb, but she reminded herself that she hadn't actually come here to shop. It was all part of the elaborate instructions contained in the sealed orange envelope that Bunny had presented her with.

At any other time, she'd be starting to feel as if she were caught up in some sort of elaborate practical joke, only she knew that Bunny understood there was nothing funny about her current situation. Despite now knowing that the circumstances in which they had originally met had been a lie, she had decided to trust him. More than anything, her decision had been based on the fact that she felt far too bewildered and exhausted not to. He was all she had left.

The instructions on a piece of card in the envelope had managed to be both highly precise and nonsensical. Still, she found rules comforting, and these were those. They read as follows:

One – leave wherever you are staying with no more than what you would take with you on a typical day out shopping (handbag, et cetera). If possible, wear black. No hats!

Two – proceed to O'Connell Street where you will buy a bag of bonbons from the Bus Stop newsagents near the O'Connell monument. If bonbons are not available, cola cubes. Failing that, almost anything will do. No toffees!

Three – proceed to Clerys and head for women's clothing on the second floor. Spend approximately ten minutes browsing and select three different items to try on.

Four – once ten minutes have passed and you've selected your items, head into the changing rooms and take the second last stall on the left-hand side. If it's occupied, take one of the other stalls and wait for the second last stall on the left-hand side to become available.

Five – when you are in that stall, hang up your items on the wall and wait for approximately one minute.

Six – after a minute, say in a loud clear voice, but do not shout, "This would look better in turquoise."

When she'd first read the words, Rosie had turned over the piece of card, expecting there to be something more, but that was it. Thankfully, the second last stall on the left hand side of the changing rooms had been free straight away. She entered it and, feeling faintly ridiculous, had stood there, bag of bonbons in hand, watching the timer on her digital watch race towards sixty seconds. When it hit the mark, she cleared her throat and announced, "This would look better in turquoise."

She felt even more ridiculous when nothing happened. She was just coming back round to the idea that perhaps this really was some sort of terribly inappropriate practical joke, when the previously solid-looking wall to the rear of the cubicle slid away. It revealed a short woman dressed as a nun, standing in a dark, narrow hallway and holding a finger to her lips.

Rosie, faced with the inexplicable, froze. The nun started motioning for her to step through the wall. Rosie made to leave then stopped herself. While she hated the unknown, she didn't want to go back to her apartment either. She took a deep breath, turned back around and stepped through the gap in the wall.

She found herself standing in a narrow, dusty, unilluminated walkway. The large panel of missing wall was actually being held up by another nun who was standing to the left of the opening, and who was herself rather large – in all respects. The shorter nun guided Rosie out of the way while the larger one carefully moved the section of wall back into place, plunging them into absolute darkness.

Both nuns simultaneously clicked on torches and the shorter one crooked her finger to indicate that Rosie should follow her. As she did so, she could sense the other nun walking in lockstep behind her. They'd travelled about fifteen feet when the leader stopped and turned around.

"I am Bernadette," she whispered. "She is Assumpta. If anyone should ask, you are Sister Irene."

"Can I—"

"No, you cannot. Give Assumpta your handbag and your jacket."

Rosie complied and, with a friendly smile, the larger nun placed the items inside a large Clerys carrier bag.

The little one held out a black overcoat. "Put this on." Again, Rosie complied, then bent down to allow Bernadette to place a wimple over her head.

Bernadette took a step back and ran her torchlight up and down Rosie before giving an approving nod. "It'll do. Follow me, Assumpta will stay behind us. Don't speak unless spoken to. Walk normally. Don't do anything silly like clasping your hands together. You're walking through a department store, you're not on a retreat to Lourdes. Clear?"

Rosie nodded.

"Do you have a mobile phone?"

Rosie fished it out of the pocket of her black jeans and handed it to Bernadette, who instantly passed it to Assumpta. Rosie watched in horror as the larger nun swiftly disassembled the phone and dropped it into a bucket of water that was sitting on the floor. "No!"

"Non-negotiable," said Bernadette. "Right, off we go."

They resumed walking in the same direction for another twenty feet or so before turning right, then left. Then Bernadette came to an abrupt halt. She placed her hand on a lever and listened intently at a section of wall for a few seconds. Seemingly satisfied, she nodded at Assumpta and they turned off their torches in unison.

"Wait," whispered Rosie.

Both torches clicked back on again and Bernadette glowered up at her. Rosie held up the bag of bonbons. "What are these for?"

Bernadette rolled her eyes. "Assumpta likes bonbons."

"Oh." Rosie turned and awkwardly handed the bag of sweets to Assumpta, who favoured her with a broad smile.

"Now," said Bernadette, "if you don't mind." She nodded at Assumpta and the two torches switched off again.

After a brief second came a clicking noise and the section of wood panelling opened outwards. As the trio passed through, a strong smell of disinfectant hit Rosie before anything else. They were now gathered in a large cleaning cupboard, surrounded by mops, large bottles of bleach, polish, and big plastic bags full of dusters. Rosie started to sneeze and Assumpta grabbed her nose.

They stood frozen that way for a few seconds, until Rosie felt the urge pass. She nodded and Assumpta released her.

"Here we go," whispered Bernadette.

She opened the cupboard door and the three of them trooped out in single file. They walked on the marble floor for a few feet then turned left. Rosie was taken aback to realise they were in the toilets – the gents toilets, as evidenced by the half-dozen urinals set against the wall. If she showed her surprise, it was nothing compared to the shock on the face of the lone man who was availing himself of the facilities.

"What the— You can't be in here!"

Bernadette walked steadily onwards. "Oh, do be quiet. I'm a nun. My total lack of interest in what you're holding is one of the main reasons I signed up."

And with that, the habit-clad trio walked out of the door of the gents customer toilets in Clerys, and Rosie Flint disappeared.

Chapter Thirty-Two

YOU CAN'T MAKE AN EGG WITHOUT BREAKING SOME OMELETTES

Bunny stepped out of the lift and walked towards the reception desk, which was a symphony of chrome, glass and funky lighting. It looked as if it cost more to build than *Apollo 13*. The woman behind it beamed a warm smile that didn't look like it came cheap either. Around the room, several people were reading magazines and pointedly not talking to one another.

"Hello, sir," the receptionist greeted him. "Do you have an appointment?"

"Actually, no, but ... Sorry, do you have any idea what that song is?" he asked, pointing back the way he'd come.

"I'm sorry?"

"The song," Bunny said again. "In the lift. It's playing a song only, 'tis not a *song* song, it's, like, a Muzak version of the song. I was only in there for a minute but it's in my head now, and for the life of me I can't figure out what it is."

The woman shook her head and continued smiling. "I'm afraid I've never noticed it."

"Lucky you. You'd know it, though. It goes, *na na na – na na – na na na-na.*"

She looked at him blankly.

"*Na na na – na na – na-na na-na,*" he repeated.

"Sorry," she said, her eyes beginning to shift around the room, which Bunny recognised as the "can anyone help me if this nutter goes off the deep end" look. He'd seen it before.

"I don't suppose there's anyone we could ask, is there?"

"About the music in the lift?" she said, her tone making clear her exact thoughts about the question. "No, not that I can think of. Is there anything else I can help you with?"

Bunny decided it was best to move on. "Actually, yes. I'm here to see a friend of mine – Martin Bush."

"I'm afraid there's nobody working here with that name."

"Oh, no – sorry. He's a patient."

"All patient details are strictly confidential so I can't even confirm or deny that somebody is a patient here."

"Right. No, of course. Sorry – I should have made clear. I'm an old friend of Martin's, and his wife, Diane, sent me here to offer him moral support."

"Really?" the receptionist asked, doing nothing to keep the disbelief from her voice.

"We're very good friends."

She raised her eyebrows as far as whatever cosmetic procedure she'd had done would allow her to. "Yes, I'd imagine you must be. His wife ..."

"Sent me here for moral support," finished Bunny. "Yes." He leaned in and spoke in a conspiratorial whisper. "Marty gets nervous in situations like" – Bunny waved a finger in the air – "this. You know – unfamiliar environments."

"I thought he was a guard?" asked the woman, before realising her mistake. "Not that I'm saying he's a patient here."

"Relax," said Bunny, pulling out his Garda ID. "I'm a guard too."

She nodded, as if the realisation had just dawned on her. "I see. What's your name?"

"Bernard McGarry."

"Right. And you're here to ..."

"Lend him a hand."

The receptionist looked horrified. "Excuse me?"

"Morally, I mean. Help keep his spirits up."

"I see. I'll just check …"

"Absolutely. Do tell him it's an emergency, though."

The receptionist stopped midway out of her seat. "It's an emergency?"

"By which I mean it's very important that I see him to offer moral support. Tell him Diane said it was very important that he talk to me."

"Right. That makes sense," she said in a way that made it very obvious it definitely didn't.

Two minutes later, the receptionist showed Bunny into a much smaller waiting room where Martin Bush was sitting alone. He looked considerably less than pleased about his new visitor.

"Marty. Great to see you."

Martin attempted a smile for as long as it took the receptionist to leave the room, then grabbed Bunny's arm. "What the fuck are you doing here?"

"Jesus, Marty," said Bunny, taking the seat beside him, "you seem very tense."

"I am very fucking tense. This place alone would make me tense, but, inexplicably, you are here. How did you find out where I was?"

"I dropped by the house and Diane told me."

Marty shook his head in disbelief.

"I told her it was really important that I talk to you urgently – and it is."

Marty pinched the bridge of his nose, shoving his glasses up his face as he did so. "I can't believe this. How is it my wife seems to think the sun shines out of your arse?"

"It's because—"

"I know why it is," snapped Marty. "Billy bloody Walsh grabbed her arse at a dinner dance fifteen years ago and you punched his lights out."

"It was very poor behaviour," said Bunny. "Entirely unacceptable. He had it coming."

"I know he did. And, as I have said innumerable times since, I'd have done it, only I was in the bathroom at the time. Would it have killed you to have waited until I got back?"

"It was a sort of spur-of-the-moment thing," said Bunny. "The punch, I mean. Although, I'd like to at least think that Billy didn't plan his actions beforehand either. Still claims he never did it. Gropey gobshite."

"Still, though – I can't believe she told you I was here."

"Relax," said Bunny. "So, you're at the doctors. It's nothing too serious, is it? Diane didn't say."

Marty gave Bunny an incredulous look. "Did you not notice what this place actually is?"

"She just gave me the address and then I hit the button in the lift. By the way, you didn't happen to catch the song they play in there, did you? It goes, *na na na – na na – na-na na-na* ... For the life of me, I can't remember what it is." Bunny noticed the look on Marty's face. "But let's not worry about that now. Why? What is this place exactly?"

Marty spoke through gritted teeth. "A fertility clinic."

"Oh," said Bunny. "As in ..."

"Yes."

"Right." Bunny winced and spoke more to himself. "Lend him a hand ..."

"What?"

"Nothing. So yourself and Diane are trying to have a kid?"

"Yes."

"Fair play to you. She'd make a great mum, and you would be a fine father, I'm sure."

Marty tugged his earlobe irritably. "Thank you for the vote of confidence."

"So, you're having a bit of trouble, I take it?"

"I would really prefer not to discuss this with you."

"Understandable," said Bunny. "Not that there's any shame in it.

Very common thing these days. I believe a lot of lads have lazy swimmers now ... Or, I dunno, do women have, like, lazy eggs? I'm not sure how it works. Fast eggs probably makes more sense? Picky eggs? Boiled eggs? Harder to get through? Scrambled eggs?"

"Bunny."

"Sorry. I sort of got stuck in an egg loop there. So is it yourself or herself?"

"That's what we're here to find out," snapped Marty. "Although I was expecting it to be just me here, if I'm honest."

"Absolutely. I'm very sorry to intrude but ..." Bunny caught himself, then pointed at the other door in the room – the one he hadn't come in through. "So, if you don't mind me asking – do you have to go in there and ..."

Bunny did the mime.

Marty glared at Bunny.

Bunny stopped doing the mime.

"Right," he said. "I mean ... Did you know that falcon breeders let the birds copulate with their heads?"

"What?"

"'Tis true," continued Bunny. "I mean, the breeder's wearing a hat at the time. Bit of protection. We had a weird animal-facts round in the table quiz I'm quizmaster for down at O'Hagan's."

"Great," said Marty, testily.

"So, how do you do it?" asked Bunny, nodding back at the other door. "I mean, I know how you do it, but ..."

"I believe they give you some reading materials to look at."

"Right. To get you in the required mood."

"Yes."

"Do they give you, like, a menu of certain things you can choose from?"

Marty placed a hand on his forehead and a very faraway look came into his eyes. "Am I having a nightmare? I think I must be having a nightmare. That makes more sense than the fact that I'm sitting here, waiting to go into a room to do something my mother once assured me would make me go blind, into a specimen pot, and before I do, I'm sitting here discussing the process with Bunny fucking McGarry. Either I'm having a nightmare or I crashed on the way here and this is actually hell."

The two men sat there for a few seconds and Bunny drummed his fingers on his knees. "Would you like me to go?"

"More than you could possibly imagine."

"Fair enough. I'll cut to the chase, then – I need a favour. I need to have a quick chat with a certain minister, and I need to do so discreetly. Seeing as you're a senior boyo in the Special Detective Unit – and congrats on the promotion, by the way – I was wondering if you'd help me out?"

"You'd like me to compromise the security of a member of the cabinet?"

"I'm not trying to assassinate somebody, Marty. I just want a quiet word."

Martin Bush looked very unsure about this.

"I'll never tell anybody that you told me – you have my word. Plus, you telling me will mean I'll get out of here and you can focus on matters in hand. No pun intended."

———

Two minutes later, Bunny stepped back into the lift, having got all the information he needed. As the doors closed, he threw a parting wave to the receptionist.

———

Forty-five seconds later, the doors to the lift reopened and Bunny stuck out his head.

"'Do You Know The Way To San Jose'," he exclaimed, looking around the room excitedly. "In case anybody else was wondering. The song in the lift," he added, pointing up at the speaker, "'Do You Know The Way To San Jose'."

A sea of confused and irritated faces looked back at him.

"So," he said, stepping back into the lift. "I guess it might have just been me on that one."

Chapter Thirty-Three

JAILBREAK

Bunny slotted the Porsche into a parking space between a minibus and a tractor, and killed the engine. He picked up his phone, which had been bleating at him insistently for the last twenty minutes, took a deep breath and answered. "DI O'Rourke, to what—"

"Where the hell is she?"

"And who would this be?"

"Don't piss me about, Bunny. I'm really not in the mood. And while we're on the subject, when I ring you, you answer the damn phone."

"First," responded Bunny, "I'm not currently working for you. And second, I couldn't answer the phone because I was driving the car."

"Pull over next time."

"I couldn't. I'm on narrow country roads and there's no room. It's not like I'm telling you something you don't know, Fintan – two of the boys have been following me for the last couple of days, so you know I'm down in Kerry."

This resulted in a slight pause at the other end of the phone before O'Rourke spoke in a more measured tone. "I'm not aware of any tail on you."

"Oh, please. Pull the other one – it's got my sweaty knackers attached to it."

"Given that you're still technically a serving member of the Garda Síochána, we really shouldn't have to put a tail on you. Theoretically, you should actually be assisting us."

"I am," insisted Bunny. "Sure, didn't I even slow down on my way through Offaly to let the lads catch up with me after they got stuck behind a tractor pulling a load. I'm nothing if not cooperative."

"Whatever. To go back to my original question – where the hell is Rosie Flint?"

"I don't know."

"Bullshit."

"Actually," said Bunny, "it's one hundred percent the truth. I take it you've lost track of her?"

"You bloody well know we have. At five o'clock yesterday she went into the changing rooms in Clerys, then apparently disappeared off the face of the earth. Quite aside from anything else, that might win some kind of award for the most Irish disappearance in history."

"And as you well know, seeing as you've had me followed for the last two days, I was nowhere near Clerys at that time."

Bunny had noticed the tail as soon as he'd left Rosie's apartment for the second time yesterday, having delivered the note from the Sisters. The reason he'd kept it was because it provided him with a rock-solid alibi. He had every intention of losing it now that purpose had been served.

"I didn't say you were anywhere near Clerys," O'Rourke continued. "Still, you know where she is, don't you?"

"Actually, hand on heart, I don't."

Bunny felt good about being able to say that, as it happened to be the truth. All he'd done was hand Rosie the envelope given to him by Sister Bernadette.

"If you'd like to be sure, I'm happy to leave the car unlocked for the next twenty minutes. The two lads in the blue Volkswagen can come up and check I haven't got her stashed in the boot. It's small, but you can fit a man in it." Lev hadn't looked comfortable, although, to his credit, he hadn't complained.

"Thanks," replied O'Rourke. "Please do. That poor woman has people trying to kidnap her, and God knows what else, and if you're to be believed, she's disappeared off the face of the Earth."

"Look, as you know, for better or for worse, she wouldn't take the police protection. She wanted to go somewhere away from all of this. If it's any consolation, if neither you nor I know where she is, whoever the hell was after her must not know either."

"They'd better not," snarled O'Rourke. "So help me, if she turns up dead, I will hold you personally responsible."

"Much appreciated," said Bunny drily. "So, how is the investigation going?"

O'Rourke laughed. "I'm not telling you a damn thing and, just so you know, neither will Detective Cassidy. I've ordered her not to communicate with you in any way – although I got the distinct impression she wasn't going to, even before I told her not to. She isn't your biggest fan these days either. And while we're on the subject, what the hell are you doing in Kerry?"

"Well, seeing as you asked so nicely ... I'm down here because one of the lads from my team is away at a Gaeltacht college. I thought I'd drop in to see him, and then later on, I'm off to a party."

O'Rourke grumbled something unintelligible.

"What was that?"

"Nothing. Enjoy yourself and try not to get into any scraps with wading birds."

After hanging up the call, Bunny got out of the car and stretched his limbs. While owning the Porsche had been the fulfilment of a life-long dream, it wasn't the most comfortable of rides for a man his size. Once his blood had started to circulate to all parts of his body once more, he headed towards the door to the school.

Exhausted as he was, after talking to Marty Bush yesterday he'd decided that his best course of action was to go home, get something approximate to a decent night's sleep, and then travel down here first thing. He'd made good time – door to door it had been four hours between closing his front one and knocking on this one.

Five minutes later, he was being shown in to the headmaster's office by the school secretary. The man sitting behind the desk had that kind of weary, beaten-down expression acquired from spending a lifetime trying to fill young minds with information they did not want in there.

"Thank you, Mairéad. How can we help you, Detective?"

"You have a student here by the name of Declan Fadden."

The man's wince told its own story. "We do."

"I need him for important police business."

Chapter Thirty-Four

FINDING STUFF IS HARD

DI O'Rourke stood in front of the desk and considered his options. Waking the most senior guard in Ireland from the deep slumber into which he had fallen while sitting behind his desk seemed like a very bad idea. What seemed like a worse idea, however, was sneaking back out of the room, having been called there by the most senior guard in Ireland.

It occurred to him while considering these two options that there was an even worse one – namely, the most senior guard in Ireland waking up to find him standing there watching him sleep. And so it was that DI Fintan O'Rourke took his career prospects in his hands and cleared his throat as loud as seemed sensible.

Ferguson shot upright so fast that O'Rourke stepped back and gave a rather unmanly yelp in the process. The Commissioner scanned the room for a moment before focusing his attention on his visitor, his expression making it clear that he wasn't an entirely welcome one. He held up one finger while he ran his sleeve across his face. Then he picked up a nearby cup of tea and drank from it, his grimace indicating it might have been lacking in the temperature stakes. O'Rourke couldn't help but notice that the pattern of the leather blotter on the Commissioner's desktop was clearly visible on the man's face.

"Fintan," Ferguson growled. "Wonderful to see you, as always."

It was 3pm on a Saturday. A Saturday O'Rourke was definitely not supposed to be working, and it was a Saturday at the end of what had been an incredibly long week. He felt exhausted. It was the only way Fintan O'Rourke, a man who prided himself on a normally razor-sharp ability to assess a situation, could explain to himself what on earth went so wrong in that moment that he decided to attempt to take a seat without being asked. To his credit, his arse was still hovering a few inches above the seat when he caught the Commissioner's look and realised the spectacular error he was making.

"Yes," said Ferguson archly. "Do take a seat. Can I get sir an aperitif? Some finger food? A foot rub, possibly?"

O'Rourke stood to full attention but the damage had already been done.

"No, I insist, Detective Inspector. Do pull up a chair and explain to me how your team – your task force, in fact – managed to lose track of the university professor with pink hair who you were supposed to be protecting?"

"It was undeniably a massive fuck-up, sir."

"Not at all. I believe the women's changing rooms in Clerys is both immense and labyrinthine. I'm just glad your men made it out alive."

"With respect, sir, and I'm not trying to excuse the failure here, but it is difficult to protect somebody who repeatedly turns down the protection."

The Commissioner slammed his fist on the desk. "We are a national police force – the entire job is essentially protecting people who don't think they need it." He leaned back in his chair and vigorously rubbed his hands up and down his face. Once he'd finished, he looked up at O'Rourke. "You look almost as tired as I feel. For God's sake man, sit down."

"No, thank you, sir. I'd —"

"Sit!"

O'Rourke's backside was in the chair before his brain had a chance to give him an option.

"Have you managed to get hold of our friend Mr McGarry?"

"Yes, sir. Reading between the lines, while he asserts he doesn't know where she is, he does seem convinced that she's safe."

Ferguson wrinkled his nose. "And I guess we just take his word for that, do we?"

In the absence of any kind of a decent answer to that question, O'Rourke decided to leave it hanging.

Just then, the phone on the desk rang and Ferguson snatched up the receiver. A moment passed. "Yes, of course – put her through." Ferguson turned in his chair and his face fell into an expression that O'Rourke had never seen before. The Commissioner's voice then dropped to a soft tone O'Rourke had never heard before either. "Hello, sweetheart. I'm afraid there's no news yet, but ..." Ferguson leaned forward, somehow looking much smaller than he had done just a minute ago. "Don't cry, my love. We're doing all we can. As soon as I hear anything ..." He took the receiver away from his ear and held it in front of him, the continuous beep of a disconnected call clear to hear. He turned back around and returned it to its cradle.

"No luck?" asked O'Rourke.

Ferguson shook his head slowly. "Not for the want of trying. While I resisted the urge to mobilise the might of An Garda Síochána to the cause, Carol did have a brainwave in that regard. Currently, every Boy Scout, Girl Guide, Sea Scout and Cubs outfit within twenty miles of our house is on the lookout for Kevin."

"I'm sure you'll find him."

"Yes," said Ferguson. "Unfortunately, several of them are sure that they've found him already. This morning alone, I've had to smooth over three situations in which the overexcited youth of Ireland have kidnapped a Labradoodle that is not our Kevin. Not to mention a three-legged Collie in Sandyford. The Scoutmaster for that particular troupe informed me that the kid in question, while keen, is not the sharpest tool in the box – as if that wasn't obvious. At this point it's the toss of a coin as to what happens first – we find poor

Kevin or I cement my reputation as the new Cruella de Vil. Anyway, I didn't call you in here for that. How goes the rest of the investigation?"

"I have officers scouring the CCTV footage from anywhere near the Grand Parade, hoping that we get a shot that might show us the faces of those involved. As predicted, the burned-out van is a forensic wasteland, but we're going door to door round the dump site in Ballyfermot to see if anybody caught the vehicle that the men swapped over to. We've checked all hospital admissions, but again, as expected, while we believe that at least one of them picked up a broken bone, they have, unsurprisingly, refrained from seeking assistance from the Irish health service."

"While I'm delighted, of course, to hear we are ticking all the boxes, please tell me we actually have made some meaningful progress?"

"Well," said O'Rourke, choosing his words carefully, "I also have a couple of people going through anything and everything Rosie Flint has said publicly. Looking for some kind of clue as to why these people are so interested in her."

"Go on."

"She gave an interview – on a university student radio show of all things – in which she did make a rather pointed remark about powerful men in the world of politics who are, to quote her exactly, 'appalling hypocrites in the attitude they take to legalising sex work'."

"Interesting," said Ferguson. "Less and less does it seem that all of this kicking off while the country chooses its next leader is a coincidence."

"Indeed," said O'Rourke. "By the way, in the last hour, the field has narrowed to two – Catherine Royce and the Arsehole."

For the first time, Ferguson actually looked a little cheerful as his eyes widened. "Really?"

"Yes, sir. By all accounts, it's on a knife edge."

The Commissioner's eyes were wild now as he drummed his fingers excitedly on the desktop. "Perhaps I did call this putt a little early. While I didn't think paying for it sounded particularly like something the Arsehole would do, being a hypocrite of the highest order is much more up his street."

"Yes, sir."

Ferguson picked up a pen and deftly twirled it between his fingers. "So, a female taoiseach looks like it might be a real possibility?"

"It does," confirmed O'Rourke. "So much so that I caught a radio show on the way in where people were discussing how her husband would cope with having to entertain the wives of world leaders."

"Oh, for Christ's sake – I thought it was a new millennium. That Thatcher woman had a husband – I seriously doubt he was taking the girls out for shopping and cocktails."

"I seem to recall he played a lot of golf."

"Well," said Ferguson. "Take it from me – there are worse things you can do as a husband."

Chapter Thirty-Five

DANCE LIKE NOBODY IS WATCHING

Bunny slotted the Porsche in the space the man in the hi-vis jacket waved him into. It had been a longer drive here from Kerry than he'd expected – not least because in order to get Deccie on board with the plan, he'd been forced to make an unscheduled stop for chips. Their break had lasted longer than the time it had taken to lose their tail, which had been embarrassingly easy.

He'd half hoped a gob full of chips might stop Deccie from expounding on his theory that an international drug-running ring was being operated from the Gaeltacht he'd been attending, but no such luck. It had to be said that while the staff were probably not doing that, they had been alarmingly willing to part company with Deccie – to the point where a delirious conga line almost followed them out of the building. Bunny was still trying to get through the fake story he'd come up with, and they were pushing him out the door. He was more aware than most that the lad was an acquired taste; it was fair to say it looked as if they'd taken to Deccie even less than he'd taken to them.

Bunny tried to focus his attention on the matter in hand. The questionably fertile Marty Bush had told him that getting near a certain politician would be all but impossible. At a political convention the delegates would be surrounded by security. At that point he realised that he didn't need to get close to the candidate at all. They were throwing a birthday party for a family member, and judging by the number of cars parked in the temporary car park opposite the house, it was a rather large party at that. A massive banner wishing Marie a happy sweet sixteen hung above the front gates.

Bunny had never been to a sweet sixteen party. He was pretty sure that they hadn't been a thing in Ireland until very recently. The whole tradition smacked of an American institution that rich Irish people had imported because they couldn't think of any other way to spend their cash, and judging by the house opposite, the people throwing this party had no shortage of funds.

As Marty had told him in their short impromptu briefing, the family was loaded, which was why the protection afforded to ministers by the Garda Síochána was only part of the package. They had private security to complement it. Irony of ironies, they'd be worried about the possibility of kidnapping. Since the Good Friday Agreement, the IRA were at least officially out of the kidnapping business as a way to fund their operations, but their previous successes had firmly established the practice as a little cottage industry on the island of Ireland. While not as popular as it once was, you were nobody here until somebody tried to snatch a relative to exchange for a suitcase full of cash.

As Bunny sat in the car and watched the other partygoers making their way towards the house, he realised he might have made a rather large miscalculation. In his mind, he'd dismissed a sweet sixteen as a children's birthday party. Deccie Fadden was many things – a child being chief amongst them. Ergo, Deccie would provide the perfect cover for Bunny to get into the party. However, the glamorous girls walking by, who looked closer to thirty than to thirteen, made the twelve-year-old sitting in the passenger seat in trackie bottoms and a jumper his granny very possibly had knitted seem terribly out of place. It wasn't Bunny's biggest problem, but he also noticed that everybody else was carrying beautifully wrapped presents. All Bunny had in the car was a copy of a GAA magazine and half a bag of chewy toffees that had been there too long and were now the wrong kind of chewy.

They'd just have to wing it.

Bunny turned to Deccie. "Right. Remember what we discussed. I'm going to do the talking."

"It's not the best use of our resources," countered Deccie, "but if you insist."

"I do."

With that, they exited the car and joined the queue of people at the front gates.

At the front of the line, the little fella dressed all in black with a clipboard and headset did little to hide his scepticism as Bunny and Deccie stepped up. He glanced across to the shaved gorilla in a tuxedo as if to say, "Get ready to start looking ominous."

"Hello, gentlemen. Invitations, please?"

Bunny gave a broad smile. "Howerya. You'll have to forgive me, I'm the eejit who left the invite at home in Dublin."

Headset nodded, as if this confirmed everything he knew about the world in one sentence. "Yes, I'm afraid this event is strictly invitation only."

"Oh, I know that," said Bunny. "I have an invite, we just forgot it. My son used to go to school with Marie."

"Really?" said Headset, rolling out his most withering of looks. "He's very short for sixteen, isn't he?"

Bunny went to speak but Deccie beat him to it. "That's right. I am extremely short. That's mainly because of the cancer." He jabbed a thumb in Bunny's direction. "As you can see, my father here is a very tall man, but yes, I'm a short arse thanks to all the cancer. That, or the treatments. You'd have to ask my doctors. Very kind of you to bring it up, though. Nobody's ever mentioned it before. I guess most people are a little more wary than you are of ripping the piss out of a kid with months to live."

Bunny tried to maintain a fixed expression, which was more than could be said for Headset, who looked like he'd just lost a game of pass the parcel with a grenade.

"I ... I obviously ..."

"No," said Deccie, holding up a hand. "Fair is fair. We drive all this way but, I mean, it's not like it's an official Make-A-Wish thing. More of a goodwill gesture. It's my own fault, really. I should have left the invitation where it was, but I kept taking it down and looking at it. When you're going through all the treatment, you've gotta find stuff to cling onto. Things to look forward to, y'know?"

"Now all I've got is that interview with the *Mirror* on Monday. I think they were hoping I was going to make a big deal about being invited to this party by a kind-hearted politician, but I guess it goes to show that there's no such thing, is there?"

Deccie reached out and took Bunny's hand. "Come on, Dad. Let's stop wasting the nice man's time. Maybe I'll live long enough to grow a couple of inches so I can at least get my other wish of getting to ride a rollercoaster before, y'know, the end."

Forty-five seconds later, Deccie and Bunny were walking up the driveway towards the house, the gravel crunching beneath their feet.

Bunny spoke without looking down at Deccie. "You are seriously going to have to stop doing that."

"It worked, didn't it? *Dad,*" he added for emphasis.

"Have you heard of karma, Deccie?"

"Is he that new Brazilian Arsenal just signed?"

"Never mind. And, while I didn't approve ... fair play. That rollercoaster bit was inspired."

"I was particularly proud of that bit alright, boss."

As they entered the house, Bunny had to reluctantly hand over his coat to the guy taking them at the door. In his head, he decided to stop referring to it as "a house". A mansion – that's what it was. A bloody mansion. And not a small one. There were columns in the entrance hall, which was itself large enough to park a bus in. It needed to be that big, too, given that most of the teenagers in Ireland and a fair few of their parents appeared to have been invited.

Dance music was pumping from the stereo in the front room to the left, where groups of teenagers were standing around, dancing, and chatting and preening. The occasional female screech could be heard over the din as the individual in question met someone who looked fabulous.

Deccie pulled on Bunny's sleeve. "What is *that*?" There was an unmistakable air of awe in his voice as he pointed in the other direction, to where the cohort of older guests had gathered.

"That, Declan, is what rich people call a buffet." Bunny looked down as his pretend son sniffled. "Are you alright?"

"Sorry – I've just never seen anything that beautiful before."

"You can go and just ..." Bunny trailed off as he realised he was speaking to thin air.

Deccie Fadden had descended on the buffet like a pint-sized locust and Bunny decided to leave him to it. Presumably somebody would inform the lad that it was considered common courtesy to use a plate.

To his right, Bunny noted the sweeping staircase that led upstairs. He also noticed the gent in the tuxedo standing guard at the bottom of it. Bunny walked over casually, only to have his way blocked in the most polite manner possible.

"I'm sorry, sir. The upstairs area is off limits."

"I'm just looking for the toilets."

"No problem," said the man with a smile. "If you just go round to the right there, you'll find one bathroom, with another on the far side of the kitchen, and there are some Portaloos out beside the marquee."

Bunny leaned in. "The thing is," he whispered. "This is a bit embarrassing, but I have to drop the kids off at the pool, and it's a large brood. I don't think I can entrust it to the kind of water pressure you typically get in a downstairs toilet. I'm sure you understand."

The look of distaste on the man's face gave the impression that he didn't give a shit, and apparently had never needed to have one. "The downstairs facilities will be fine, sir."

"I mean ... I wouldn't like to see you get into any trouble. I did try and warn you."

The man refused to dignify Bunny's words with a response, but merely pointed in the direction of the downstairs bathrooms.

Bunny moved off and subtly scoped out the rest of the downstairs. While the ground floor was considerable in size, annoyingly, there appeared to be only one set of stairs leading to the first floor. It wasn't as if Bunny had a detailed plan, but getting upstairs was the one part of it that was actually crucial. He had a theory – a wild theory, possibly – but he would never be certain without any evidence.

Out of his pocket, he took the picture he'd ripped from the front page of yesterday's *Irish Times*, and studied it again. He could be wrong but every time he saw the image his gut instinct grew stronger.

He needed to get upstairs.

He watched an elderly woman look on with a sort of horrified fascination as a certain someone attempted to eat six spring rolls in one go.

What he needed was a distraction.

———

Bunny stood over in the corner beneath the stairwell and tried to act casual. He picked up something coated in breadcrumbs from his plate of finger food and took a bite. The mouthful didn't reveal to him what the thing was, but it did at least make clear to him the fact that he didn't like it. He gagged and considered the potted plant by his side. He noted somebody else had already spat a masticated morsel in there – clearly these things were going down a storm. He manned up, swallowed, and glanced in the direction of the front room. As if on cue, somebody started clapping along rhythmically with the song and the other partygoers took it up instantly. Two guests walked past him.

"What's going on?"

"Some little fat kid is breakdancing," came the response. "It's incredible."

More guests started moving towards the front room because nothing draws a crowd like a crowd.

Bunny could observe the security guard at the bottom of the stairs unobtrusively from where he was. He watched the man craning his neck to see what was going on, before curiosity got the better of him and he moved across the wide sweeping hallway to see what the fuss was about.

When he looked back to his abandoned post, the guard didn't see anything. He definitely didn't see the door to one of the upstairs bedrooms closing.

———

Creeping about in somebody else's private space felt deeply unpleasant to Bunny, but needs must. He was standing in what he could only assume was the master suite. The bedroom alone took up more space than the entire downstairs of his house.

He made his way over to a pair of doors on the far side of the room. Opening one, he found it to be a walk-in wardrobe. He stepped inside and looked around. Two walls were taken up with women's clothing; the other two with men's. Through the other door was the ensuite bathroom, which featured his-and-hers vanity units. Bunny stood at the sink that was clearly the his and found what he'd been looking for.

———

Two minutes later, while keeping a careful eye on the security guard at the bottom of the staircase, Bunny closed the bedroom door softly. As he started to make his way down the stairs, a voice behind him said, "Hello."

He spun around to see a man standing in a doorway further down the hall. The man held up his glass. "Bunny McGarry, I assume. You look like you could use a drink."

Chapter Thirty-Six

A DRINK BEFORE THE WAR

It wasn't as if Bunny made a habit of prowling through other people's houses, but in his limited experience, when people caught you doing so, they generally didn't take it as well as Gerald Royce appeared to be doing. The two men were standing in what Bunny assumed you could call a study. Royce waved Bunny towards a leather chair then made his way over to the amply filled drinks cabinet in the corner to refresh his drink.

Gerald Royce was probably knocking on the door of seventy but he wore it well. He had that healthy look about him, like someone who took care of himself. His build was slender and his complexion was the rosy kind you got from long country walks and not from large drinks like the one he'd just poured. He had that strong, pronounced jawline too.

Bunny turned down the offer of a drink but Royce returned with one for him anyway, handing it to him before taking a seat in the leather chair opposite.

"I don't remember you being on the guestlist for my granddaughter's birthday party," Royce said, "but then again, there were so many names, you could have been."

From a distance the man looked a picture of relaxed composure, but Bunny had noticed the tremor in Royce's hands as he'd passed him the heavy cut-glass tumbler containing a generous measure of no doubt expensive whiskey.

"What should we drink to?" Bunny noted the slight slur in Royce's speech. "I suppose this isn't really a toasting situation, is it?" Royce knocked back his drink in one. His rheumy eyes took in the room around him for a few seconds before they settled on Bunny. He offered an apologetic smile.

"In case you were wondering, Roger Plummer called after you spoke to him."

Bunny looked surprised to hear this.

"He didn't sound well on the phone," Royce continued.

"No," said Bunny. "He's not a well man at all. He all but told me he has only a few months to live."

"Great shame. Roger is a good man." Royce waved his glass-holding hand in Bunny's direction. "I'd appreciate it if whatever happens now, we try and keep his name out of this."

Bunny shrugged. He was still far from sure what was actually happening now.

"He said you'd come here. That you were the type never to let something go."

"A woman's life is in danger," said Bunny flatly.

Royce looked as if he'd just been slapped in the face. He turned away and studied a painting on the wall, of a stag with two arrows in its side, as if seeing it for the first time. Eventually, he turned back to Bunny. "Can I ask – what do you have in your pocket?"

Bunny hesitated then pulled out the hairbrush he'd picked up from the bathroom and held it up.

Royce stared at it in honest confusion. When the realisation hit him, his head jerked up. "Ah. Of course. DNA." He nodded repeatedly, as if happy with his conclusion. "It's amazing what they can do these days, isn't it?"

"It is."

"It won't be necessary." The older man looked down, as if

gathering himself, then returned his gaze to Bunny. "Rosie Flint is my daughter."

While it confirmed what Bunny already suspected, there was still something shocking in hearing it said aloud.

"Do you know, I think that might be the first time I've ever spoken those words out loud? I mean, Roger suspected, I assume, but we never confirmed it. When I heard of Rosie's mother's death, I asked him to step in and keep an eye on the girl. Make sure she wanted for nothing."

"Well," said Bunny, "except a family."

Despite the situation, Bunny still felt bad when he saw the wounded look in Royce's eyes as the dig landed.

Royce looked away. "That's ... fair. Not that it excuses anything, but if you'll allow an old man, I'd like to explain?"

Bunny nodded. He still had plenty of questions.

Royce cleared his throat and did his best to sit up straight. "I loved Anna Flint. I was a foolish, weak man but I honestly did love her. Catherine and I were going through a rough patch. A very rough patch. Honestly, I was all set to leave her, and all that that entailed. It would have torn the family apart, not to mention the business, but I was a man in love. Then, Catherine found out and confronted me. More than that, she went to Anna directly. Confronted her."

Royce licked his lips. "My wife has always been a fighter, long before she ever got into politics. She wanted me back, and Anna wanted nothing to do with breaking up a family. After the two women had made their respective choices, I sort of ... 'went with the flow' doesn't seem like quite the right way of putting it, but I trust you know what I mean. Since then, Catherine and I have worked on our marriage and, honestly, we've been in a good place for a long time. I only strayed the one time, and it's been decades since we spoke of it."

"And what about Rosie?" asked Bunny.

"I didn't even know of her existence until Anna died and I received a letter out of the blue. She was always so well prepared. She'd left letters with a friend. I suppose she must have had an inkling about what was to come. Awful business. Poor woman. When

I think of her dying that way ..." Royce trailed off and his eyes glazed over. Lost in memory. As quickly as he'd drifted off, he snapped back, remembering where he was. "Catherine has done a lot of work to improve things for victims of domestic violence." He tilted his head and squinted. "Sorry, where was I?"

"Letters."

"Ah. Yes. Anna informed me that Rosie was mine, and said that Rosie would be receiving a similar letter explaining that I was her father and it would be up to her whether she decided she wanted anything to do with me. She made it clear the choice was entirely Rosie's. I waited, but nothing ever came. I never understood why."

Royce noticed Bunny's confused look. "What is it?"

"Rosie has no idea that you are her father."

"What?" Royce looked stunned.

"Absolutely none. As far as she's concerned, her biological father died when she was a few months old."

The older man's mouth hung open. Bunny could see this piece of news bouncing around in his head, changing his perspective on everything. "But ... the letter from Anna ... It said that Rosie was going to find out."

"I don't know what to tell you," said Bunny. "Something must have happened, but I'd bet my life she never got that letter."

"My God." Royce's voice was a stunned whisper. "All this time, I assumed she wanted nothing to do with me. That's why I had Roger ... Catherine was a TD at that point and we knew Roger well because he handled our security. I went to him and asked him to keep an eye on Rosie for me. We had a private arrangement. He'd check in on her and then report back to me. He had a quiet word here and there, made sure she got the best that she could from the foster service and what not. When she got arrested at a couple of protests as a student, he made sure her record was never an issue. That kind of thing. Truth be told, there wasn't much I needed to do for her." An odd look of pride came across his face. "She's such a clever girl. Scholarships and all that. I've followed her career eagerly. Read everything she's published. I even attended a lecture. I've been honestly thrilled to see her doing so well."

"Did your wife know about her?"

"Absolutely. I realise how ridiculous this must sound in the context, but Catherine and I no longer have secrets from each other."

"And how did she feel about her?"

Royce shrugged. "How would anyone feel? I mean, it's not like we spoke about it a great deal." Royce's eyes widened as the penny dropped. "Sorry, I've just realised what you're getting at. Catherine had ... has no resentment towards her. She understands that Rosie is blameless in this."

"That being the case," said Bunny, "can you explain why somebody's trying to kill her?"

Royce worked his jaw as if he'd just taken a punch and was checking it still worked. He shook his head several times then looked Bunny in the eye. "Honestly, never in a million years did I think we'd be here. Catherine would have no idea either – I assure you of that."

Bunny resisted the impulse to ask further questions – he sensed Royce was going somewhere.

"My wife has been a brilliant public servant for decades. I know I'm biased, but I'm telling you now – that is a fact. She has worked tirelessly, and in that time, frankly, she has seen numerous others with a fraction of her integrity, intelligence and dedication ascend to the highest office while she has stood by in lesser roles. She found her calling late in life. She concentrated on raising the children before she even thought about entering politics. If you have a spare afternoon, go back through some press clippings and count the number of times she's referred to as 'a safe pair of hands'. That's political speak for someone who is good at their job but not seen as a threat by those higher up. The arrogance of these pompous bastards." He jabbed a finger in Bunny's direction. "And the things I could tell you about certain other candidates she's been running against for the leadership."

Royce paused and looked away for a second. Bunny guessed he

was realising how that sounded in the circumstances. When the politician's husband spoke again it was in a much quieter voice.

"Couple of years ago, an approach was made. Was Catherine interested in becoming Taoiseach? I mean, ask that of any politician and the answer is obvious. But ... these parties ... individuals. Actually, no – it would be more accurate to describe them as companies. They were prepared to invest in her – that's the phrase they used, 'invest in her' – to make it happen. Who wouldn't want that?"

"Doesn't look like you're short of a few quid," observed Bunny.

"Well, no, but ... this is a different sort of thing."

"I'll bet. And what were they looking for in return for their investment?"

Royce chewed his bottom lip. "You're probably aware that there's oil and gas off the west coast of Ireland – possibly a great deal of it – but nobody's been willing to grant full exploration rights because of the environmental concerns." He looked at Bunny then carried on quickly as if jumping in to refute an accusation he assumed was coming. "Yes, I know how that sounds, but the case can be made that it's good for the economy. It would provide a lot of jobs. People need jobs."

"Sure," said Bunny. "It would still be massively unpopular, though."

"They said that when she was in power ... They said they had a plan to help manage that."

"I'm sure they did. So, you make this deal with the devil and, in return, your wife becomes Ireland's first female taoiseach?"

"You can judge all you like, but we wouldn't have agreed to it if we didn't think it was for the greater good."

Bunny could see the layer of resentment and anger bubbling below the surface of Royce's veneer of politeness.

"How did we get to where we are now, then?" he asked.

"We weren't naive," replied Royce. "At least, not totally naive. To achieve what they said they could, we knew there'd have to be some ... dirty tricks. At the time, we had a newly elected Taoiseach with a healthy majority riding high in the polls. Who'd have known back then that we'd be here now?"

"Your new friends, apparently."

"Well ..." Royce twirled his glass in his hand. He spoke without taking his eyes from it. "You have to understand – it's very rare for the opportunity to step in directly as Taoiseach with a majority. The gloves were off on all sides."

Bunny was becoming irritated by it all. The justifications. "I'm pretty sure the boys behind you and the missus weren't wearing any gloves to begin with. But what I'm still not seeing is where Rosie comes into the picture?"

Royce met his gaze again. "While they were doing their research on everybody else, they were obviously doing it on us too. And they are good. Very good. The payments to Roger were funnelled through an offshore account, but they still found them. They came to me and demanded to know what they were for." Royce hung his head, and this time Bunny could see tears in the man's eyes. "God help me, I told them. As I made clear, it had never been a problem. Rosie seemed to want nothing to do with us, so it was all fine."

"I'm guessing they felt differently," said Bunny drily, "seeing as they've had her followed for months. I'd imagine her showing up on TV wasn't well received either." He slapped his hand against his forehead. "Oh, for fuck's sake – of course."

"What?"

"Christ, I'm slow," muttered Bunny. "I've only just put it together. Sabina LeFèvre – one of the two people your associates killed a couple of days ago— Sorry, my mistake, one of the three. She was a high-end courtesan who supported Rosie's work, and there was a bidding war for the rights to her memoir. They jokingly referred to it as *The Book of Revelations*."

"These pricks must've assumed that Rosie had possibly told her about you – and that was one of the revelations. Everything they've done makes sense if you consider they're pulling out all the stops to make sure the campaign of their hand-picked puppet candidate isn't derailed at the last minute by her husband having an illegitimate child. Never seemed to dawn on any of you fucking idiots that the girl herself has no idea – not one single clue – that you're her real father."

Royce got to his feet and headed towards the drinks cabinet, stumbling a bit as he did so. "What a mess."

"Yes," agreed Bunny. "Three people are needlessly dead, and it looks like it'll all come to nothing."

"I don't suppose I could convince you to—"

Bunny shot out of his armchair, sending his untouched glass of whiskey tumbling to the floor. A nasty dark stain bloomed on the thick cream carpet. His mind flashed back to Mark Smith's apartment. "Don't bother trying to bribe me. My opinion of you couldn't sink any lower." He turned towards the door.

"Wait," said Royce, in such a pleading tone that Bunny stopped in his tracks and turned round. "I ... Please tell Rosie that honestly, I never thought for one second that things would go this way. I would rather die than see her get hurt."

"Well, she's okay – no thanks to you – but the man she loved and a couple of her friends are dead, so don't expect any nominations for Father of the Year any time soon."

With shaking hands, Royce poured himself another drink. Both men looked towards the door as spontaneous applause and cheering erupted downstairs.

"Oh God," said Royce. "She must be home from Dublin. Catherine doesn't know about any of this yet. I swear she has no clue that any of those deaths were related to us. I didn't until I spoke to Roger. Could you ... Could you please give me time to explain it to her before ... whatever happens next, happens?"

In truth, Bunny didn't know what was going to happen next. He was going to leave here and make a call – that much he knew. Catherine Royce's unlikely run at the premiership would come to a premature end and her political career would be left in tatters, but it was hard to say what the legal ramifications would be. The Royces couldn't be held directly responsible for the murders, and as for everything else, good luck to anyone who tried to turn dirty politics into a conviction.

All of that was somebody else's problem. What mattered to Bunny was making sure that Rosie was safe.

"How do I contact these 'friends' of yours?" he asked Royce.

"You can't."

"Bullshit."

"I'm serious. We could never contact them even if we wanted to. This man we'd never met before – we didn't even know his name – just came to us, and over the space of a couple of meetings, laid the whole thing out. If he needs to get in contact with us, he rings me, but it's not like I have a number to call him back on. We don't even know the companies he represents. I guess they figured it was better we were kept in the dark until she got into power. That way, either it happened or it didn't, I suppose."

"In which case," said Bunny, "the fastest way for me to make Rosie safe is for the world to know that your wife is very definitely out of the race."

"Just … give me a little time," Royce pleaded.

Bunny considered the request. "I'm ringing the gardaí as soon as I leave here. You've got until 10am tomorrow to make a public statement confirming she's out of the running, or I'll be screaming everything I know from the rooftops by ten fifteen."

"Thank you," said Royce.

Bunny opened the door. "You're not welcome. Sorry about the carpet."

Chapter Thirty-Seven

GLUTTONY LOVES COMPANY

Bunny finished speaking and waited. The silence at the other end of the line went on for so long that he checked his phone's display to make sure he hadn't somehow been disconnected while delivering his detailed account of what he'd learned from talking to Gerald Royce.

"Holy shit," said DI Fintan O'Rourke, confirming that he was still there. "What a mess."

"You can say that again."

"I'd better get somebody down there before the Royces get their heads together and start changing their story."

"Well, that might happen," said Bunny, "but some things they can't change. Rosie is still his daughter."

"Does she know that yet?"

"No," said Bunny, "and I'm not looking forward to being the one to tell her. She's been through enough heartache this week to last a lifetime. The last thing she needs is this."

"I thought you didn't know where she was?" said O'Rourke, his tone noticeably less accusatory than it had been when they'd last discussed the subject.

"I really don't," responded Bunny. "But I know a woman who might. Anyway ..."

He was distracted from what he was about to say next by the sound of Deccie Fadden throwing up. They'd pulled over in a layby on the road back to Kerry. Bunny had needed to make the call anyway, so Deccie needing some "fresh air" was just an unfortunate coincidence. Well, unfortunate for Deccie, very fortunate for the interior of Bunny's car.

"What the hell was that?" asked O'Rourke.

"Have you heard the expression 'you can take the Deccie out of the buffet, but you can't take the buffet out of the Deccie'?"

"No."

Bunny winced as Deccie puked again on the grass verge. "Well, that's because it turns out you can. In fact, it'll come hurtling out of him."

"I just had a bad prawn," moaned Deccie.

"Did you, Declan? Or did you have forty-seven good ones?"

"I reckon they poisoned me at that Gael—" The rest of his sentence was lost to an unhappy moment of purge.

"Is everything alright there?" asked O'Rourke.

"'Tis fine. The poor lad is just learning a valuable lesson about the perils of gluttony." Bunny's phone vibrated in his hand – a text message telling him he had a voicemail. "If that's all, Detective Inspector, I'd better be getting on."

"Oh," said O'Rourke, "that will most certainly not be all, but it'll do for right now."

"If you wouldn't mind, Fintan – can you let Butch know that I tried to ring her first?"

O'Rourke tutted. "Yeah, alright. You still might need to buy her flowers, though."

"As always, Fintan – your advice is much appreciated."

Bunny hung up. "Seriously, Deccie – are you okay?"

"I think most of it" – he retched – "is out."

"Right," said Bunny, thumbing his phone, "it'd better be. If I'm forced to choose between you and the car, you might not like how it goes."

"I may have overdone it a bit."

"D'ye think?"

"But I regret nothing."

Before Bunny could retrieve the voicemail, the phone rang in his hand. He didn't recognise the number but the dialling code was Galway.

"Hello?" he answered.

"We have a problem," came the voice of Sister Bernadette.

"What kind of problem? Is Rosie okay?"

"What she is is impossible. We have had a serious breach of trust. You need to pick her up and get her out of here."

"Okay. As it happens, things have been more or less resolved. Where is 'here' exactly?"

Bernadette reluctantly gave him directions, then hung up without another word.

"Deccie," shouted Bunny. "Time to go. Get in the fecking car."

Once Deccie was in, Bunny floored the accelerator and the Porsche took off with a squeal of tyres.

"Now this is more like it," said Deccie. "At this speed we'll be back in Dublin within the hour."

"We're not going to Dublin. We're off to Connemara."

"What's there?"

"By the sounds of it – trouble."

"Sounds serious," said Deccie, his voice muffled.

Bunny guided the car around a steep bend then looked across at his passenger, who was sitting there eating a sausage roll. "Jesus, Deccie! You just finished throwing up!"

"I know, boss. That's why I need to get the taste out of my mouth."

Chapter Thirty-Eight

THE WILD, WILD WEST

Deccie *ooh*ed dramatically as the car hit yet another pothole and its undercarriage scraped sickeningly against the stony ground.

"Will you stop doing that?" snapped Bunny.

"All I'm saying is your suspension is going to be knackered."

"I'm very well aware of that, and I don't need you pointing it out every time we go over a pothole. Just ... look out the window and enjoy the scenery, will ye?"

"There's nothing to see. We're in the middle of nowhere."

"Nothing to see?" echoed Bunny. "You're in Connemara, Deccie. Widely believed to be home to some of the most magnificent natural beauty on this planet."

Deccie sniffed dismissively. "It's just grass and rocks and that."

Bunny paused at the sound of yet more expensive damage being done to the undercarriage of a Porsche 928 S LHD then repeated, "Grass and rocks and that?"

"Yeah. It's not even been mowed. You'd think that if they were so proud of it, they'd tidy the place up a bit. And loads of it looks very brown."

"It's a bog, Deccie."

"Ugh," replied Deccie with undisguised revulsion. "I knew

country people were a bit rough, but I didn't realise they shat outside."

"Not bog as in toilet, you ignoramus – bog as in bog. As in a bog. As in where turf comes from."

"Are you telling me that turf is made out of shite?"

"No. What are they teaching you in school?"

"Nothing worth knowing, boss. That's why I keep saying I should leave. I get my education from the street."

"Right," said Bunny. "To prove it, I'll let you out when we pass through that town on the way back. By the way, this whole area is a Gaeltacht."

"I should have guessed," muttered Deccie, with a disapproving shake of his head. "If they weren't so busy speaking Irish so that no one could understand them, they might have had time to tidy up the place and build some loos. Animals."

Thankfully for Bunny's blood pressure, they turned a corner and ahead of them in the distance sat the yellow house on a steep hill that Bernadette had told him to keep an eye out for. "This is the place."

"Thank God," said Deccie. "I need a shite, and I don't care what anybody says – I'm doing it indoors."

The car sounded increasingly unhealthy as it made its way along the undulating track towards the house. There was now a fresh rattling noise that would no doubt prove costly, but right at that moment, Bunny didn't really care. All he wanted was to get Rosie into the car and drive her back to Dublin. Even if she had to spend the night in a Garda station, by 10am tomorrow, she'd be safe.

He parked up beside a battered Ford Cortina at the bottom of the hill, and he and Deccie got out.

"There's no stairs," said Deccie.

"There's a path to walk up."

"What? We're mountaineering now?"

"Ara, will you shut up?"

They trekked up the path, Bunny endeavouring to conceal the fact that he was struggling. The house was about thirty feet above the car parking space and he doubted it had been built there with wheelchair accessibility in mind.

When they reached the top, they stopped and looked around.

Remote really didn't do the place justice. Standing there, as the summer sun hung low over the wild Atlantic to the west, Bunny could appreciate just how out of the way the place was. The nearest town was three miles away over the rugged landscape and rocky outcrops that jutted up from amongst the clumps of gorse bushes and long grass. The house itself was perched on a hill that sloped steeply on three sides. On the fourth side, behind it, the ground fell away sharply at the cliff edge, and the ocean could be heard crashing against the rocks far below.

It wasn't as if Sister Bernadette was renowned for having a sunny disposition, but as soon as she opened the door, Bunny could see just quite how annoyed she was. Wordlessly, she ushered the pair inside. On one side of the kitchen table sat Rosie, drumming her fingers on the tabletop and staring at the worn linoleum floor, while Assumpta sat on the other, flicking through a puzzle book.

"Jesus," said Deccie. "Is it me or is it tense in here?"

Bunny winced. "Beautifully diplomatic as always, Declan."

Bernadette looked down at Deccie. "Why is there a child here?"

"You said come immediately." Bunny shrugged. "I came immediately. He happened to be with me."

"If it's any consolation," added Deccie, "I don't want to be here either. Now, can I use your shitter?"

"Declan! Manners!"

"Sorry, boss. May I please use your shitter?"

Bunny tried to look apologetic as Bernadette pointed down the hall. "The toilet is the second door on the left."

With a nod Deccie moved off.

"He seems ..." started Bernadette.

"Yes," replied Bunny. "He certainly is." He turned his attention to Rosie, who had continued to stare at the floor the whole time he'd been there. "So, would somebody like to tell me what happened?"

A long pause followed, which Rosie did not attempt to fill.

Eventually, with a tut, Bernadette stepped in. "We got here late last night. Today, after lunch, Rosie and Assumpta went out for a walk, only Ms Flint inexplicably took off running. We are here to help her, to keep her safe, and she decides to bolt, as if we're somehow keeping her prisoner."

"Rosie," said Bunny in a soft voice.

Rosie simply turned her head and stared at a different spot on the linoleum. Her fingers didn't miss a beat.

"After looking for her for a couple of hours, I headed into the nearest town to ring you, and that's where I found her. She was just coming out of the phone box having, I assume, made a phone call, but she will not tell us who she rang. Although she has asked us repeatedly to leave her here on her own."

"I see," said Bunny. "I'm sorry about this. Obviously, we've all got off to a bit of a rough start. Would you mind if Rosie and I had a word in private, please?"

Bernadette didn't seem terribly happy about the suggestion. However, after a moment she nodded, and she and Assumpta left the kitchen, closing the door behind them.

Bunny took Assumpta's place at the table. Rosie's face was gripped by a series of blinks that he let pass before he started to speak.

"It's alright, Rosie," he said, trying to keep his voice as calm as possible. "What's going on? You said that you wanted to go somewhere safe where nobody could find you. Take a look at this place – it's exactly what you asked for. I know Bernadette can be a bit much, but her heart is in the right place and, more importantly, she knows what she's doing."

Rosie shifted in her seat and made an effort to look at Bunny's shoulder. "I'm sorry. I'm sorry about everything."

"You've nothing to apologise for."

"They need to leave. So do you."

"I appreciate you feel like you need to be on your own – you've been through a lot. I understand."

Rosie raised her eyes to meet his briefly before she looked away again. "No, you don't understand."

"I—"

"You don't understand," she repeated, nearly shouting the words. "I've made a decision. These people – whoever they are – they killed Mark, they killed Sabine, they killed Henry. They will kill anyone I am close to and they will not stop."

"They will. I ... Look, I need to explain to you. There have been some developments. I finally know what's going on."

"It doesn't matter," she said, rubbing the heel of her hand against her eye. "It's just like my mother all over again. The only way you can defend yourself is by being the one to take action. All of you need to get out of here now."

"But just let me ..." Bunny felt sick to his stomach but tried to keep the panic from his voice. "Who did you ring, Rosie?"

She said nothing.

"Rosie, who did you ring?"

"I rang Duncan, my assistant. I let him know I was fine."

Bunny pursed his lips. "Duncan? Right. Anyone else?"

"I rang my office."

"Why would you do that?" Bunny closed his eyes for a second. When he opened them again, he stared up at the ceiling. "You told me you thought somebody was listening to your phone calls. So you left a message on the answering machine with directions to where you are, didn't you?"

Rosie shifted her hands and Bunny noticed the glint of steel under her right sleeve. He reached across the table and grabbed her wrist. She tried to resist but Bunny drew the steak knife carefully from where she had concealed it.

"Give me that back," she said, snatching it out of his hand. "I need it. And you need to get out of here and leave me alone." Tears were streaming down her face. "I've been running from people like this my whole life. It ends now."

"We all need to get the hell out of here," Bunny snapped, before he threw open the kitchen door and rushed outside. In the distance, a jeep was roaring along the road he and Deccie had just driven up, its headlights on in the waning light.

Bernadette joined him. "What's ..." she started, but trailed off when she caught sight of the headlights.

Bunny's mouth was suddenly dry. "They're here."

Chapter Thirty-Nine

FIREWATER BLUES

Bunny crouched down behind the low stone wall at the front of the property as, beside him, Sister Bernadette surveyed the scene below through a pair of birdwatching binoculars.

"Well?" he asked.

She didn't lower the binoculars as she spoke. "Three men, semiautomatic weapons, and what I would imagine are night-vision goggles."

"Great," muttered Bunny. "I was worried they didn't have enough advantages."

His only inkling of a plan up until this point had been the idea that perhaps he could delay the interlopers long enough for the others to sneak away across the bog. Now that he knew these bastards had night vision, that was a non-starter. They'd be slow-moving fish in a barrel, waiting to be picked off. He turned his attention to the shotgun propped against the wall next to Bernadette.

"How much ammunition do you have for that thing?"

She lowered the binoculars and looked down at the gun. Bunny couldn't be sure, but the expression on her face was possibly the closest thing Sister Bernadette had ever come to looking embarrassed. "Two shells. I forgot to pack the box of ammunition before we left. Not my finest hour."

"Well, at least you didn't walk a twelve-year-old into a bloody trap."

"You weren't to know."

Somehow, Sister Bernadette trying to offer him words of comfort only emphasised to Bunny how desperate the situation was.

"I'm sorry about Rosie doing this—"

"Stop that. Clearly the girl isn't thinking straight. More importantly, we have no time to dwell on it now. We need to focus on dealing with the situation at hand. We know what they have. What do we have?"

"Not a great deal," admitted Bunny. "This place has no landline or even the slightest whiff of a mobile phone signal. There's nobody around for miles, that jeep is blocking the only road out of here, and neither of the vehicles we have would get more than ten feet if we were to try to go cross-country around here. And that's if we could even reach them. From what you've told me, any escape by sea isn't viable, so we're trapped and they know it, which is why they're taking their time."

"I didn't ask you what the problem was," snapped Bernadette. "I asked what we have to help fix it."

"Alright. Keep your hair on. Let's see – we hold the high ground. We have a shotgun with two shots, so a couple of those boys are going to have to share. There's you, me, and three non-combatants."

"Assumpta is nobody's non-combatant," Bernadette scoffed. "No offence to your male ego, but I'd rather have her than you in this situation. Hell, I'd rather have her than those three and their machine guns. The reason she doesn't say much is that she's too busy thinking."

Before Bunny could respond, Assumpta came running at an awkward crouch around the side of the house and stopped beside them, sweating profusely and panting heavily.

"Well?" asked Bernadette.

Assumpta nodded and smiled. She pointed at the three metal

barrels that were sitting to the right of the front door. Bunny had checked them out on his way past – all they contained were rocks.

"Time?" asked Assumpta, which came as a shock to Bunny, who had come to the conclusion that the nun never spoke.

"Very little," said Bernadette as she glanced over the wall again. "Oh, look – they're disabling our vehicles."

"Ara, for feck's sake," exclaimed Bunny. "I just got it abled."

Bernadette ignored him. "They'll be spreading out imminently, to come at us from all three sides."

"Need time," said Assumpta.

Bernadette considered this for a few seconds then snatched up the shotgun and fired one shot in the direction of the figures working on the cars below.

"Jesus!" Bunny peered over the wall and saw the three men scramble back to the jeep and duck behind it. "What was the point of that? You were never going to hit them from here, and now we've only one shot left."

"I wasn't trying to hit anybody. I was sending a message. Now they know we're armed. Barely, admittedly, but they don't know that. They'll be a little bit more careful in their approach now, as nobody wants to walk into the business end of a shotgun. If it were me, and I was dealing with an opponent with no hopes of escape, I'd wait until darkness had fallen completely, to take full advantage of my night-vision capabilities." She looked up at the sky and the cross of the sun that had all but sunk below the horizon. "I reckon that might buy us about thirty minutes at most." She looked across at Assumpta. "Enough?"

Assumpta merely shrugged, as if Bernadette had asked her when the next bus was due. She tapped Bunny on the shoulder and indicated that he should follow her.

After detouring to the kitchen to grab Deccie, Rosie and a torch, Assumpta led them to a rudimentary stone structure sitting about thirty yards behind the house. In the gloom, Bunny could make out the edge of the cliffs and the roar of the Atlantic crashing against them far below. Assumpta pushed open the wooden door. Bunny already had a very good idea what would be inside, but his suspicions were confirmed when she shone the torch into the darkness.

"What's that?" asked Deccie.

"A poitín still. 'Tis a way of turning barley into something a lot less healthy and a lot more fun."

"Mental. I heard that stuff can make you go blind. Can I have some?"

"No."

Bunny took the torch off Assumpta and stepped inside the structure, ducking to avoid the low roof. He inspected the various barrels with pipes running between them, and the collection of glass bottles sitting in the corner. Whoever's still this was, they were producing a fair quantity of it.

"Rosie. Deccie. We need bedding, towels – anything you can find. Go. Now."

He looked back at Assumpta, who had an odd grin on her face.

He was starting to see Bernadette's point.

Chapter Forty

GREAT BALLS OF FIRE

It took them only twenty-three minutes in the end, to prepare for their plan. In truth, as Bunny sat there, leaning his back against the stone wall, night falling around him, he knew it wasn't much of a plan at all, but then again, somebody had once said that no plan survived contact with the enemy. What they had was a starting point – after that, it was a case of hoping for the best and a bit of luck. Maybe a whole lot of luck. This would be jazz, not a regimental march.

Sister Assumpta sat to Bunny's right, with Deccie in between them.

Deccie tugged on Bunny's sleeve and spoke in a whisper. "I have to admit something, boss."

"What?"

"There is one good thing about the country."

"What's that?"

"The sky. I noticed it at the Gaeltacht. All them stars that they have out here – they're amazing."

"See – I knew we'd find something eventually."

"Wait and see. You can't see them now, but give it about half an hour. It's bleedin' spectacular. Do you know all the names of the consolations and that, boss?"

"I do know the constellations, as it happens." Bunny peeked over the wall, checking there was not yet any movement down below. "When we get out of this, I promise you I'll teach them to ye."

"Cool," said Deccie, nodding over and over again. "When we get out of this," he repeated, as if reassuring himself.

"Listen, Deccie – I'm sorry for dragging you into this. If I'd had any idea, I'd obviously never have brought you with me."

"Ah, still beats people trying to teach me to speak Irish."

"You're a lost cause, Declan. A lost cause." He shifted around so that he was face to face with Deccie and put his hand on the lad's shoulder. "Right, now, pay attention – this is important. As soon as everything kicks off, you look for a gap and you run. Don't look back. Don't try and do anything. We don't need you to be a hero. Just get yourself out of here. These guys aren't worried about you."

Deccie shoved Bunny's hand away angrily and jabbed a finger in his face. "How dare you say that to me. After all we've been through. You're always telling us about the importance of teamwork. I'm not going back to the lads with them knowing I ran away and left you here so some pricks from the country could slap you around the place."

Bunny was taken aback by the ferocity of Deccie's response. "Right ..." He stole a glance over the wall again. "Well, for a start, Declan, these boys are not from the country. Odds on, they're English."

Bunny regretted his words as soon as they were out of his mouth.

Deccie's eyes grew wide with outrage. "English? Sure, that's worse. This is basically an invasion."

"Just— Listen to me. Whatever happens, after the season we've just had, the team needs your leadership more than ever. Please, for me – get out of here."

"Alright," said Deccie reluctantly.

"Good lad. I need to get in position." Bunny ruffled Deccie's hair then pulled him into a tight hug.

"Get off me. You're embarrassing me in front of the nuns."

Bunny released him and moved off into the darkness.

Once Bunny was out of earshot, Deccie turned to Sister Assumpta and drew his hand from behind his back, holding up the two fingers that had been crossed the whole time. "Doesn't count."

———

Bernadette stared into the face of Rosie Flint. "Can you do this?"

"I ..." started Rosie. "I just wanted to say how sorry—"

"There's no time for that. I need you to do your job – can you do that?"

Rosie gave a weak nod and was shocked when Bernadette gently took her face between her hands.

"Look at me."

With considerable effort, Rosie did. Her eyes blinked rapidly.

"What matters is the next thing. We are not defined by what is done to us. We are defined by how we respond to it. Just keep moving forward. How you get through it is to just get through it. Alright?"

Rosie jutted her chin and nodded.

"Good. Wait for my signal."

With that, and being careful to stay low, Bernadette hurried the twenty or so feet to the north wall, the lighter sweaty in her hand. The good thing about using a house with an old-school turf-burning poitín still out the back was the collection of lighters in the kitchen drawer.

Her post was the north wall, Rosie's was the south, and Assumpta would handle things at the front east wall with the assistance of the boy. She looked around. This small area was theirs to defend. It didn't look like much, but people had fought and died for less.

She stared intently through the gap that she had made for herself between the stones in the wall. The slope up to this side of the house was the most gradual and easy to traverse. It was why she had installed herself here. If this plan had any chance of working, it would be down to her being able to determine when they were coming. Bunny, as was his way, had referred to it as the Grand Old

Duke of York moment – when they were down wouldn't work, and when they were up would be far too late. They needed to catch them when they were only halfway up.

She held her breath.

Was that movement?

Was this that moment?

———

Furkser turned his night vision off and then on again, surveying the target. It should be straight forward, but then the whole bloody thing should have been straight forward and not the damnable mess it had become. He double checked his weapons. As a rule, he didn't like Uzis, but it was what they'd been given. The Uzis and his trusty Glock. They would do the job.

He'd left Buchanan at the bottom of the hill with the jeep, sent Marshall to the north side, and he was covering the south. Buchanan's right eye had all but closed over since the pummelling he'd received from Smith, and Furkser had been forced to reset Marshall's broken right arm himself, while Marshall had bitten down on a leather belt.

He knew he shouldn't let any emotion in, as it risked clouding his judgement, but damn it, Furkser was really looking forward to killing Rosie Flint and that McGarry idiot. Thanks to her, Mark Smith was dead, and thanks to McGarry, it had been Furkser who'd had to do it.

After tonight, he was going to put his retirement plan into operation. He had more than enough squirrelled away to get himself that bar in Thailand. By morning, he'd be out of this godforsaken country and as far away from the Spider as was humanly possible. He knew better than anybody how the man dealt with other people's failure. It hadn't bothered Furkser before, but then he'd never failed before. Maybe he was getting too old for this?

He winced as the headset in his ear beeped. Previously, all operational control on the ground had been left to him, but this time, once they'd found out Rosie Flint's location, the Spider had insisted on taking a more "hands-on" approach. Not close enough to get those hands dirty, but close enough to get on Furkser's tits.

"Why haven't you gone yet?" came the Spider's voice over the radio.

With these comms he could be anywhere within a ten-mile radius. Furkser guessed he was quite a lot closer than that – up in the mountains, most probably. If there was one thing he knew about the Spider, it was that he liked to look down on people.

Furkser held the button on the unit on his belt. "We're waiting for optimum darkness. They know we are here and they are armed."

"You have waited long enough. Go. Go. Go."

———

Buchanan stepped out from behind the jeep and started to move up the slope, the rudimentary path to his left, the two disabled vehicles to his right. The ground was rock with vegetation springing up from it at random points. He moved at a slow, steady pace – alternating between looking down at his feet and up at the target. The slope was about a forty-degree angle. Nothing he couldn't cope with, of course, but it always paid to watch your footing.

As he reached the halfway point, he noticed movement at the top of the hill. He crouched down and trained his gun on the top of the wall. Something large appeared. A metal barrel.

"I've got— Woah!"

The exclamation was because the barrel had just burst into flames. Buchanan dived to his right as the fire-soaked thing hurtled down the slope towards him. As it whooshed past, the edge of it rolled over his foot, sending spikes of pain shooting up his leg.

"For fuck—"

The barrel thudded into the side of the jeep, but a quick glance over his shoulder told him that it wasn't a concern. The container had material wrapped around it that had been set on fire using some accelerant, but the foolish amateurs had miscalculated, and the flames had gone out before it reached the bottom of the hill.

He stood up gingerly, tested his foot and raised his head just in time to see the second barrel come flying over the wall. On this occasion, he stepped out of the way and fired a burst of shots in the direction from which it had come.

Furkser's voice came over the radio. "Buchanan. Report."

"They're sending down barrels on fire. Not a problem."

When the third barrel came down the hill, they hadn't even managed to get it lit. Buchanan didn't fire. Instead, he moved left and onto the path. His change in position confirmed that his foot was sore but nothing more. The third barrel careered away into the darkness, nowhere near him, thumping to a stop somewhere below.

The Spider's voice entered his earpiece. "Other two. Move in."

"Stay off comms," snapped Furkser.

"I'm in command."

"Negative."

Buchanan shook his head. This whole thing was descending into amateur hour. He decided to get moving, and started to make his way up, slowly skirting the side of the track. The sooner these idiots were dead the better.

―――――

Marshall pulled out his earpiece and swore under his breath. He'd had more than enough of this shit. He moved around the large boulder he'd been using for cover and headed up the slope towards the north wall, pulling a flash bang off his belt as he went. A few more feet and he'd be within range. One of these, and whoever was up there wouldn't even see the bullets that would come immediately after.

He cursed again as the flash bang fell to the ground. Bloody cast. He fumbled around for a few seconds before he managed to locate it. He drew himself upright and was just pulling the pin when he caught the bloom of flames out of the corner of his eye. He looked up to see a

Molotov cocktail sail over his head and crash into the boulder behind him.

"What the—"

Before he had time to formulate a thought, a second Molotov cocktail came hurtling through the air. This one landed in front of him and exploded on the hard ground. Flaming liquid splashed out in all directions. His combat trousers caught alight.

He slapped at them briskly to put them out. In his panic, he didn't notice that he'd also pulled the pin on the flash bang, which was why he never saw the third Molotov coming.

———

Buchanan caught sight of the explosions and flames, first from the south side, quickly followed by a trio from the north. Furkser returned fire instantly and a female scream from that direction ripped through the night air, followed quickly by what sounded like Marshall screaming somewhere to his right.

"What is happening? What is happening?" screeched the Spider in his ear.

The damned fool. Buchanan pulled out his earpiece. The guy's bleating was making it hard to—

Something heavy hit Buchanan from behind and sent him sprawling forward. Before he could turn around, a big man was on top of him, pinning him to the ground and sending ferocious punches raining down on his head.

He heard a male voice – a single word accompanying each blow as it landed. "Don't. Shoot. At. Kids."

Just before he lost consciousness, Buchanan realised that perhaps the third barrel not being on fire had been more deliberate than it had appeared.

———

Marshall was rolling around now, oblivious to everything except the flames that were engulfing his body. He looked up to see a blanket being tossed over him, which was followed by a multitude of blows to his form, seemingly trying to put the fire out while also giving him a solid beating. He had the presence of mind to fumble for his sidearm but something smashed against his broken arm and caused him to scream in pain again. He managed to fight his way out from beneath the blanket just in time to see the flames illuminate the demented face of a diminutive elderly nun before her steel-toed boot connected with his head.

———

Bunny had the submachine gun in his hands and was attempting to drag it off the man he'd just rendered unconscious. He was making hard work of it, as the strap was caught under the man's body. Bunny wasn't feeling his best, and was still a touch dizzy. Being sent hurtling down a hill in a barrel will do that to a person, even when the side of the barrel against which their head is braced doesn't hit a rock somewhere along the way. He was concussed and pissed. Part of him considered throwing up, but he didn't have the time right now. While his attention was entirely focused on liberating the gun, he was aware that most of the world around him was currently on fire. He needed to—

Before he could finish the thought, a bullet thumped into the ground beside him. To his left, at the top of the hill, stood Rosie Flint. A tall man stood behind her, his left hand grabbing a fistful of her hair, his right holding a handgun.

"Let go of the Uzi," the man barked at him.

Bunny recognised the guy. Last time he'd seen him, he and Mark Smith had been rolling around on the ground, which had ended badly for poor Smith.

Bunny looked down at the machine gun. As it happened, the weapon was pointing directly at the unconscious man.

"How about you drop yours or I—"

A second bullet smashed into the unconscious man's head. Bunny was no doctor but given that half the guy's skull was now missing, he didn't reckon he'd be coming round any time soon.

Bunny dropped the gun and looked up in revulsion. "Ah, for feck's sake."

Flames were spreading behind them, licking the side of the house. He noticed that Rosie was bleeding heavily from a wound at her left shoulder. He presumed she must've taken a bullet while trying to throw one of the improvised Molotov cocktails.

"I'm going to guess your name is Furkser," Bunny said to the man, who was still holding Rosie by the hair. "Mark Smith mentioned you."

"Shut up and put your hands in the air," ordered Furkser, shoving his gun under Rosie's chin.

Bunny complied.

"Who else is here?"

"Nobody."

Furkser fired a shot that skated off the rocks near Bunny's feet, then placed his gun to Rosie's temple. "Try again."

"If you were going to go for the 'just come out with your hands up and nobody will get hurt' approach, I'd maybe not have shot your own man in the head first."

"He'd fucked up one too many times."

"Have you ever heard the phrase, 'With friends like you ...'?"

"Do you know what?" said Furkser, "I'm going to enjoy shooting you almost as much as this annoying bitch."

"Lovely," said Bunny. "If you do that, though, I'm not going to tell you who else knows who her father is."

Furkser paused. "What?"

"What?" echoed Rosie.

"You still shouldn't play with matches," said Bunny loudly. "Still."

"Stop talking bullshit," snarled Furkser.

"What are you talking about, Bunny?"

With the flames behind her, he couldn't make out all of Rosie's face, but her tone of voice was enough to paint a picture of her bewilderment.

"My father is dead," she continued.

"I'm afraid not. This isn't exactly how I wanted you to find out, Rosie, but your real father is Gerald Royce – the husband of the woman who is *not* becoming Taoiseach tomorrow."

Before Rosie could say anything else, Furkser shoved the barrel of the gun hard up under her chin again.

"Tell me who else knows – now."

"Do you want an exact list of names or just a general number?"

Furkser drove the butt of the gun into the side of Rosie's head with a sickening smash, causing her to wobble on her feet. "Last chance."

Bunny took a step towards him but stopped when Furkser turned the gun in his direction.

"You're some kind of arsehole."

"Names!"

Fifteen yards behind Furkser, through the flames, Bunny noticed the unmistakable figure of a twelve-year-old of his acquaintance giving him a double thumbs-up as he ran across the yard and dived over a stone wall.

"Tell me or—"

Furkser was cut off by the monumental explosion of a poitín still that had been ignited by the aforementioned twelve-year-old. Deccie had lit a Molotov cocktail and tossed it in there in what he would later go on to describe as the greatest moment of his young life.

As Furkser spun around, Bunny took off running towards him.

Rosie Flint guessed this was her last and only chance. She withdrew the steak knife that was still in her pocket and rammed it deep into her captor's thigh.

Furkser screamed and released his grip on her hair, pushing her away from him and turning the gun in her direction. Before he could shoot, Bunny put his entire weight into tackling him to the ground. As Furkser attempted to throw him off, Rosie grabbed the wrist of the hand holding the gun and held on for dear life.

Furkser rammed an elbow into Bunny's throat and tried to shake Rosie, who was now biting his knuckles in an effort to get him to drop the gun. From out of the darkness, Assumpta landed hard on top of Furkser, knocking the wind out of him and giving Bunny enough time to throw a vicious left hook at his unprotected jaw. Then, because you don't change a winning formula, Bernadette arrived on the scene and her steel-toed boot thumped hard into the side of his head.

After all of this, Furkser lay face down on the ground, out for the count.

Given the circumstances, there was no need for Deccie to launch a vicious kick from behind straight into the man's testicles, but in his defence, Deccie didn't like running at the best of times, and there was no way he was going to waste such a beautiful run-up on not booting some gobshite in the nuts.

———

Three minutes later, both Furkser and a crispy-round-the-edges-but-otherwise-alive Marshall were sitting against the stone wall. Their hands had been bound behind them using a number of cable ties found in one of Furkser's jacket pockets. Bernadette was training a gun on them, and Assumpta was tending to Rosie's wound while Deccie gave everyone an unasked-for and unwanted blow-by-blow account of his involvement in proceedings.

Bunny considered the blaze behind them and decided there was no point trying to save the house. It was already well aflame. On the upside, he guessed that even as remote as they were, somebody would notice this much fire and come looking.

A faint sound reached his ears, and he scanned the ground around him in an attempt to discover the source. It was coming from the earpiece attached to the walkie-talkie that had fallen off Furkser in the fight. He picked it up.

"Furkser," barked an irritated voice. "Furkser. Respond. Furkser."

Bunny pulled the cable for the earpiece out of the walkie-talkie and pressed the red button on the side. "I'm afraid Mr Furkser can't come to the phone right now. He's unavoidably detained – I'm guessing for a good forty years to life."

There was a long pause on the other end before the voice spoke again, trying to sound nonchalant. "Mr McGarry, I assume?"

"That's right. And what would your name be?"

"That isn't relevant."

"Fair enough. I'm sure Mr Furkser and his buddy here will give it up soon enough."

"Sadly for you, they don't know it. It pays to keep the hired help in the dark, don't you agree? Especially when they turn out to be so incompetent."

"Harsh but fair."

"Still, well done on your little victory."

Bunny looked at the walkie-talkie. "Thanks very much. Given the range on these things, I'm guessing you're not too far away. How about you drop over and congratulate me in person?"

His invitation garnered a laugh from the other end. "I must regretfully decline. My days of getting my hands dirty with the likes of you are in the past. I'm really more of a big-picture person now."

"That's a shame," said Bunny. "By the way, to update you on the aforementioned big picture – tomorrow morning Catherine Royce will be dropping out of the race to become Taoiseach."

"What?" asked the voice, suddenly sounding much less jovial.

"I'm sorry, were you a big fan of hers? I believe she'll be retiring from politics entirely, owing to family concerns, not to mention the odd legal issue."

The voice tried to go back to sounding nonchalant. "You win some. You lose some."

"Very true," said Bunny. "You've lost big here, haven't you?"

"Laugh it up. I'll be out of the country in a matter of hours and I live to fight another day."

"Fair play to you. Still, if you look off to the west there, you can see the majestic Irish coast, which isn't going to have any massive rigs on it any time soon. Do you reckon your employers will be very understanding about your total failure to make that happen?"

For a couple of seconds Bunny heard breathing on the other end, followed by a beep, then the channel went dead.

Bunny dropped the walkie-talkie and looked over at Bernadette. "Must have been something I said."

Chapter Forty-One

WHILE YOU WERE SLEEPING

Bunny awoke with a start.

"You alright there, sleepyhead?" asked Butch from the driver's seat.

He looked around him and realised they were back in Dublin – on the Navan Road, to be exact, the old Phoenix Park Racecourse to their right. "Jesus, sorry – I must have nodded off, and it looks like I've been out a while."

"You certainly have," she responded.

While Bunny wouldn't go so far as to say that their relationship was back to normal, things were certainly a lot less frosty between the pair, as evidenced by Butch's offer to drive him back to Dublin from Connemara, after he'd finished answering an awful lot of questions.

He'd told the police what had happened, although the dramatis personae was rather radically altered. Assumpta had managed to fix the Sisters' car and they'd made good their disappearing act before the authorities had showed up. Luckily, Furkser and his henchman were saying nothing, so nobody had been able to contradict Bunny and Rosie's version of events. There was, of course, another witness, but Deccie's account had been quietly discounted, seeing as it involved him delivering numerous roundhouse kicks to considerably more opponents than appeared to have been present.

"I'll tell you something else, boss," came Deccie's voice from the back seat of Butch's car, "did you know that you talk in your sleep?"

"Oh, really?" said Bunny, feeling suddenly nervous. "I didn't say anything too embarrassing, did I?"

"Well," said Butch, "I didn't know you had such strong feelings about Willie Nelson."

"Are you pulling my leg?"

"Might be."

"Yeah," agreed Deccie. "Ye didn't say much that we could understand, and the talking was a refreshing change from the snoring."

"I don't snore."

"If you don't," said Butch, laughing, "then I'm gonna have to get this car seen to, because the engine is making a shocking noise. Do you have any mechanics you could recommend?"

"Don't," was all he said.

His Porsche had been put on a tow truck at great expense, and was on its way back to Dublin. He'd mentioned to O'Rourke about the gardaí perhaps paying for that, but the suggestion had not been received warmly.

"The snoring wasn't too bad really, boss," continued Deccie. "I mean, not compared to the farting. So much farting."

"Ara, stop. The two of you are just trying to wind me up."

"I wish we were," said Butch. "I've had the windows open since Athlone."

"It really says something when your arse stinks worse than the countryside."

"Indeed," agreed Butch. "Is now a good time for us to have another of those chats about your diet?"

"God, no. Not after the week I've had."

Butch guided the car around the roundabout beside the Halfway House pub and continued on. "Okay. But we shall be returning to it in the future."

Bunny nodded. He didn't say anything, but he was relieved to know that after all that had happened, his and Butch's friendship still had a future.

"So," he said, "any updates?"

Butch shook her head. "Like O'Rourke said, the thing has stopped being criminal and is political now. Catherine Royce has resigned as a TD, citing health reasons. My guess is that the entire thing gets hushed up."

"Most likely. Does this mean what's-his-face is going to be Taoiseach now?"

"I'd imagine so."

"Unfortunate."

"Yeah," agreed Butch. "He always struck me as being a bit of an arsehole."

"Language, Pamela! There are children present."

"I don't know if we can really call Declan here a child any more, given what he's been through. He's offered to come down the dojo with me, give me a few tips."

Bunny turned and raised his eyebrows at Deccie. "Really?"

"Don't mention it, boss. It's a dangerous world out there. Women need to know how to protect themselves."

"Ain't that the truth," said Butch.

"Speaking of which," said Bunny. "Any news on Rosie?"

"The hospital says the shoulder wound isn't too bad, considering. Apparently, Gerald Royce is going to see her later today."

"Is he now?" said Bunny. "That's going to be one hell of a family reunion."

"Technically, I don't think you can use the word 'reunion' there. It's only—"

Before she could finish the thought, Butch slammed on the brakes and all three of them surged forward against their seat belts.

"Jesus!" exclaimed Deccie.

They'd come to a stop just past the entrance to Cabra Convent Girls' School. A couple of cars behind them honked their horns furiously. Butch pulled over to the side of the road, stuck a hand out the window and indicated for the angry motorists to go around them. As one of the vehicles did so, the driver offered some choice hand signals of his own, but Butch ignored him.

"Is everything alright?" asked Bunny.

Butch looked in the rear-view mirror. "Just open the glove compartment there and hand me the flyer inside it."

Bunny did as instructed then watched as Butch studied the picture of a dog on it and looked intently in the rear-view mirror again. "Right," she said softly. "Deccie, I want you to very carefully open the back door on the passenger side."

He did as he was told.

"Here, Kevin," she shouted. "Good boy. Here, Kevin."

Before Bunny could ask any further questions, a rather bedraggled Labradoodle leaped into the back of the car and started licking Deccie's face.

"Sweet. Can I keep him?"

Bunny reached back and quickly closed the door.

"No," said Butch, "you most definitely cannot. I'm afraid that dog is wanted for questioning."

"What's he done?" asked Deccie.

"Fingers crossed, he's got me a promotion."

EPILOGUE ONE – I TOLD YOU SO

Morgan Byrne turned off his boat's engine and waited.

He swore to himself that this would be the last time. He did that every time, but this time he meant it. That was the problem with getting into bed with international drug dealers – they didn't respond well to being informed that you were hopping back out again. He'd merely hinted at it to Vernon, and the guy had started to put the pressure on him.

He looked out across the water and waited. After a couple of minutes, a light off the coast flashed three times. He responded with his own torch – two long flashes followed by two short ones. The agreed signal that everything was okay.

He then fired the outboard motor back into life and headed out to meet the boat coming towards him. He'd take their delivery and hang on to it for three days, until Vernon turned up with the van to take it away. For the entire seventy-two hours, Morgan would barely sleep as the worry ate away at him.

Just as the boats reached each other, all hell broke loose. Bright lights and loudhailers seemed to have appeared from nowhere and were hurtling towards them. There were boats – seven or eight of them – and a helicopter with a searchlight.

In the absence of any chance of escape, Morgan raised his hands, stayed where he was and followed the instructions of the coastguard.

Within two minutes, he was in the back of a different boat, his hands cuffed behind him.

Dazed as he was, he turned to one of the gardaí.

"How ... how did you find out?"

The guard looked down at him, his nose wrinkled. "Anonymous tip-off."

"Oh," said Morgan. "Right."

"Yeah." The guard leaned down and jabbed a finger into his chest. "You should be ashamed of yourself. It's bad enough running drugs, but using a Gaeltacht as cover? You're going down for a long time. *Slán abhaile!*"

EPILOGUE TWO – WE BEGIN AT THE END

The Spider sighed.

The room was indeed smoke filled, and most of it was coming from the soldering iron that one of the men had been applying to his skin. Their interrogation, in his expert opinion, had been poor overall. Then again, they seemed to suffer from a lack of direction. Clearly, they'd been instructed to work him over rather than to extract any particular information from him. He knew all manner of useful information, just nothing that would help him in his current predicament.

He'd taken every precaution, used every trick in the book. After the debacle in Ireland, he'd endeavoured to disappear. Given his line of work, he'd had preparations for such an eventuality in place for years. He'd thought his plan had covered every angle. Evidently not.

He heard a door open behind him and footsteps approaching across the concrete floor. He was in a warehouse. Right at that moment, he couldn't remember in what country. He'd moved so many times and they'd still found him.

A man appeared in front of him and lifted the Spider's chin. Weakened as he was, he recognised the face.

"Hello. Do you remember me?"

He nodded and spoke through parched lips. "Stringer."

"That's correct. It's so nice to see you, Mr – well, what should we call you? You've used so many names. Do you even know which is the real one any more?"

"Doesn't matter."

"As you wish," said Stringer. "I just wanted you to know that you were right."

"Was I?"

"Yes," he said, waving a hand to indicate the other men in the room. "The men I had to hire to kill you after your failure were indeed expensive but, as you suggested they would be, they were worth every penny."

"Killing me would be counterproductive."

Stringer tilted his head and smiled. "And why is that?"

"I know things."

"You do," agreed Stringer. "But what was it you said to me the last time we met? That's right." He leaned in. "Knowledge isn't power. Knowledge coupled with failure equals an unacceptable liability."

Stringer straightened up and held out his hand. Somebody gave him a gun, which he hefted, looking thrilled. "We don't need you any more because, as you see, I have decided to become you."

The Spider found himself laughing. Stringer did not enjoy this.

"Shut up."

He tilted his head back and laughed some more.

Stringer shoved the gun against his forehead. "Exactly what is so funny?"

"Oh, nothing."

"What?" he demanded.

"It's just ... I was far better at being me than you'll ever be, and look where I've ended up."

Stringer cocked the hammer on the gun.

"Take a look around the room," said the Spider with a smile, "because I guarantee that one of these men will one day be sent to kill you."

The last thing the Spider saw was the sudden doubt in Stringer's eyes.

Human nature was his business, in all its grubby glory.

FREE BOOK

Hello again reader-person,

I hope you enjoyed *Firewater Blues*. Thanks for buying it and taking the time to read it. Bunny's USA saga will continue later in 2022, but if you need a Caimh fix before then, make sure you've signed up to my monthly newsletter for free short stories, audio stories and the latest goings on in the Bunnyverse.

You'll also get a copy of my short fiction collection called *How To Send A Message*, which features several stories featuring characters from my books. To sign up go to my website:

www.WhiteHairedIrishman.com

The paperback costs $10.99/£7.99/€8.99 in the shops but you can get the e-book for free just by signing up to my newsletter.

Cheers muchly and thanks for reading,

Caimh

ALSO BY CAIMH MCDONNELL

Visit www.WhiteHairedIrishman.com to find out more.